PETE

DEATH BY

ERIC ELRINGTON ADDIS, aka 'Peter Drax', was born in Edinburgh in 1899, the youngest child of a retired Indian civil servant and the daughter of an officer in the British Indian Army.

Drax attended Edinburgh University, and served in the Royal Navy, retiring in 1929. In the 1930s he began practising as a barrister, but, recalled to the Navy upon the outbreak of the Second World War, he served on HMS *Warspite* and was mentioned in dispatches. When Drax was killed in 1941 he left a wife and two children.

Between 1936 and 1939, Drax published six crime novels: *Murder by Chance* (1936), *He Shot to Kill* (1936), *Murder by Proxy* (1937), *Death by Two Hands* (1937), *Tune to a Corpse* (1938) and *High Seas Murder* (1939). A further novel, *Sing a Song of Murder*, unfinished by Drax on his death, was completed by his wife, Hazel Iris (Wilson) Addis, and published in 1944.

By Peter Drax

Murder by Chance
He Shot to Kill
Death by Two Hands
Tune to a Corpse
High Seas Murder
Sing a Song of Murder

PETER DRAX

DEATH BY
TWO HANDS

With an introduction
by Curtis Evans

DEAN STREET PRESS

Published by Dean Street Press 2017

Introduction copyright © 2017 Curtis Evans

All Rights Reserved

First published in 1937 by Hutchinson & Co. Ltd.

Cover by DSP

ISBN 978 1 911579 59 5

www.deanstreetpress.co.uk

INTRODUCTION

ERIC ELRINGTON ADDIS, aka "Peter Drax," one of the major between-the-wars exponents and practitioners of realism in the British crime novel, was born near the end of the Victorian era in Edinburgh, Scotland on 19 May 1899, the youngest child of David Foulis Addis, a retired Indian civil servant, and Emily Malcolm, daughter of an officer in the British Indian Army. Drax died during the Second World War on 31 August 1941, having been mortally wounded in a German air raid on the British Royal Navy base at Alexandria, Egypt, officially known as HMS *Nile*. During his brief life of 42 years, Drax between the short span from 1936 to 1939 published six crime novels: *Murder by Chance* (1936), *He Shot to Kill* (1936), *Murder by Proxy* (1937), *Death by Two Hands* (1937), *Tune to a Corpse* (1938) and *High Seas Murder* (1939). An additional crime novel, *Sing a Song of Murder*, having been left unfinished by Drax at his death in 1941 and completed by his novelist wife, was published in 1944. Together the Peter Drax novels constitute one of the most important bodies of realistic crime fiction published in the 1930s, part of the period commonly dubbed the "Golden Age of detective fiction." Rather than the artificial and outsize master sleuths and super crooks found in so many classic mysteries from this era, Drax's novels concern, as publicity material for the books put it, "police who are not endowed with supernatural powers and crooks who are also human." In doing so they offered crime fiction fans from those years some of the period's most compelling reading. The reissuing of these gripping tales of criminal mayhem and murder, unaccountably out-of-print for more than seven decades, by Dean Street Press marks a signal event in recent mystery publishing history.

Peter Drax's career background gave the future crime writer constant exposure to the often grim rigors of life, experience which he most effectively incorporated into his fiction. A graduate of Edinburgh Academy, the teenaged Drax served during the First World War as a Midshipman on HMS *Dreadnought* and *Marlborough*. (Two of his three brothers died in the war, the elder, David Malcolm Addis, at Ypres, where his body was never found.) After the signing of the armistice and his graduation from the Royal Naval College, Drax remained in the Navy for nearly a decade, retiring in 1929 with the rank of Lieutenant-Commander, in which capacity he supervised training with the New Zealand Navy, residing with his English wife, Hazel Iris (Wilson) Addis, daughter of an electrical engineer, in Auckland. In the 1930s he returned with Hazel to England and began practicing as a barrister, specializing, predictably enough, in the division of Admiralty, as well as that of Divorce. Recalled to the Navy upon the outbreak of the Second World War, Drax served as Commander (second-in-command) on HMS *Warspite* and was mentioned in dispatches at the Second Battle of Narvik, a naval affray which took place during the 1940 Norwegian campaign. At his death in Egypt in 1941 Drax left behind Hazel --herself an accomplished writer, under the pen name Hazel Adair, of so-called middlebrow "women's fiction"--and two children, including Jeremy Cecil Addis, the late editor and founder of *Books Ireland*.

Commuting to his London office daily in the 1930s on the 9.16, Drax's hobby became, according to his own account, the "reading and dissecting of thrillers," ubiquitous in station book stalls. Concluding that the vast majority of them were lamentably unlikely affairs, Drax set out over six months to spin his own tale, "inspired by the desire to tell a story that was credible." (More prosaically the neophyte author also wanted to show his wife, who had recently published her first novel, *Wanted a Son*, that he too could publish a novel.) The result was *Murder by Chance*, the first of the author's seven crime novels. In the United States during the late 1920s and early 1930s, recalled Raymond Chandler in his essay "The Simple Art of Murder" (originally published in 1944), the celebrated American crime writer Dashiell Hammett had given "murder back to the kind of people who commit it for reasons, not just to provide a corpse; and with the means at hand, not with hand-wrought dueling pistols, curare and tropical fish." Drax's debut crime novel, which followed on the heels of Hammett's books, made something of a similar impression in the United Kingdom, with mystery writer and founding Detection Club member Milward Kennedy in the *Sunday Times* pronouncing the novel a "thriller of great merit" that was "extremely convincing" and the influential *Observer* crime fiction critic Torquemada avowing, "I have not for a good many months enjoyed a thriller as much as I have enjoyed *Murder by Chance.*"

What so impressed these and other critics about *Murder by Chance* and Drax's successive novels was their simultaneous plausibility and readability, a combination seen as a tough feat to pull off in an era of colorful though not always entirely credible crime writers like S. S. Van Dine, Edgar Wallace and John Dickson Carr. Certainly in the 1930s the crime novelists Dorothy L. Sayers, Margery Allingham and Anthony Berkeley, among others (including Milward Kennedy himself), had elevated the presence of psychological realism in the crime novel; yet the criminal milieus that these authors presented to readers were mostly resolutely occupied by the respectable middle and upper classes. Drax offered British readers what was then an especially bracing change of atmosphere (one wherein mean streets replaced country mansions and quips were exchanged for coshes, if you will)—as indicated in this resoundingly positive Milward Kennedy review of Drax's fifth crime novel, *Tune to a Corpse* (1938):

> I have the highest opinion of Peter Drax's murder stories.... Mainly his picture is of low life in London, where crime and poverty meet and merge. He draws characters who shift uneasily from shabby to disreputable associations.... and he can win our sudden liking, almost our respect, for creatures in whom little virtue is to be found. To show how a drab crime was committed and then to show the slow detection of the truth, and to keep the reader absorbed all the time—this is a real achievement. The secret of Peter Drax's success is his ability to make the circumstances as plausible as the characters are real....

Two of Peter Drax's crime novels, the superb *Death by Two Hands* and *Tune to a Corpse*, were published in the United States, under the titles, respectively, *Crime within Crime* and *Crime to Music*, to very strong notices. The *Saturday Review of Literature*, for example, pronounced of *Crime within Crime* that "as a straightforward eventful yarn of little people in [the] grip of tragic destiny it's brilliantly done" and of *Crime to Music* that "London underworld life is described with color and realism. The steps in the weakling killer's descent to Avernus [see Virgil] are thrillingly traced." That the country which gave the world Dashiell Hammett could be so impressed with the crime fiction of Peter Drax surely is strong recommendation indeed. Today seedily realistic urban British crime fiction of the 1930s is perhaps most strongly associated with two authors who dabbled in crime fiction: Graham Greene (*Brighton Rock*, 1938, and others) and Gerald Kersh (*Night and the City*, 1938). If not belonging on quite that exalted level, the novels of Peter Drax nevertheless grace this gritty roster, one that forever changed the face of British crime fiction.

Curtis Evans

CHAPTER ONE

CHALK STREET was crowded from end to end and from pavement to pavement with a slow-moving jostling crowd. Costers' barrows lined the gutters.

It was lunch-time on a frosty day in November, and business was brisk among the office and warehouse workers in the district. Office boys staring, and sucking bars of chocolate. Girls from a near-by box factory, squealing and laughing, arm in arm in twos and threes. All were hatless. It was a custom of the midday crowd in Chalk Street.

Here you could be cured of every disease for threepence; could satisfy any thirst with sarsaparilla, blackcurrant or lemon juice for tuppence; could buy studs, mouse traps, wire puzzles or embrocation. Not dully as in a shop, but gaily, adventurously, for you never knew what you'd be buying next. That was the attraction of Chalk Street.

If you were broke there was entertainment enough to make any one forget the hunger pangs of a lunchless lunch-hour.

For the serious and medically minded there was usually a lecture in progress given by an elderly gentleman wearing mutton chop whiskers, a high choker collar and a stock. Professional jealousy had forced him to leave Harley Street, or so he said.

With the help of a highly coloured diagram of the "innards" of the human body, he traced the origin of all ills.

A box of his pills would cure them and if you didn't choose to pay the price—three brown coins to you, sir—well, it wasn't no good coming back and blaming him if you died in the night. And he wasn't no blinking quack. Here to-day and gone to-morrow. He'd be on this stand at the same time next week and the week after.

Behind a barrow piled high with open boxes of silk stockings a young man held forth in a voice that could have competed ably with a dance band trumpet.

"'Ere y'are. Hevery one guaranteed. Not a ladder in a boxful. Pick 'em where you like. Got every shade. 'Ere y'are. Hevery one guaranteed—"

Alongside him an earnest little man in a greenish bowler and a very large muffler croaked over a load of gramophone records.

"Turn 'em over, gents. Turn 'em over. Dances four-pence. Red labels a bob. Turn 'em over. No, sir, I don't think I has got a Caruso. Getting very scarce them Carusos is. I 'ad one only last week but the blinking kid put his foot on it. Just after I'd bought 'im a new pair of boots."

A little farther on a man with a mouth which was always wide open yelled the virtues of chocolates. He dived a dirty hand into a box of "assorteds" and held them up to view.

"Tuppence a quarter! Tuppence a quarter! Best quality. Cost a tanner anywhere else. Who wants? Who wants?" The crowd surged round the chocolate merchant, fascinated by the never-ceasing flow from his india rubber mouth. Tuppences, slyly proffered, were thrown contemptuously into a cardboard box. A quarter was weighed and wrapped. And another, and another.

Nearly every stall or barrow had its attendant crowd except that of Mr. Rivers. He never shouted. He never waved his arms about or told the story of an adventurous life, to catch the attention of the crowd.

He stood behind his barrow with his hands thrust deep in the pockets of his tightly buttoned overcoat. He was wearing a flat cloth cap. A cigarette hung limply from his mouth.

"Everything in the tray tuppence. Everything in the tray tuppence. Pick 'em where you like."

The tray was filled with pieces of iron and steel of every imaginable shape. Padlocks, nails, screws, key-rings, hinges, screw-drivers, gimlets, bradawls.

There was a painted plate dangling from a stick which read: "Keys cut while you wait."

A man came up to Mr. Rivers from behind and touched him on the arm.

"Barney's back."

"O.K."

Mr. Rivers did not turn round as he asked: "Where is he?"

"Up by the Gink's barrer, doing his stuff."

Mr. Rivers looked up and down the street and then said out of the side of his mouth to a melancholy-looking man by his side:

"I'll be back in a minute. You stop here."

Joe Kemp edged along the pavement to the position which Mr. Rivers vacated, and took up the chant.

"Everything in the tray tuppence."

Mr. Rivers made his way slowly through the crowd to where an oldish man in a wide black felt hat was standing in the gutter between two barrows.

Round the brim of the felt hat crawled two mice. One was fawn and white and was called Fanny. The other, her husband, was a portly brown and white gentleman mouse called George.

The outer circuit of the hat was rigged up with jumps made of tape and match-sticks. Two squares of cardboard bore the words "start" and "finish." Cheese rubbed on the jumps induced the plethoric George to clamber up and over. Fanny was "expecting" so did not exert herself.

Ninety per cent of Barney's audience watched the mice. The remainder listened to his story of an adventurous life at sea, about girls in Rio, girls in Pago Pago, girls in San Francisco.

Barney was an avid reader of American True Life Romance Magazines.

He was coming to the point when he was going to offer for sale bottles of an elixir which had given him strength in his youth to battle round the Cape, when Mr. Rivers came along.

He stood on the pavement until Barney had made his sales, then he took a step forward and touched him on the arm.

"All right. I'm a-coming to you in a minute."

"Back again?"

Barney swung round nearly bringing Fanny to an early death. She held on to a jump with her tiny pink feet.

The smile was wiped off Barney's mobile features, then it came again.

"Yes, here I am, Mr. Rivers. Back for the winter season."

"Got anything?"

Barney, with his head on one side, nodded three times.

"I don't fancy it's much in your line, but—"

"I'll see you at Joe's place to-night."

"O.K."

Mr. Rivers walked away and Barney turned to find his audience had melted in the way that London crowds do.

Mr. Rivers went back to his stand. Joe made way for him.

"All right, you can carry on. I'm going to have some chow."

He turned away from the noise of the market down a quiet street. A hundred yards on he stopped outside a café and looked in over a dirty lace curtain.

The place was crowded. Mr. Rivers kicked open the swing door and walked up to a counter.

"Coffee and ham sandwich," he ordered, and leaning on an elbow ran his eye over the tables. There was no one there he knew.

"'Morning, Mr. Rivers."

Spike Morgan moved out from behind a screen. He was a man of about twenty-five, his eyes were a cold blue, and there was a hardness in his face that put ten years on his age. He was wearing a stained raincoat and a light fawn felt hat with a green band.

"What cheer, Spike. I thought I'd run into you here. Busy?"

"Not so as you'd notice it."

Mr. Rivers nodded and felt in his pocket for money to pay for his meal.

"Come over here." He picked up his cup and plate and walked to a table in the far corner of the smoke-clouded room. "Do you want a job?"

"I don't mind," Spike answered carelessly. Though he hadn't the price of a bed in his pocket, he didn't intend to give anything away. Mr. Rivers was not deceived. He opened his sandwich and dabbed it liberally with mustard.

Spike asked: "What sort of a job?"

"Don't know yet. A smash most likely."

"Where?"

"In the country."

Spike drew in a lungful of smoke and coughed it out. Then he looked down at the toes of his shoes. Mr. Rivers went on eating his sandwich. When he had finished it, he took a gulp of coffee, wiped his mouth and lit a cigarette. Spike's gaze wandered round the room.

"Thought I'd let you know in case you were thinking of getting fixed up. Here's a quid to go on with." Mr. Rivers took a note from his pocket and laid it on the table. Spike picked it up carelessly.

"What's the cut?" he asked.

"A corner for you."

"Who else is in on this?"

Mr. Rivers ignored the question and, dusting some crumbs off his waistcoat, got up and pushed back his chair.

"I'll send word when I want you."

"O.K." Spike waited till Rivers had gone, and then he called to the woman behind the counter, "Sausage an' mash twice and coffee."

He hadn't eaten that day and, when the plate was put before him, he walked into it like a schoolboy. Crime hadn't paid any dividends for the past few weeks.

Mr. Rivers walked to the end of the street. Then he saw Leith and stopped. Detective-Sergeant Leith had a disconcerting habit of asking questions which were awkward to answer. He was walking slowly through the crowd, his hands thrust deep into the pockets of his Burberry.

Though seldom mistaken by his clients for anything else than what he was—a busy, a flat, a split—yet James Leith was successful in his work of filling the dock at the West Street Police Court.

He was familiar with the witness boxes in the Old Bailey Courts. He called Judges by their Christian names when they weren't present. He knew every opening.

"On the night of the 29th January, in consequence of information revived, I visited No. 99 Blank Street. There I found the prisoner in bed. I took him into custody."

Thus baldly he would recount events which formed the first chapter of a sordid story, which had for its ending a melancholy drive to Wormwood Scrubs in a police van.

To Leith these visits to the Old Bailey were welcome breaks in the routine of police work, but they only came, on an average, once every nine months. On these days he would lunch luxuriously on a steak in a near-by restaurant which existed on the patronage of the respectable hangers-on of crime—barristers, solicitors, police officers and witnesses. His meals on these occasions tasted all the better for the knowledge that a four-word entry in his diary was all that was required to account for his day's work.

"Attended Central Criminal Court."

On one occasion he had had the pleasure of seeing Mr. Rivers in the dock, charged with receiving goods, well knowing them to have been stolen. Later he had the mortification of seeing Mr. Rivers leaving the Old Bailey unescorted. Ever resourceful, Mr. Rivers had told a story that is so old that jailers sink into a coma when it is told. It was new to the jury. They were interested in the circumstantial account which Mr. Rivers gave them of the man who had sold Mr. Rivers the goods in question, and they were so misguided as to accept the explanation at Mr. Rivers's own valuation.

On the day of Barney's return, Leith had lunched lightly and indigestibly off a packet of sandwiches. Consequently he looked at the crowd with a certain amount of loathing. Then he saw Barney and stopped to listen to him. He liked the old man, though he had the gravest doubts as to his honesty. But then Leith suspected every one with a fair impartiality.

When Barney came to the end of his address and had dispersed the crowd quite successfully by the simple process of asking them to buy something, Leith approached him.

"Got a licence yet?"

Barney's face creased and he laughed so that his shoulders shook. George clung to the brim of the hat with all his strength.

"Licence, Mr. Leith! At my age! Why, it would run away with all my profits and what with overheads—"

"I suppose you mean the mice?" The corners of Leith's mouth twitched with the hint of a smile.

"That's right. They has to be fed."

"I haven't seen you for a time. Where've you been?"

"In the country. For me health. Nothing like a bit of fresh air to set you up for the winter."

Leith half-turned to walk on, when he saw Mr. Rivers standing by his barrow. He jerked his head in his direction and asked:

"Do you know him?"

"Who?" Barney looked in the direction but, as he was a good four inches shorter than most of the crowd, he couldn't see who Leith meant to indicate.

"Rivers," Leith replied, and saw a guarded look come over Barney's face.

"Rivers. Oh, yes," he said, after a slight hesitation. "Yes, I knows him in a manner of speaking, but not to speak to. You see, he's private and I'm public. A penny off the pint counts and it tastes the same whichever bar you uses."

"Yes, I suppose so," Leith said absently. He was thinking of Rivers.

"What does he do for a living?"

"Works the markets. An' he's got a shop too."

"Yes, I know that. He runs a car."

Barney said he didn't know nothing about that, in a tone which showed quite plainly that he did not intend to give Leith any information about Rivers.

When Leith disappeared Barney shuffled along to Rivers's stand.

"He was asking after you," he said, and as he spoke his lips barely moved. The words were meant for Rivers's ears alone.

"What'd he say?" Mr. Rivers asked without turning his head.

"Wanted to know what else you did besides working round here. I told him I didn't know."

"Right. I'll see you up at Joe's to-night. You'd better move."

Mr. Rivers was careful not to be seen talking to men like Barney and Spike Morgan. When he did a deal in stolen property the matter was usually arranged at some windy street corner or on the back seat of a bus.

Barney stowed George and Fanny away in his pocket, where they settled down to a frugal meal of biscuit crumbs. Then he looked in at the shop to see the time. It was a quarter past two. The lunch-hour customers had gone and there were several hours before he had to meet his niece, Alma, at Waterloo. It was too cold to hang about.

"Think I'll look in at Larry's," he mumbled to himself.

Alma Robinson was excited at the prospect of going to London. She had been brought up by an aunt and had spent all the twenty-four years of her life in the wilds of Surrey. The aunt had been old-fashioned, and Alma, meek to her dictates, had lived a quiet country life, never painted her lips nor cut short her long chestnut hair, which, parted in the middle, waved down low on either side of her oval face. When the aunt died, Alma found that she was in the fashion again and reaped the reward of obedience.

Will liked it like that, too. She had always been fond of Will Dorset, and he was fond of her in his slow, unimaginative way. They had been walking out for seven years—ever since Alma first put up her hair.

When Alma announced that she was going to leave the village of Crowley on the slope of Hascomb Hill, Will Dorset woke up. His brain, however, moved but slowly, and before he had come to the point of asking Alma to marry him, there she was standing waiting for him to walk down to the village with her to catch the bus. She was going to get a train at Guildford.

"I'll carry your bag."

Alma smiled at him as she handed over her little basket trunk bound with clothes-line.

"Thanks. I'm afraid it's rather heavy."

Will picked it up and put it on his shoulder.

"That's no weight."

They walked down the road for a hundred yards or so in silence. Then Will asked a little gruffly, looking straight ahead:

"Coming back soon, I suppose?"

"No. I don't think so. I don't know really. I'm going to stop with my uncle."

"You mean that—" Will was going to say "that queer little cuss what wears the black hat and keeps them mice." He stopped himself. Alma took offence easily.

The narrow escape from making a fool of himself put Will off his stroke. He had meant to work up to the subject of marriage, but now he couldn't even start.

"It's cold."

Alma agreed.

They walked on.

"Seems like we're too soon." Will dropped the trunk on the footpath outside the post office.

"It'll be along in a minute, but don't you wait."

"Oh, it's all right." Will groped in his pocket and found a squashed packet of cigarettes. Alma looked longingly up the road for the bus. Will made further researches in another pocket and brought out a box of matches.

"You'll find London a bit different to here." Will sucked hard at his cigarette and rolled it between his fingers until it drew evenly.

"Yes, I suppose I will." Alma nodded slowly. "It'll be a nice change. I've always wanted to get away to London."

"I'm coming up on Friday."

"I didn't know that. Why didn't you tell me before?"

"Didn't know till this morning. The boss wants me to take the van up."

"What time?"

"In the morning."

"We might meet somewhere."

"Can you think of any place?" Will asked.

"No. I've only been in London twice before in my life." Alma thought for a moment. "I tell you. When I get settled in with uncle I'll ask him where's a good place and drop you a line."

Will brightened. "Be sure and not forget."

"I won't. Oh, there's the bus," said Alma in a tone of relief. Will picked up the trunk and when the bus drew up he followed Alma up the two steps and slid it under a seat. Then he retreated and stood in the roadway.

"Got your money?"

Alma opened her bag and made sure that she still had the few shillings which Barney had given her. She refastened the catch and held the bag tight on her lap.

"Yes, thanks. Oh, and, Will, tell them at the farm that I won't need any milk to-morrow. I paid the money but forgot to say anything. It's a job to remember every little thing."

The conductor, who had been having a quiet smoke and talk with the driver, returned to the rear of the bus. He looked up and down the street. Then he jumped on board and pressed the bell twice.

The bus started off with a jerk. Alma leaned forward and waved out of the open door. Will waved back and remembered all he had meant to say. He hadn't even asked her what her address would be in London. His interest in Alma grew in inverse ratio to his chance of seeing her again. The girl at the post office who had attracted him mildly at one time passed right out of the betting. It was Alma first. The rest of the field nowhere.

CHAPTER TWO

NUMBER THREE Napier Terrace was one of a row of seven houses looking over the Regents Canal to a coal yard. At night the silence by the canal side was complete, broken only at intervals by a bus rumbling over the bridge a couple of hundred yards away.

Eighty years or so ago the canal ran through fields, and the householders of Napier Terrace walked between green hedgerows to the point where the horse bus started for the city.

It was different now. The skyline was jagged with the outline of a derelict warehouse and mounds of coal which never seemed to grow less. Great steel lighters, towed by a squat puffing tug, brought further supplies. Half-ton grabs emptied the lighters while a conveyor with its endless grimy belt poured coal into the furnaces of the North London gas works.

Joe Kemp stabled the barrow in the back yard of Mr. Rivers's shop. He did not see the lighters, nor the coal heaps, nor the cock-eyed broken windows of the warehouse, as he slouched along the cinder path above the canal. There was only one thought in his mind. Supper and beer, or maybe it was beer and supper. Anyway, he was hungry and thirsty and his feet were tired.

He rapped on the door of No. 3. A minute passed before he heard shuffling footsteps within. A bolt was shot back and a key turned. The Kemps did not keep open house. "You're early." Mrs. Kemp opened the door grudgingly. She was a great barrel of a woman clad in a dirty and enveloping overall which fell in straight lines from her bosom to her feet. She was coarse featured, but her wide mouth opened easily in a smile. When she laughed huskily she showed a double row of broken teeth. She was easy to get on with and good company when things were going well—that is, when they went the way she wanted them to go.

"Yes. I finished early. Rivers has got something on."

Mrs. Kemp shut and locked and bolted the door and followed her husband down the narrow passage, her heelless slippers flapping and dragging on the oilcloth.

Joe kicked open a door which led into a small square room full of light and heat; light, blinding white from a naked incandescent gas mantle over a table on which was spread a red and white chequered cloth.

A high grate was banked up with red hot coals. The window was shut and closely curtained.

Joe felt in his pocket for a packet of cigarettes. He stared unseeingly at the fire.

"Rivers is coming in to-night."

Mrs. Kemp's heavy face brightened.

"Well, he'll be company. Cheer things up. What's he want?"

"Barney. He's coming too. Rivers wants to see him."

Mrs. Kemp nodded.

"Has he heard of anything?"

"Barney? I suppose so. He's bringing a girl with him."

"Yes, I know. That's all fixed up."

Mrs. Kemp stared at her husband for a minute or two and then said:

"You'd better go and clean yourself up an' put on a collar. It's on the back of the door." She waited until she heard Joe climb the stairs and enter the front room. "Chuck us down a couple of pair of shoes. My best and the ones you says is too tight for you."

She worked out in her mind a complicated sum. Three bob, the shoes'd fetch, and with what she had already, which was one and threepence halfpenny, she'd be able to get two jugs of beer and a pound and a half of sausages. There was the best part of half a loaf of bread in the bin and enough tea and margarine and sugar. Well, just enough sugar, if she and Joe held off. Entertaining in Napier Terrace was a complicated business.

"I'm going to get the doings, see. Make up the fire when you come down."

A grumbling noise, which may have been an assent, came from the front bedroom. Joe didn't like being made to wear a collar.

Mrs. Kemp was back in the house before Barney and Alma arrived. They had taken a bus to the canal bridge and, as Barney led the way down the path, a fresh wind sprang up and drove spatters of rain in their faces.

"Mouldy spot, ain't it?" Alma glanced down at the soot-black ditch below. A bus crossing the bridge made a swiftly changing pattern of yellow light on the water. She could feel beneath her feet the vibration set up by the bus.

Barney was muttering to himself or maybe to his mice. His head was bent forward as his long legs covered the ground in swinging strides. Alma had almost to run to keep up with him.

"I say, go easy." Her bag knocked against the railings. She grasped his arm with her free hand. He shook it off.

"It's all right, we're there." Barney stopped suddenly and opened the gate at the end of the short path leading to the front door of No. 3 Napier Terrace.

Alma followed him slowly, and tried to push a damp, straying wisp of hair under her hat.

Barney knocked twice, waited a few seconds and knocked again. A minute passed before he heard the sound of Mrs.

Kemp's dragging footsteps and called out: "Come on, open up. It's wet out here."

The door opened a crack.

"Is that you, Barney?"

"Who'd you think it was calling at this time of night? The blinking Lord Mayor?"

The door opened further.

Barney stepped in through the door sideways and pulled Alma after him.

"It's perishing cold out. This is Alma."

Mrs. Kemp shut the door. Then Alma felt her hand grasped firmly. It was like a man's grip.

"You go along, Barney. You know the way." Mrs. Kemp took Alma's bag and carried it as though it were feather light. Alma rubbed her aching wrist and made further efforts to tidy her wind-blown hair as she followed in the wake of Mrs. Kemp up the bare wooden stair. The treads seemed to creak in unison with Mrs. Kemp's corsets.

Alma wished that she hadn't left Crowley. She hated this house. She was tired and cold and her hair was wet.

"This'll be your room." Mrs. Kemp put down Alma's trunk, struck a match and lit a naked gas jet. "There's water in the jug if you want to wash. I'll get you some soap."

Alma pulled off her hat and bent to a glass. She took out her handkerchief and wiped her face. Then she opened her bag and searched through it for a brush and comb.

Mrs. Kemp returned with a wafer of pink soap. "Don't be too long. We're going to have supper as soon as I can get it ready." She shut the door behind her.

Alma looked out her nightdress and laid it on the bed. She poured some cold water into a tin basin and made a hasty wash. The soap wouldn't lather. It slipped through her chilled fingers.

Miserable as she was, she hesitated before she at last made up her mind to go downstairs. The landing was almost dark, lighted only by a stray beam from the gas jet in the passage below.

She felt her way downstairs by the shaky handrail, and as she reached the bottom she heard Barney's laugh and took heart.

The light and heat of the living-room made her eyes water as she opened the door. Barney was sitting by the heaped fire.

There was another man beside him who looked up as she came in. He got up and said:

"Come along. I expect you're cold." Joe jerked his head towards the chair he had been sitting on.

"I'll sit here, thank you." Alma pulled a chair from the table and sat on the edge of it, spreading her hands to the hot coals.

Barney looked up and winked.

"All fixed up?"

Alma nodded.

"You'll be all right here. Always a good fire and plenty of eats."

Mrs. Kemp came in with a pile of plates which she set out on the table. Alma looked up at her and then quickly back at the fire. There was something too obviously appraising in the two black eyes fixed on her.

Barney was playing with a fat fawn and white mouse. Mrs. Kemp's gaze strayed to him. "Put that damn' brute away." Barney laughed. The mouse was crawling across the chequered table-cloth to a loaf on a plate.

"Come you out o' that. D'ye hear?" Fanny sat up and began to wash her face with tiny pink paws.

"You never does do what I tells yer." A large grimy hand scooped Fanny up and returned her to her bed-sitting-dining-room, where George was supping off a few crumbs of soft biscuit.

"When do we eat?"

"Any time now." Mrs. Kemp sliced a loaf quickly and efficiently. "Mr. Rivers is coming in later."

"Yes, Joe told me."

"Did he tell you he'd got a new winger?"

"No, who's that?" Barney tilted back his chair and put his feet on the mantelpiece.

"Spike Morgan. He's hot."

"He'll have to be. The last one's getting a chance to cool off all right. A seven stretch on the Moor, wasn't it?"

"Five," said Mrs. Kemp shortly. "And it's Maidstone."

"Along with the nobs. Maidstone's classy these days. Got to be a gent to be sent there."

Mrs. Kemp sat down on a hard chair and folded her arms.

"It wasn't Mr. Rivers's fault. He did all he could. Got a good mouthpiece and sent him all sort of stuff when he was at Brixton."

"And I'll bet that did him a power of good. Where's his wife an' kids?"

"They're being looked after."

Barney felt in an inside pocket and took out a pouch of fine cut tobacco and a packet of papers. His thick fingers rolled a cigarette deftly, and as he wet it with his tongue he looked at Mrs. Kemp.

"Spike used to work round these parts, didn't he?"

"That was a year ago," said Joe. "He's been on the south side since then."

"Was he the kid the Tibbetts had working for them?" Joe nodded.

Barney lifted a small hot coal from the fire with the tongs and puffed at his cigarette. Straggling ends of tobacco flamed up.

"Spike's no blooming good," he said.

Mrs. Kemp's thick neck reddened.

"He's all right."

"What's he done?"

"Nothing much yet, but as soon as Mr. Rivers gets on to something good Spike'll make a clean job of it."

Barney grunted his disagreement with this statement. Mrs. Kemp looked at a cheap tin clock ticking loudly on the mantelpiece. "Didn't know it was that late," she muttered and heaved herself to her feet. She nudged Alma with her elbow. "Here, you make yourself useful and toast this little lot." She stretched out her hand for the plate of sliced bread and put it behind Alma. "There's the fork hanging up by your right hand."

Barney watched Mrs. Kemp until she had left the room then he leaned forward and touched Alma on the arm. "How d'you like the place?"

"All right, why?"

"I wasn't sure how you'd take the old woman. She's not so bad when you get to know her. Got funny ways, but she won't let you down if she can help it, and that's saying something."

Barney brought George out of his pocket and dusted biscuit crumbs from his whiskers. "Her only trouble is that she don't like mice. That's why I don't stop here."

"Where d'you live?"

"At the settlement. With the Tibbetts."

"Couldn't I come with you?"

"But you said you liked the place."

"I didn't know you wasn't going to stop." Alma shielded her face against the heat of the fire.

"You'll be all right. Give it a try for a day or two and if you want a change then, I'll see what I can do."

Alma didn't like Mrs. Kemp, but she was too sleepy to argue.

"What'll I have to do if I stop here?"

"Give her a hand. That's about all. Clean the place and—"

Mrs. Kemp came shuffling into the room. She was carrying a frying pan in which were a dozen sausages and a lump of lard.

"Here, Joe. Get on with these on the fire and save the gas."

Joe took a pan unprotesting and raked the coals to make a flat place for it.

"How's that toast coming along?"

"Not much more to do," Alma replied.

Mrs. Kemp sat down and stared at her.

"Barney said you'd want to stop here. Is that right?"

"Yes, I think so." Alma did not look round as she spoke.

"Tomorrow'll be time enough to make up your mind. Five bob a week an' your keep."

"That'll suit her all right," Barney put in before Alma could reply.

"There might be a chance of making a bit more. Mr. Rivers said the other day he was looking for a girl to give him a hand in the shop, but we'll see about that later."

Mrs. Kemp looked at the sausages and then at the clock. She lifted a kettle from the grate and put it on the fire.

Supper was well on its way when there was a double knock on the street door. Mrs. Kemp put down a forkful on the way to her mouth. "That'll be Mr. Rivers. Go and let him in, Joe." She turned in her chair and took from a cupboard behind her a bottle of whisky and a glass.

There was a sound of muffled conversation in the passage outside, then firm footsteps advanced.

"Come along in, Mr. Rivers." Mrs. Kemp was smiling, showing every one of her crooked front teeth.

Mr. Rivers, in a neat blue serge suit, collar and flowery tie, looked much more respectable than he had done earlier in the day at the market. He had shaved and his grizzled black hair was neatly brushed.

He stood quite still for a moment or two while he nodded to Mrs. Kemp, Joe and Barney. Alma tried to keep her eyes on her plate but failed. She had to look up. Mr. Rivers smiled at her.

Mrs. Kemp said quickly: "This is Alma. Barney brought her. She's his niece."

Mr. Rivers, still smiling, held out his hand to Alma who took it shyly and smiled back at him.

"Come and sit down, Mr. Rivers." Mrs. Kemp pushed forward a chair and cleared a place. "Do you fancy a banger?"

"No, thanks, I've fed, but I could do with a drop of that." He pointed at the bottle of whisky.

Mrs. Kemp poured out a generous measure. "Get some water, Joe."

Mr. Rivers sat silent until the water was produced. He poured a little into his glass and drank, slowly, appreciatively, pouting his lips.

Mrs. Kemp finished her meal and pushed her plate on one side.

"I hear you've got Spike," she said conversationally. "At least Joe said you had." Her tone implied her complete distrust of Joe as an informant.

"I've seen him, yes." Mr. Rivers replied cautiously.

"You couldn't do better than Spike."

"Maybe not. We'll see." He had no intention of discussing Spike with Mrs. Kemp.

He looked at Alma. "You look tired," he said. "Have you had a long day?"

"Yes. I was up early."

"If I was you I'd go straight to my bed," said Mrs. Kemp. She knew what Rivers was getting at. He wanted the girl out of the way before he had his talk with Barney. "Come along and I'll get you settled in."

Alma was glad to be out of the over-heated room and went gladly upstairs. Mrs. Kemp's idea of settling her in was to ask if she'd got everything, and to leave the room before Alma had time to think of anything she wanted.

When Mrs. Kemp got back to the back room, Rivers asked if Alma was all right.

"Nothing the matter with her," Mrs. Kemp replied; "tired, that's all. What's Barney got to say?"

"Yes. Come on, let's have your news." Rivers put down his glass and filled his pipe.

Barney grinned. "News, Mr. Rivers? I don't think I've got much in your line."

"What do you know?" Mr. Rivers's smile disappeared and his eyes hardened.

"There's a house in Sussex, near Petworth. It might be worth a try, but I don't know much about it."

"That's something. Anything else?"

"Lord Sanborne's giving a party in May."

"Too far ahead."

Barney moved uneasily in his chair. He felt like a fly on a scientist's pin, helpless, wriggling. He took a drink of tea.

"You said at the market you'd got something. Come on, out with it."

"It's an idea, that's all."

Mr. Rivers tapped impatiently on his glass.

Barney smiled foolishly and said quickly:

"There's money running about loose, down at a little place called Crowley. Running about waiting to be picked up. I didn't tumble to it at first until a man I was talking to said they was worth a packet. A tenner a piece. Sometimes more."

"Talk sense, Barney," Mrs. Kemp snapped.

Mr. Rivers touched her arm.

"Let him alone. Go on, Barney. Running about, you said." He knew Barney and his way of approaching a subject from an odd angle.

"Foxes," said Barney. "Black foxes with white tips to their tails. There's a bloke of the name of Harding has hundreds of 'em, and makes a good thing out of the skins, so they tell me. A dozen of 'em would be worth having." Mr. Rivers, suspicious of a joke against himself, stared woodenly at Barney. There was silence for a full minute then Mrs. Kemp started to clear the table noisily.

She retreated to the back kitchen with a pile of dishes. Mr. Rivers waited till she had gone and then poured some whisky into a glass and pushed it across the table to Barney. He knew how to manage him.

"Here's how!" Barney drank the neat spirit slowly, tasting every drop.

"Here's to the next job!" Mr. Rivers finished the remains of his drink and sat back in his chair with his thumbs in the arm-holes of his waistcoat.

"Now, let's cut out the funny stuff and get down to it."

"It's right enough what I said," said Barney. "Black fox skins sell easy. When I saw them brutes running about I said to myself: 'It's funny no one ever thought of having a crack at 'em afore.'"

Mr. Rivers was mildly interested.

"Skins are all right, but it's got to be skins. How the hell d'you think we could handle live foxes?"

"Yes, that's right. I see what you mean." Fanny, tired of biscuit crumbs, poked her twitching little nose out of Barney's pocket. He let her crawl on to his hand and put her down on the table. "They're pelting 'em this month."

"Where is this place Crowley?" Mr. Rivers asked.

"Not far out. It's between Snailsham and Guildford. The farm's up at the back of the village on the hills. The land's mostly bracken and pine, and there's not many people living thereabouts."

Barney broke off a crumb of bread and set it down before Fanny who sniffed at it and began to nibble.

Mr. Rivers refilled Barney's glass.

"Drink up."

"Thanks."

"What else do you know?"

"They're sending 'em up in a van on Friday. I know the bloke who drives it. At least Alma does. She told me."

"Alma?"

"That girl who was at supper. She's my sister's kid. I could find out anything from her. That is, if you're interested."

"I'll think it over." Mr. Rivers got up and knocked on the kitchen door.

"I'm going."

Mrs. Kemp came in, drying her hands on a dish cloth.

"Already? Why, I thought you'd be able to stay and have a little chat." Her face was wrinkled in a smile. She held the bottle up to the light. "There's plenty more."

"Another night, Mrs. Kemp."

Mr. Rivers pushed his chair into the table. "That girl," he said; "do you think she could come round in the morning and give my place a clean up? I haven't got any one at the moment."

"I'll speak to her, Mr. Rivers. I'm sure it'll be all right."

"Then I'll say good night. Good night, Joe. Ten o'clock to-morrow. Good night, Barney."

He went out through the kitchen to the back door, which Mrs. Kemp hurried to unlock. She held it open until he reached a gate in the wall at the end of the garden. He turned left-handed down a narrow alleyway between two blank walls to a corner. Then right, along a cobbled street to a yard at the back of his shop.

CHAPTER THREE

MR. RIVERS'S rooms were over his shop and he lived in them, though his income would have run to a modern flat with a re-frigerator and the use of a liveried porter. He had long since decided that such ostentation was to be avoided; he did not wish to draw attention to his visitors. Most of them wore scarves in the place of collars, and would have felt out of place in a brightly lit entrance hall.

The approach to the stairway which led up to the rooms over the shop was through a yard. Packing cases in various stages of disintegration were littered about.

In one corner stood the barrow on which Joe carried part of the contents of the shop to the street markets where Mr. Rivers had a stand.

Mr. Rivers shut the gate behind him and placed three wood-en tea chests in such a position that an intruder would be sure to fall over them. His hearing was good, and boxes kicked across cobble-stones made quite an efficient alarm.

The larger of the two rooms at the top of the narrow stairway was furnished stuffily and had the oppressiveness of a Victorian dining-room which late in life had tried to turn over a new leaf.

A mahogany sideboard, which almost covered one wall, creaked and quivered when any one crossed the room. It creaked to-night when its owner walked over to it to mix himself a whisky-and-soda; an array of china cats and bits of Goss china chattered on the marble mantelpiece beneath a wide, spotted looking-glass. In each corner of the mirror there was painted a pink rose and a cluster of leaves.

So far so Victorian. The other furniture was of a later period. A deep arm-chair was drawn up to the fireside. Rugs covered a floor of oak boards—Persian rugs which lay like silk cloths without a cockle or a curl; and in the centre of the room was a circular walnut table. It was bare of ornament except for a glazed china figure of a boy sitting on a log. His hands were clasped round his bare knees; his head was thrown back and he was laughing, laughing as only a child can laugh, without restraint.

He had come to Mr. Rivers as one item in a haul, and his transfer to the top room had been lamented by his late owner and also by a syndicate of underwriters at Lloyds.

The laughing boy had started life with Mr. Rivers beside a china pig on one end of the mantelpiece. Then gradually he was brought to the centre, and later to the walnut table, which, after him, was the joy of Mr. Rivers's heart, if he had one. The man who sold him the table doubted it, with a fluency which Mr. Rivers ignored.

Mr. Rivers turned on the electric fire with his toe and sat in the arm-chair. His mind was running on what Barney had said about the foxes. At first he had thought Barney had been trying to make a fool of him, but there might be something in it, he decided. Furs of that sort did sometimes fetch a big price. Barney had said they'd be worth a tenner apiece. Ten times a hundred was a thousand. Four hundred pelts was the yearly output of the Crowley farm. Four thousand pounds. The figures excited Mr. Rivers. Four thousand pounds!

He pulled himself to his feet and began to wander about the room. Already his brain was working on the details of the job. Spike could do it, but he'd need some one else to help him. Some one to drive the car. Would it be safe to use his own bus or would it be better to get Spike to knock one off? He'd have to see Spike about that and talk it over.

His eyes focused on a picture before which he was standing. It was a dry-point of the sacking of a great sailing ship. Smoke and flames were pouring upwards from her hold, destroying the sails hanging from the yards. In the foreground an open boat, filled with a villainous crew, was breasting a long swell; pirates returning to their own vessel.

His thoughts returned to the project he had in mind. He must get on to Spike and get him to come along right away. He picked up the receiver of his telephone and dialled a number, heard the calling buzz-buzz and waited impatiently till a voice said: "Who's that?" . . . "Is Spike there?" . . . "I'll see. Hold on."

Mr. Rivers could hear faintly the sound of many voices and then footsteps and Spike's voice.

"That you, Spike? Rivers speaking. Can you come along to my place?"

"It's late."

"I want to speak to you. It's important."

There was a moment's silence, then Spike said: "O.K."

Mr. Rivers put down the receiver slowly, and picked up his glass and drank.

Fifteen minutes later he went down to the yard and moved the boxes away from the gate. There was no one in sight. He stood under the lee of the wall to shelter from the driving rain and cursed himself for not having put on a coat. He had almost made up his mind to go back to the house to get one when he heard a man coming down the street, walking quickly. It was Spike.

"Wait a minute till I fix this." Mr. Rivers unfastened the catch of the gate and took a flash light from his pocket. "Follow me and watch your step."

Spike took off his felt hat and shook the water from it as he walked into Mr. Rivers's room. Then he slipped off his coat and walked over to the fire and stood with his back to it.

"Well?" he said sulkily. "What's up?"

"I've seen Barney."

Spike laughed and there was a sneer in his hard blue eyes. "Barney, eh?"

"He's not so dumb as he looks. I've had one or two good things out of him."

"He's barmy."

Mr. Rivers looked at Spike for a few seconds before he replied. "That's only his way. He talks more sense than a lot of people." He turned to the sideboard, poured out a drink and handed it to Spike, who took it without a word.

"I want you for a hold up."

Spike's fingers tightened on his glass and he drew in sharply on his cigarette. There was silence for a minute and when he spoke there was a hard edge to the word. "Where?"

"In the country."

"That's out of my line."

"Yes, I know." Mr. Rivers lay back in his chair, his eyes fixed on the ceiling. "But it's all the better for that. Safer. In fact, this is the softest job I've known. Lonely spot. All you've got to do is to hold up a van, unload the stuff into your car and beat it back here."

"How far out is it?"

"Twenty, twenty-five miles."

"A hell of a chance I'd have of getting through. Every road'd be watched."

"Not if you work it right. If there's no alarm there'll be no one to stop you. You could tie the bloke up. Run the van off the road. It's all open country there."

"Sounds like a two hundred job, if not three."

"That's what I wanted to talk to you about. Wait a minute." Mr. Rivers was across the room before Spike realized that he'd stopped talking.

The door opened a crack.

Spike put his glass down on the hearth and drew in his legs, ready to move. Mr. Rivers held up a hand and looked out and down into the yard.

Suddenly he shouted: "Who's that?" and Spike heard some one kick a box and swear. Mr. Rivers shut the door and turned his head. "It's Leith. Better get out. Through the front room and the shop. The stairs are on the right." Spike looked round for his hat, found it and ran across the room on his toes. He took care to avoid the bare boards.

Mr. Rivers waited till he heard Spike on the front stairs; then he opened the door and walked boldly on to the landing, over-looking the yard.

"What's the matter, Mr. Leith?"

"I'm coming up."

Mr. Rivers went back into the room. He fluffed up the cushions on the chair by the fire, emptied the ashtray Spike had used and was at the door when Leith walked in.

"Got a visitor?"

"No, Mr. Leith."

"Mind if I squat?" Leith took off his dripping raincoat and looked round for a peg.

"I'll put it in the hall," Mr. Rivers said.

"Thanks. It's a filthy night. All alone?"

Mr. Rivers nodded over his shoulder and Leith took a pipe from his pocket. He frowned at the fire as he filled it; then he rolled up his pouch and looked round the room. "You've got this place fixed up all right," he said. "I like that piece." He took the laughing boy from the table and turned it in his hands. "Looks like something good. What did it sting you?"

"Thirty shillings."

Leith looked at Rivers for a moment.

"Here, you put it back. I might break it. When did you start going in for art?"

Mr. Rivers smiled and moved to the sideboard. "Whisky?"

"Beer if you've got it."

Mr. Rivers stooped and opened a cupboard door. When the glass was full, Leith took it and said: "I saw a bloke along that back street. I fancied he came in here."

"You mean into my yard?"

Leith nodded and wiped his mouth.

"I thought he did. I had a look round but everywhere else is locked up. You ought to do the same."

Mr. Rivers drew up a Windsor chair and sat down. "I'm not frightened of burglars. I've got nothing to lose."

"I saw Barney to-day."

Mr. Rivers shifted his position on his chair and crossed his legs before he answered. "Yes. He was in the market. I saw him myself."

"I wonder what he's up to?"

"What d'you mean?"

"Well, trouble always seems to start when he's around. You wouldn't have noticed it, but—"

Leith stopped talking as though he had said too much. He took a deep draught of beer and sat staring at the fire. When he spoke again it was about football. Mr. Rivers wasn't interested, but was polite and agreed with Leith in everything he said.

At eleven o'clock the detective got up. "Well, I'll have to be moving."

Mr. Rivers made a half-hearted protest as he went to get his coat and hat.

"I'm glad I haven't got your job. 'Specially in this weather."

Leith buttoned up the collar under his chin and put his hands in his pockets.

"I'd put a lock on that gate if I were you," he said.

"Yes, I will. Good night."

Rivers watched Leith until he was out of the yard. Then he locked and bolted the door and called out: "Spike!"

There was no reply. He walked quickly into the passageway, and, looking down the stairs, called again. He could hear the rain driving against the window of the shop. He switched on a light and ran down the stairs. The street door was shut, but not bolted. It was as well that Spike had gone. He shot the bolts and turned the heavy lock. "Wants a drop of oil," he muttered to himself and went up to bed.

Barney, with all his belongings in a handkerchief, left No. 3 Napier Terrace shortly after Mr. Rivers. He said he'd be round in the morning to see Alma. It was something to get her settled, and as he strode along the cinder path he hardly felt the rain nor the wind which drove in his face.

Mrs. Kemp would look after Alma much better than he. He had nothing to bother about now but to find a bed. The handful of coppers in his pocket weighed heavily and jingled as he walked. There was enough there to buy a doss if the Tibbetts weren't back yet. Eightpence for a bed. Fourpence for breakfast.

A cold pin-point touched his fingers and a warm, furry little body wriggled into his hand. It was George. Fanny was more stand-offish. She was curled up in a corner, sleeping off a surfeit of biscuit.

Funny that people, especially women, should shudder at the sight of a mouse. Trusting, affectionate little blighters. So small, so helpless, and they demanded so little.

Barney laughed and chuckled to himself as he strode along, up the rise to the bridge. He was thinking now of Mr. Rivers; of his face when he'd first mentioned the foxes to him. Thought he was being made a fool of and not too sure even now. This was only one of the many good things he'd put in Rivers's way, and what had he got out of it all? A few shillings and a grudging word of thanks. That was Mr. Rivers's way. He took all and gave as little as he dared.

Barney pushed his way through the evening shopping crowd on the lamp-lit pavement. Trams with bells clanging ground their way along. There was movement here. Life! To Barney it meant nothing. He shut it out from his mind.

He swung off left-handed, short of a public house. A man, infinitely sad, was playing a cornet. Barney didn't give him a glance as he plunged down the slope of a dark street. His feet slipped and slithered over the greasy cobbles.

At the end of the street a path ran into blackness between high board fences. Barney did not slacken his stride. He could smell wood-smoke driven back on the wind. Not far now. In the shelter of the fence he raised his head and saw clear cut against the sky the roof of a caravan. He sighed his relief. Tibbett was there. There was no mistaking his crooked chimney. He could tell it anywhere, for he himself had helped to beat it out of biscuit tins.

A dog barked, low pitched and warning. White teeth showed between lips drawn back in a snarl.

"That you, Captain?"

Barney put out a hand. The snarl turned to a welcoming whine. A warm muzzle was thrust into his hand. He talked to the dog.

"Got here all right, you old scoundrel? And how'd you like it? Bit of a change, ain't it?"

Captain jumped up pawing at his coat.

Barney pushed him off. "Easy on. You'll scare Fanny."

A square of yellow light showed against the black bulk of the caravan. Barney struck a match and found the door. The ladder was drawn up and he had to reach up on tiptoe to knock on the panel of the door.

There was a startled movement inside the caravan and a shrill voice asked who was there.

"Open up. It's me."

The upper half of the door swung outwards and Barney could see Mrs. Tibbett.

"Is that Barney?"

"None else and perishing cold."

A bolt shot back. "Coming down. Catch a hold."

Barney caught the ladder as it fell and clambered up.

Mrs. Tibbett pulled up the ladder and shut and bolted the door as Barney came, blinking, into the tiny room.

Mr. Tibbett, with a pair of steel-rimmed spectacles on the end of his nose, looked round a newspaper. With his scrubby beard he had the look of a startled, and slightly cross, brown bear.

"Oh, it's you," he said in a high-pitched voice. "We'll be wanting some more wood for the fire, Maria. Well, where have you been?" Mr. Tibbett lowered his paper, pushed back his glasses and looked at Barney.

"You've still got Captain?"

"Sure, we've got him. Lucky for you he didn't pin you."

Barney grinned as he edged along the seat to make room for Mrs. Tibbett. "He knows me." He felt in his pocket, groped around and produced Fanny. "Don't want anything to happen to her. She's going to have a family."

Mr. Tibbett sniffed his disapproval of Fanny and her family to be.

"Where've you come from to-day?" Mrs. Tibbett asked as she took up her needles and began to knit.

"Working, and fixing Alma up at Kemps'."

Mrs. Tibbett stopped knitting.

"Alma at that place! Why did you take her there?"

"Sal's dead and Alma had nowhere else to go."

Mrs. Tibbett pursed her lips as her needles flashed into action.

"Mrs. Kemp's all right," Barney said defensively.

Mr. Tibbett crumpled his paper and put it to one side.

"When did it happen?"

"Last week." Barney took his day's earnings from his trouser pocket and spread the pennies out on the table.

"There's not enough there to keep two. Alma's got to earn her own living."

"Still—" Mrs. Tibbett continued to show her disapproval of the arrangement.

The pennies clinked as Barney's fingers played among them. "You see, it isn't as if she had any training. She couldn't take a place."

"Mrs. Kemp won't keep her for nothing. She's not that sort."

"Alma can learn what's wanted. She might get a job with Rivers later on."

"Him!"

Mrs. Tibbett's face wrinkled on a frown of disgust.

"She's right," Mr. Tibbett said shortly. "Rivers is no good. You know that, Barney, as well as we do."

Mr. Tibbett reached up to a shelf and took down a short, blackened clay pipe. He filled it slowly, carefully, packing in each stray string of tobacco with a stubby forefinger.

Mrs. Tibbett nodded twice. "Why you have any truck with that man, I don't know, Barney. One of these days he'll leave you flat."

Barney gathered up his pennies and put them back in his pocket.

"I've often thought of it, breaking with him, but it's not so easy. It would mean shifting my beat, and I can't do that. I've been working round these parts too long to try new ground."

Mr. Tibbett put his elbows on the table and puffed fiercely at his clay.

"What's the matter with you, Barney, is, you haven't any guts. You should tell Rivers to get some one else to do his dirty work."

"It's not so easy as all that." Barney sought to change the subject. "D'ye hear anything of Spike Morgan these days?"

"Never heard no good of him. He's broke and came asking for the loan of a dollar. Captain got him, near as a toucher, he did." Mr. Tibbett took his pipe from his mouth, chuckled and choked.

"Captain knows him, don't he?"

"He knows Spike all right. Knows him too blamed well for Spike's liking."

"It was only a week ago he was round," said Mrs. Tibbett. She put down her knitting and turned up the wick of the lamp over the table. "And what Roger says about him is right enough." She sighed. "I know I tried with him hard enough. Mended his clothes and tried to make him save his money, but it weren't no good."

"Where is he now?" Barney asked.

"Southwark," snapped Mr. Tibbett; "and if he don't fetch up in jug afore long, then I don't know nothing."

He relit his pipe and cocked an eye over the match flame at a clock on a shelf. "Time for a game. Hand us them cards down, Maria. The board's behind you, Barney."

Mr. Tibbett shuffled the cards as Barney stuck two matches in the holes of the cribbage board.

"Tuppence on the game?" suggested Mr. Tibbett.

Barney agreed.

"What was you asking about Spike for?" Mrs. Tibbett asked.

Barney didn't answer for a moment. "Spike?" he said when he'd gathered up his hand. "Oh, I dunno."

"You've been hearing something about him," accused Mrs. Tibbett. "What was it?"

"Two for his boots," said Mr. Tibbett.

"King," said Barney, thumbing his first card.

Mrs. Tibbett, who had no respect for the game, repeated her question.

"What was it you heard about Spike Morgan?"

Mr. Tibbett glared at her.

"Mr. Rivers said something about him," Barney replied.

"What did he say?"

"Just that he'd seen him. That was all."

Barney played his second card quickly, as though to avoid further questioning, but Mrs. Tibbett was not to be put off so easily.

"Then what Mrs. Benson told me was right. Spike *is* working for Mr. Rivers." Mrs. Tibbett nodded several times to herself and went on with her knitting.

When the game finished and her husband had pocketed his winnings, she wound up her wool.

"Bed, and time too," she said. She stepped into a curtained-off pantry and took a straw palliasse from a locker.

"There's your bed, Barney. If there's anything you want, you've only to ring." She laughed at her little joke, as she had done a score of times before.

Barney went into the pantry and Mr. Tibbett hung over the half-door finishing his pipe, while his wife made his bed. When it was ready, he took off his coat and slippers and lay down.

"Ready, Maria."

Mrs. Tibbett put out the lamp.

"'Night, Roger."

"'Night, Maria. 'Night, Barney."

Two minutes later the caravan was filled with a rhythmic high-pitched snore. Mr. Tibbett was asleep.

CHAPTER FOUR

NEXT MORNING Mr. Rivers told Joe to take the barrow to the market. He helped him load it.

"You start off on your own. I'll be along about dinnertime." Rivers went back into the shop and put on a collar and dickey. He clipped a tie, which was knotted on a wire frame, into place and buttoned up his waistcoat, took a hat from a peg and let himself out into the street.

Two buses took him to Aldgate. He walked eastward for a hundred yards or so, then turned left up Houndsditch and, at the corner by the Feathers public house, right-handed into a narrow street, crowded with children playing.

He went into a shop where half a dozen women were sewing and chattering and laughing. They were black-haired and dark-skinned. One of them looked up from her work and said in a sing-song voice, "Good morning, Mr. Rivers. Lovely day, is it not?" The others laughed.

Another, older than the rest, turned her head and called out, "Mr. Hy-ams. Mr. Hy-ams. Mr. Rivers is here." A door at the back of the shop opened, and a little man came through it, fussily, bustling. He raised his two hands and smiled broadly, his neat moustache narrowing to a black line across his upper lip.

"Mr. Riverss." He added at least one "s" to Mr. Rivers's name, hissing it through his even white teeth. "Come along. Come along. With me." And he put an arm round Mr. Rivers's shoulders. "And you girls! You get on with your work."

Mr. Rivers went into Izzy Hyams's office. It was a bare, dirty little room, furnished with a wooden desk, a high stool, and two chairs upholstered shindy and hardly with black horsehair. For decoration there were two tradesmen's calendars, and cuttings from fashion papers of impossibly thin women wearing fur coats which fitted them like wet bathing dresses.

Izzy knelt before a safe standing on the floor, opened it, and took out a box of cigarettes.

"It is the boy I have to help me. He steals them," he explained, with a hunching of his shoulders, and a broad white-toothed smile.

Mr. Rivers sat down on one of the horsehair chairs. He lit a cigarette, and talked about business. It was terribly bad, Mr. Hyams said, and the weather was also terrible. As Mr. Hyams saw little of the sky and practically nothing of the sun even when it shone, his interest in the subject soon died. There was a pause. Rivers coughed, and looked at the door.

"There's something I want to talk to you about," he said. "Private."

"That is all right. It is a thick door, and they talk so much they do not have time to listen, even to each other. Women are all like that."

Rivers made no comment on the scathing criticism of women. He wasn't interested in them.

"I may have a parcel of skins coming my way one of these days. Are you in the market?"

Izzy's mouth set in a line, and all expression was wiped from his face. This was business.

"What sort of skins?"

"Fox."

"Red or black?"

"Black."

"You mean real fox?" Izzy leaned forward in his chair, and his eyes grew round. He had dropped the correct business attitude, but almost at once regained it. He leaned back, and laughed, and his eyes closed to slits. He pushed his fingers through his wiry black hair.

Rivers leaned back and crossed his legs. "Yes. Real enough," he said carelessly. "Good stuff, too."

"Where are they?"

"I'll bring 'em along some time."

"Where did they come from?" Izzy showed the caution common to Scot and Jew alike.

Rivers said, "I bought them, but I'm not going to tell you where. You might try to short-circuit me."

"Shorrt circuit?" Izzy's knowledge of the English language was not complete. Russian was his native tongue. German he knew, and French a little.

"It doesn't matter. But what does matter is that I've got something to sell. Do you want to buy?"

"What were you thinking of asking, Mr. Rivers?"

"Twenty-five pounds."

Izzy laughed, genuinely this time. He laughed so that he choked and coughed. "Twenty-five pounds. For how many?"

"One," replied Rivers stolidly.

Izzy wrapped his arms about him and rocked on his chair. He wiped tears from his eyes with a dirty handkerchief.

"But, Mr. Rivers, that is ab-surd. Altogether ab-surd. Fox! Why I can buy them at the sales for fife, six, seven pounds. For a very good one perhaps I would give ten or eleven pounds. Never more."

"These are good stuff."

"Are they English?"

"Yes. Why?"

"Some of them are very poor. Not like the Can-adian fox. You see, the climate makes a lot of difference. In England it is too warm."

Rivers grasped the arms of his chair, and half got up. "If you're not interested, I'll try somewhere else."

"Interested? I am always interested in furs, but the price you name—I confess that does not interest me."

"Well, what will you give?"

"But how can I answer that? I must see them first. Yes, I must see them."

"Well, I'll tell you what. I'll send the lot round here, and we'll talk about the price then, but if we don't come to terms, I'll take 'em away again."

"That will be all right, Mr. Rivers. I'm sure we will agree about the price. You know me, and can trust me."

Rivers certainly knew Izzy, but as to trusting him, that was quite another matter. Still, he had got a place where he could store the skins, and that was something.

The talk reverted to the weather, and soon Mr. Rivers said he must be going. Izzy escorted him through the shop. His presence had a damping effect on the work-girls, who suddenly became silent, and bent their heads to their work.

Rivers sauntered along the pavement. He had fixed up one end of the job, and was easy in his mind as to completing the other arrangements. A pint of beer and a steak and kidney pudding was a fitting and comforting conclusion to the morning's work.

Time enough to-morrow to get busy on the details. Mapping out the route, arranging times, and getting a driver for the car. Better get along and see how Joe was doing. He was a fool, that man. No matter how often he was told he forgot the prices, and there was that lot of brass candlesticks, door-knockers and bowls. They were worth a bit, some of them. The thought that Joe might let them go too cheap upset Mr. Rivers's peace of mind. He forgot the thousands he hoped to net off the fur job in the fear of losing a pound. It was typical of the man, and typical, too, that he travelled by bus when a taxi would have carried him to the market for a shilling or two.

He hurried through the crowd, elbowing and pushing his way to find Joe, an apathetic figure, standing by the barrow. One swift glance told him that his precious brass was safe.

"What d'you think I'm paying you for?"

Joe shook himself out of a day-dream and began to cry his wares. Rivers added his voice. He raked through the litter of oddments, beat on a warming pan with a broken spanner. "Pick where you like. Pick where you like. Everything in the tray tuppence."

He stayed by the barrow until the lunch-hour crowds began to thin, and then, with an exhortation to Joe to carry on, he left him, and walked to Mrs. Kemp's house in Napier Terrace.

"Where's the girl?" he asked, when Mrs. Kemp opened the door.

"Alma? She's out. Gone with Spike."

"When did he come?"

"This morning. I gave him his dinner, and after that he went off with Alma. To the pictures, I think." Mrs. Kemp took out a hairpin and scratched her head. "He didn't waste much time."

"Mind if I come in?"

"Please yourself. The room's not looking too good." Mrs. Kemp had been aroused from a snooze, and wasn't feeling genial. She rolled as she walked down the passage and into the back room. It smelt. Mr. Rivers opened the window and sat with his back to the light.

"When d'you think they'll be back?"

"In time for supper, most likely. What d'you want with Alma?"

"You heard what Barney said last night."

"Barney! I never listen to him. If you ask me, he's cuckoo."

Mrs. Kemp's head was thick with sleep. She yawned and tapped her lower teeth with her fingers. "You'll have to excuse me, Mr. Rivers. We stopped up late after you was gone. Spike came in when we was getting ready for bed." She yawned again, and after a pause said, "He's a good kid. He says you want him to do a job."

"That's what I want to see the girl about."

"What d'you want her for?"

Mr. Rivers didn't answer that question. He had a faculty for affecting deafness when it suited him.

"I didn't want Spike here," he said. "When he's pulled it off I don't mind, but—well, I don't like it. He got in a jam with a girl down in the Borough."

Mrs. Kemp's slack figure stiffened.

"That wasn't Spike's fault. Another bloke tried to ride him off, and—"

"He got fresh with a razor."

"It wasn't Spike's fault," Mrs. Kemp repeated.

Rivers lit a cigarette, and turned in his chair to look out of the window. He knew that Mrs. Kemp was in a quarrelsome mood, and had no wish to offend her. She had been a useful ally to him in the past, and he might need her help again.

Spike had heard of Alma's arrival from Joe, and having some money in his pocket and nothing to do, he went to Napier Terrace.

Mrs. Kemp welcomed him, borrowed half a crown, and suggested that he should come in and have his dinner. Alma was in the back room sewing. Mrs. Kemp opened the door, and said to Spike, "Go on in. I'm going to do a bit of shopping."

"Hallo."

Alma looked up, startled at an unexpected man's voice. "Oh, hullo!" She put her work aside and got up.

"My name's Spike."

"Mine's Alma."

"Shake." Spike grinned at her with obvious interest. "You're Barney's kid, aren't you?"

"He's my uncle. Yes."

"Well, I shouldn't let that worry you." He pushed his felt hat back on his head and perched on the edge of the table.

Alma, put out by this direct advance, blushed and confusedly felt about for her mending. Spike picked up the garment and tossed it out of her reach.

"Doing anything this afternoon?"

"I don't think so."

"What about going to the flicks?"

"I'd have to ask Mrs. Kemp."

"I'll fix her."

"Then I'd like to."

"Fine." Spike, with his eyes on Alma, began to roll a cigarette.

"I don't know how you do that."

"Easy enough, when you know how. Want one?"

Alma shook her head. "I don't smoke."

Spike laughed, and she blushed again. "I'll teach you some time. I'll teach you lots of things. How long are you stopping here?"

"I don't know exactly. It depends."

They talked until Mrs. Kemp returned; she had drunk two shillingsworth of beer, and was jocular. To her, the world looked very much better. Saveloys from a cookshop had been the extent of her shopping, and comprised dinner for the three of them.

When they were finished, Mrs. Kemp, on whom the beer was having its effect, told Alma to wash up, and retired unsteadily and weightily to her room on the first floor.

Alma and Spike carried the dirty dishes to the kitchen, and together, joking and laughing, washed and dried them. Alma was beginning to lose her first fear of Spike, and when he suggested that she should go and get ready, she ran up the stairs with light tread. She hesitated on the landing debating whether to ask Mrs. Kemp's permission. A wheezy snore came from the front room. What did it matter to Mrs. Kemp if she did go? She could leave a note. She crossed to the door of her room, and her hand was on the knob when the snoring ceased abruptly. Bedsprings groaned, and the voice of Mrs. Kemp called out to know what she was after.

"I was going out with—er—Spike. To the pictures."

"All right. Don't be long."

Alma said, "No, I won't," and ran to her glass. She brushed back her wave of shining copper hair, adjusted a side comb, and looked at the effect with her head thrown back. Then she took her hat from a peg and put it on, patting it and adjusting it with unnecessary care. Spike liked her, anyway, but she didn't know that.

He called up the stairs impatiently.

She snatched her coat from the bed and put it on quickly. Her bag. She looked in it and checked its contents. Comb. Powder. Purse. "I'm coming."

One last hurried look in the glass. She ran down the stairs and tripped over the last step. Spike caught her round the waist and almost kissed her.

The path by the canal, the coal heaps, and the towering warehouse opposite did not exist for Alma. With Spike's arm in hers, and the thought of the pictures, she saw nothing but the clear sky and a red, frosty sun. This was fun. She wanted to run and sing. She looked shyly up at Spike. He smiled at her. Silly to be frightened of him. She was going to enjoy herself.

At the bridge Spike stopped and looked up the street. There wasn't a tram or bus in sight.

"We might as well walk. It isn't far."

"I'd like to."

They crossed the bridge, and came to a line of shops. Alma wanted to stop and stare at the windows, but didn't like to suggest it to Spike, who strode along so fast that she almost had to run to keep up with him.

When they left the cinema the rain had started again. Alma buttoned up her coat to her chin.

"Haven't you got a scarf, or anything?" Spike asked, and Alma shook her head. "I'll buy you a fur one of these days, when I get some cash."

"I don't like furs."

"You'll like the one I give you. There's a shop along there that sells nothing else. Come and have a look."

They crossed the road and stopped at a furrier's.

"I've never seen so many in my life," Alma said, and shyly touched a tie made up of many rabbit skins.

"That is coney." The shopman hooked it down and laid it on the counter. "Only thirty-seven-and-six."

Spike felt the few shillings he had in his pocket, and said:

"Yes, it's nice, but we were looking for something classier than that."

They spent an interesting half-hour in the shop, during which time the shopman's hopes soared, and finally crashed.

"There're lovely," Alma said, while they stood waiting for a bus. "But I never knew the good ones cost so much."

"When's your birthday?"

"June. But, Spike, I couldn't let you give me anything like that."

"Like hell you won't," Spike muttered under his breath. And then, aloud, "Come on, there's our bus."

They got off at the bridge and found Mrs. Kemp waiting at the doorway. She grinned at Spike. "Mr. Rivers is here. He's waiting for you in the back room." She caught Alma by the shoulder. "You'd better go up to your room and stop there till I calls you."

Alma nodded. She pressed Spike's arm, and said softly, "Thanks awfully. I loved it."

Mrs. Kemp saw the exchange and recognized the symptoms. She gave a wheezy sigh. That would make the fourteenth girl Spike had had since he'd been back. But what was the good of talking to him? If he didn't spend his money that way he'd soon find another.

Mr. Rivers was dozing in front of the fire when Spike went into the back room, but he was awake before Spike had time to shut the door behind him.

"I've been waiting for you."

Spike took off his coat and threw it over a chair. Then he lit a cigarette and came over to the fire.

"I've been out with that new girl. To the pictures."

"Don't you think it would be a good idea if you gave her a miss for the next day or two?"

"What! And sit around all day doing nothing?"

"We've got to get busy. On Friday morning there's a van coming up to Town from a place called Crowley. It'll have a load of furs on board. It's up to you to knock it off."

"Friday morning? A daylight job?"

Rivers nodded. "Yes. But that won't make any difference, if what Barney said is right."

"Let's hear all about it."

"This place where the stuff's coming from is in a lonely part of the country. Single-track road up to the farm, which doesn't lead anywhere else."

"And I've got to get back to Town. How far is it?"

"Twenty-five to thirty miles."

Spike laughed, and with his thumbs in the armholes of his waistcoat he walked across to the window. He had his back to Rivers when he said:

"I'm not having any."

Mr. Rivers half-turned in his chair.

"What's biting you? I thought you wanted a job. You'll get a fair cut."

Spike came back to the fire and sat on a corner of the table. "Now, look here, Mr. Rivers, I'm not scared of any joy, in reason, but what chance'd I have of a clean getaway over thirty miles? The local dicks'd call up the Yard. You know the rest."

"The locals wouldn't know."

"That'd be fine," Spike said. "How are you going to fix that?"

"It's all common land in those parts. No fences. You can run the van off the road fifty yards or so, and hide it."

"What about the bloke in it?"

"Tie him up."

"And if any one comes along, I suppose we tell 'em that we've done it for a film?"

"I told you there'll be no one about. Anyway, you can have some one on the look-out if you're windy."

"Windy be damned. I've got some sense, that's all."

"Who are we going to get to drive the car?"

"Len," Spike said. He didn't realize at first that Rivers had switched him on to a new line. "But, wait a minute. I haven't said I'm going to do it."

"That's all right. No need to make up your mind now. We'll take a run down to the place to-morrow." Rivers got up and opened the cupboard where the whisky bottle lived. He poured a double tot into two glasses. "There's no water. D'you mind?"

Spike took one of the glasses. "I like it this way."

"I don't think I know Len."

"He's O.K. A wiz with a car. He beat the dicks to it a month back at Tottenham."

Mr. Rivers showed interest. "Oh, he was in that, was he? I heard about it."

"Damn' near got squeezed between a tram and a lamp stand-ard, but he got out of it. Across the pavement. Killed a kid. That was all."

"Killed?"

"Yeah. After that he took every chance, and got clear. A bloke what was with him told me he couldn't go in a car for a month after. It shook him to hell, that drive. Len was out again that night. He's O.K. I'd go with him anywhere."

"Where does he hang out?"

"I can find him."

"What about ten o'clock to-morrow? I'll take my car to Barnes Bridge and meet you there."

"He'll want a sweetener."

Rivers took out a greasy wallet and produced a pound note.

"I'm a bit short myself," Spike hinted.

Rivers handed over two pounds and finished his drink. "We'll fix up the figure to-morrow night, when we've worked it out."

"If it will work."

"Don't worry about that. So long." Rivers picked up his hat and went out into the passage. He stopped at the foot of the stairs and called up, "Mrs. Kemp!"

She came lumbering down, making every tread creak as her weight shifted from foot to foot.

"All right, Mr. Rivers?"

He said, "Yes," curtly, and went on: "You know what the girl said to Barney about her young man coming up to Town?"

"Yes. She told me, too. But she's not that keen on him, as far as I can make out."

"Tell her to write a letter and arrange to meet him some-where. Not here."

"But if she won't do it?"

"You've got to make her. Get the letter off to-night, or to-mor-row at the latest. See there's no address on it, and get Joe to post it a mile away from here."

"All right, Mr. Rivers. I think I'll be able to manage her."

Mr. Rivers took two steps towards the front door and then stopped. "Keep Spike off her. I want him for a job, and you know what he is with a skirt."

Mrs. Kemp chuckled. "I'll do what I can, but he's obstinate."

"There's a packet of money in it."

Mrs. Kemp followed Rivers to the door and opened it. "Spike won't let you down," she said, and waited until Rivers had reached the canal path before she shut the door and shot the bolts. Then she shuffled along the passage to the back room.

Spike was sitting in a basket chair with his feet on the mantelpiece. He turned his head as she came in, and held out a hand. She took it in her pudgy palms.

"It's good to see you again," she said, "and I'm glad you're fixed up with Mr. Rivers."

"What was he saying out there?"

"Oh, nothing much." Mrs. Kemp dropped Spike's hand and made a pretence at tidying up the room. She swept some ash off the table, and pulled the cloth straight.

"What was it?"

"He said he was glad he'd got you to do this job for him."

"He hasn't. At least, not yet. I haven't made up my mind."

"You'll be a fool if you don't."

"Did he tell you about it?"

"No."

"Then what's the sense in saying I should take it on? It sounded crazy to me."

"You haven't turned it down?"

"Not yet. We're going down to the country to-morrow to have a look round."

"What d'you want for supper?"

"What've you got?"

"Eggs. You like 'em fried, don't you?"

"That'll do." Spike leaned back, and refilled his glass. "I don't know that I want much to eat."

"You go easy on the booze, son. Wait a minute while I get some water."

Spike grumbled a protest, but Mrs. Kemp took his glass away and filled it up at the tap in the kitchen. "This is no time to go on the jazz."

"Where's Alma?"

"Upstairs. I'll call her when I'm ready. I want a word with you first."

Spike groaned.

"It's about Alma. She's different from the rest."

"I know that. I took her to the flicks—"

"She's not our sort."

"She's a good-looker."

"I want you to let her alone."

Spike stuck out his under-lip in an obstinate line. "That's my business. I can look after myself."

"I was thinking of the girl."

"You've gone pi all of a sudden."

"No, it's not that exactly—oh, never mind." Mrs. Kemp opened the door, and called: "Alma! Supper!" She gave Spike a look, sighed, and went into the kitchen to prepare the supper.

CHAPTER FIVE

SPIKE SLEPT at Napier Terrace that night, and left early next morning to call on Len.

A woman with her head tied up in a duster was taking in the milk when Spike stopped and asked, "Is this number seven?"

"Who d'you want?" The woman retreated into the doorway.

"Len. He lives here, doesn't he?"

"What d'you want with him?"

Spike grinned. "It's all right. I'm a pal of Len's."

"He's asleep, I expect."

"Tell him I'm here. I've got to see him."

The woman looked at Spike suspiciously. "All right, I'll tell him. What's the name?"

"Morgan," Spike said, and was about to enter the house when the door was slammed in his face. The letter flap opened.

"You wait out there."

"Don't seem much choice," Spike said to himself, and leaned against the door jamb. He listened to footsteps ascending the stairs. A minute or two later a window opened over his head, and he stepped into the roadway and called: "It's all right, Len. It's only me."

A sleepy voice grumbled something about being down in a minute. Spike lit a cigarette and took a walk up to the corner of the street, and when he got back to the house he found Len standing by the front door.

Len Harmon had crowded more crime into the twenty-two years of his life than most of his kind, and it had bred in him a curious mixture of wariness and bravado. There were times when he was frightened to walk in the streets, and for days at a time he would lie up in his room reading magazines and smoking cigarettes.

But when the mood took him he seemed to delight in making himself conspicuous. He wasn't scared of any blooming copper. They couldn't touch him. They hadn't up to date, for Len was lucky and never lost his head when in a jam.

Leith knew Len, and could spot him a mile off by the long, light, yellow teddy-bear coat he always wore, his purple felt hat and floppy cinnamon trousers. Len liked bright colours.

"This is a damn' fine time of the morning to knock a bloke up," Len grumbled.

"I've got a job on."

"Come inside." Len backed into the narrow hall and opened the door of the front sitting-room. Spike followed him.

"You know Rivers, don't you?"

"I've heard of him."

"He wants me to do a stick-up for him." Spike gave Len the details. "What about it?"

"What's he paying?"

"I haven't fixed that yet. We're going to have a look over the ground, and if it looks O.K. we can talk about the money then."

"There's no harm in having a snoot round. When are you starting?"

"I'm meeting Rivers at Barnes Bridge at ten."

"Time to have some breakfast first. I know a place we can go."

Mr. Rivers spent an hour after breakfast tinkering about his car. He dipped the oil and petrol tanks, then he started the engine and put a rug over the radiator. When it was warm he switched off and cleaned the windscreen. There wasn't anything else to do except to find a map.

He looked at his watch. Nearly time to start. Joe was loading up the barrow.

"Anything I can do, guv'nor?"

"Did you see Barney?"

"Yes. I gave him your message. He says he'll wait for you by the bridge."

Mr. Rivers got into the driving seat. "Come back at dinner-time and open up the shop."

"When'll you be home?"

"I don't know. I may be late. Lock up at seven."

Mr. Rivers drove out of the yard into the narrow street, turned first right and then left, into the busy street which led south over the canal bridge. He picked up Barney, and went on. There was little traffic and, though he drove slowly, he arrived at Barnes Bridge ten minutes ahead of time.

Spike was waiting there.

"'Morning, Mr. Rivers. Meet Len."

Rivers slid along the seat and got out of the car. "Pleased to meet you. Care to drive?"

"I don't mind." Len got into the driving seat.

"You sit in front," Rivers said to Barney. "I want to talk to Spike."

"Where're we going?" Len asked, out of the side of his mouth.

"Snailsham. Do you know the way?"

"Turn off at the Ace of Spades?"

"Yes, that's right."

Len let in the clutch and before they had gone half a mile Mr. Rivers realized that, compared to Len, he was a shocking bad driver. The car took the rise of Roehampton Lane as though it were a down grade.

"He can drive," Rivers whispered to Spike, who grinned and said, "I told you he was a whiz, didn't I?"

They made good time along the by-pass, and south along the Chessington Road to Leatherhead. Barney talked incessantly to Len, who paid little attention to him. He didn't speak unless it was to ask for a light for his cigarette. It hung damply from a corner of his mouth.

They drove round the back of Snailsham, where new houses were being built, and on to the Guildford Road. Barney, who had walked every yard of the way at one time or another, was full of information—mostly about public houses.

The country changed when Len turned southward over the Tillingbourne. The road narrowed until it ran between high banks, topped with rank growing hedges.

Barney wanted to stop at Crowley village for a drink.

"We don't want to be noticed," Rivers said, leaning forward and gripping the back of the front seats. "Which is the road to the farm?"

"Keep right at the next fork," Barney replied sulkily.

Len slipped into third gear and raced at a steep rise, through a fir plantation into country of heather, stunted oaks and birches.

"How far?" Len asked.

"You'll come to a gravel pit soon."

The road was so narrow that fronds of dead bracken brushed either wing.

"There it is!" Barney pointed ahead to a cutting leading off the road.

Len swung the car down a rutty track and drew up as soon as they were out of sight of the road. They all got out.

"Well, what d'you think of it? Might have been made for the job," Barney said.

"It's not so bad," Rivers replied, and felt for his cigarette-case.

Spike walked back along the track they had followed. Len went with him.

"It doesn't seem to have been used lately," Spike said. "That's something."

"Would be all right if we could do it when it's dark," Len replied. Night was his friend, daylight his enemy. Rivers heard the words.

"What the hell are you grousing about? All you've got to do is to hold up the van on the road. That'll be easy enough. Then run it in here, put the stuff in the car and beat it back home."

"Yes, but if some one finds the van before we get clear?" Spike objected.

"Who's going to come looking for it in this pit?"

"Let's have a look round on top." Spike ran at the bank and clambered to the top. Len followed. Mr. Rivers walked to a place where it wasn't so steep, and joined them.

Spike walked on to the top of a small hill and looked around. He could trace the road cutting as it wound on up hill and disappeared in a belt of pines. Southward the land fell away, and in the far distance he could make out the line of the South Downs. He turned to Barney. "Where's this fox farm?"

"A mile on. You can't see it from here."

"Not a soul in sight," Rivers said. "I said it was a soft job, didn't I?"

"What d'you think, Len?" Spike asked.

"Seems O.K. It might work."

Mr. Rivers watched Len and Spike go off, and then, with Barney's assistance, he slid down the bank into the gravel pit.

"Best thing you've put me on to, Barney. If it comes off it'll mean a fiver for you."

Barney grinned and felt in his pocket for his mice, which he had left at home. Then he sat on the step of the car and took out a packet of cigarettes.

"I'm glad you've got Len in on the job," he said, as he struck a match and cupped it in his hands. "He's better than Spike."

"Spike's all right. He's got brains."

"Yes, I dare say, and he's got a nerve, too, but there's times he flies off the handle, and then there's trouble. That's why he got the chuck from that Borough mob."

Rivers asked why.

"Razor," said Barney. "He always carries one, and he used it on the wrong man. They've got it in for him. If it hadn't been for that he wouldn't have thought of working this job."

"What about Len?"

"He's all right in a car. That's the only sort of a job he does." Barney pulled at his cigarette and blew out a great cloud of smoke. It rose slowly in the still air. "Looks as if the weather's set, and time, too."

Rivers got up. "I wonder where the devil they've got to."

"Don't you worry. That's Spike's way. He walks round every job trying to find the soft spots. If he doesn't find any, you'll be all right. He'll carry it through, if any one can."

Rivers opened the door of the car, looked at the clock, and compared it with his watch.

"He can drive all right."

"Who?"

"Len."

"I reckon he was foaled in a car." Barney chuckled to himself. "Started life with a sparking plug in his mouth. It wasn't a silver spoon, anyway. Ever met his dad?"

"No."

"He's a caution. Sixty-five, and crooked as a corkscrew. Crookeder."

Rivers heard voices above him and looked up. Spike called out, "Barney! Come up here a minute."

Barney scrambled up the bank.

"What d'you want?"

"We'll want some one to keep a look out when we pull this job."

"I get you."

Spike pointed to a solitary pine.

"That's where I'll want you to stand. You can see the road both ways."

Barney nodded and then looked frightened. "I'd sooner keep out of this. All I said was that I'd show the place." Spike didn't say anything. He walked to the edge of the pit. "Mr. Rivers!"

"Hullo!"

"We'll want Barney to give us a hand. Is that all right?"

"What d'you want him for?"

"Keep a look out."

"We'll talk about that later."

"O.K. Come on, Len."

Spike slid down the bank and got into the car. Barney made for the back with Rivers. Spike sat in front.

Len pushed the starter button and raced the engine. When it fired evenly he let it idle, and pulled a map from a cubby hole in the dash.

Spike put his hand round the back of Len's seat and leaned across.

"You know the way back, don't you? Right in the village, and then—"

"Look here," Len interrupted. His forefinger traced a C-class road which ran at right-angles to the Snailsham-Guildford line. "We've got to look out for this farm. Five miles from here, about. Then straight on across the crossroads, up the hill, over the railway."

Len studied the route for a minute, folded up the map, and gave it to Spike. "I think I've got it. All right, Mr. Rivers?"

"Yes. There's nothing else to do here."

Len drove back northward down the hill to Crowley, and on to the Cross Ways farm. The road over the North Downs was little more than a cart track, rutted and scored with the flood waters of many years.

The car lurched and swayed until it topped the summit and ran down to the tarred road on the north side. Down past bungalows and melancholy chicken farms to the Leatherhead Road. Len cut across it and drove on northwards till he came to the Portsmouth Road.

Mr. Rivers lit a cigarette. "Well, thank God that's finished with." Barney, thinking of what he would be expected to do later, didn't answer. He was unusually thoughtful.

At Putney Bridge Spike asked Rivers where the stuff was to be delivered when they got it.

Rivers gave the address of Izzy Hyam's shop.

"We'll run along there now and time it." Spike looked at the clock on the dashboard. "The embankment's the quickest way, isn't it?" he said to Len, who replied, "Yes, I suppose so."

When they got to Aldgate, Rivers directed Len to Hyams's shop. He didn't stop. "All right. I've got it." Len drove on for a few streets and then stopped the car and got out. "I think I've got it straight. What day?"

"Friday." Rivers stumbled over Barney's feet on to the pavement. "You'll have to start early. Eight o'clock."

"O.K. I'll see Spike before then, and fix where to meet. So long." He turned away abruptly and ran for a bus.

Rivers drove the car back to the shop. He told Barney to come round in the morning, and waited until he had gone before addressing Spike.

"Well, that seems all straight."

"You haven't said what you're paying. Len wants a half cut."

"Come inside." The shutters of the shop were up. "Joe ought to have opened up before now." Rivers went to the front and unlocked the street door, letting in a shaft of light. "He's lazy, and he's dumb."

Spike sat down on a broken-backed chair. "What did Leith want? Did you have any trouble with him?"

Rivers looked round. "Leith? Oh, you mean the other night?"

"Yes." Spike pushed his hat back on his head.

"He saw you come in here."

"Did he know who I was?"

"I don't know. I don't think so." Rivers lifted down a shutter and stood it against the wall. Then he dusted his hands and came over to Spike. "He's always hanging round."

Spike laughed. "He wouldn't know me, anyway. I've never worked up this way—at least, not for a time."

"He's nosey as hell."

"A fiver'll fix him."

"I'm not so sure about that."

"Have you tried it?"

"No."

"He'll take it, all right. Rozzers are all the same."

"Maybe. What've you been doing with that girl?"

"Alma?" Spike grinned stupidly. "Where did the old woman pick her up? She's all right."

"You want to give her a miss."

"She's from the country, isn't she?"

"Yes, but—"

"I thought so. When I finish this job, I'm going to give her a run."

"Where are you staying?"

"At Mrs. Kemp's. It'll be handy." Spike dropped his cigarette on the floor and trod on it. "What's coming to me out of this job?"

Rivers looked down his nose and didn't reply for a minute. He got up and rearranged some ornaments on a shelf. "It's not going to mean a lot to me," he lied. "Izzy's as sticky as hell."

"Go on." Spike's eyes hardened.

"A corner to you. Same to Len."

"I'll want more. A third each."

Rivers laughed. "You've got a hope."

"Then you can count me out."

"You're a damn' fool."

"That's my business."

"If I liked to go down the New Cut to-morrow, I would get a dozen who'd do the job for my figure."

"Try it. You haven't all that time to play with. Len won't come in for less than a three-corner cut."

"All right."

Spike gave a satisfied chuck of his head and rolled off the doorpost he was leaning against. "See you to-night. That is if I'm not out with Alma."

Rivers didn't answer the challenge.

Mrs. Kemp's ambitions as a housekeeper were not high. She didn't mind a bit of dirt. In fact she had no objection to quite a lot of dirt, even in the frying pan in which she cooked a meal.

Alma had other views, and, on the day of Mr. Rivers's expedition to Crowley, she decided to turn out the back room and give the floor a good scrub.

"It's all right as it is," Mrs. Kemp said comfortably but firmly.

Alma pulled the table to one side and knelt before a settee which stood against one wall. "Look at all this." She pulled out a handful of litter. There were dish mops, cloths, too dirty even for Mrs. Kemp's use, torn aprons that she was going to mend one of these days, and papers, weeks and months old.

"Now easy on, Alma." Mrs. Kemp poured out a cup of coal-black tea from a pot which had been stewing on the hob. "There's things there I want to keep and them papers'll come in for lighting the fire."

"I'd like to make a fire of the lot. It's a chance to get things straight now Mr. Morgan's out. He said he'd be back to-night."

"Mister who?" A generous smile spread over Mrs. Kemp's face as she stayed her cup in mid-air.

"You know. Him I went out with yesterday."

"You mean Spike." Mrs. Kemp's smile broadened. She put down her cup in order to enjoy the joke. A laugh was born somewhere behind the overall. A good, hearty, deep-throated laugh. It came bubbling up, shaking Mrs. Kemp to her ample foundations.

Alma blushed. She pushed back the heap of papers and ran into the back kitchen.

"Is there any Vim? I'm going to clean up the sink."

"You come back here," Mrs. Kemp coughed out between the spasms of mirth. "And bring a cup with you and have some tea. I didn't mean to make you cross."

Alma stood still for a moment, undecided what to do. Then she picked up a cup and went back into the room.

"Sit down." The laugh was dying. Mrs. Kemp struggled for breath, drumming on her chest with a closed fist. "Fill up your cup. That's right, deary. You talking about Spike put me in mind of something I has to say." She dropped a third lump of sugar into her tea and began to break it down with her spoon. She didn't look at Alma when she said: "You know about Will Dorset coming up on Friday?"

"Yes."

"Well, how would it be if you was to ask him here for supper?"

"I wasn't going to bother about him."

"But you promised you'd write him a line and go out together, didn't you?"

"Yes, I did. But—"

"You've got Spike in your mind. I wouldn't bother about him if I was you. How long is it you've been walking out with Will Dorset?"

"Seven years nearly."

"He sounds a steady one."

"But he's so slow."

"It's the slow sort that make the best husbands," said Mrs. Kemp.

"Oh, I don't know." Alma got up and stood leaning against the mantelpiece, staring at a coloured calendar.

Mrs. Kemp went to a cupboard and brought out a sheet of cheap writing-paper, a penny bottle of ink and a pen. "The ink's dried up; I'll put some water in it." She came back from the kitchen a minute later. "That's all right now. Sit down and write him a line. You don't want to say much."

"Oh, all right. If you think I should." Alma took the pen and wrote the address: "3 Napier Terrace."

"What's the rest of it?"

"North West one."

"Where shall I say we'll meet?"

"Now let me think." Mrs. Kemp's knowledge of London was limited to a half-mile radius from the canal bridge. She looked at the clock for inspiration. The maker's name was written across the face. "J. Bulloch," and underneath "Hornsey Rise."

"Why not the Hornsey Rise Tube Station?"

"He wouldn't know how to get there," Alma objected. "Anybody'd tell him. You put that down."

Alma finished the letter and signed her name. Mrs. Kemp produced an envelope and leaned over her as she addressed it. "That's all right." She folded the letter and put it in the envelope. "I've got a stamp upstairs." On her way upstairs Mrs. Kemp took the letter out of the envelope and tore off the address, and when Joe came home that evening she sent him out to post it.

CHAPTER SIX

SPIKE SPENT most of Thursday looking for Len. He wasn't at his lodgings and his landlady didn't know when he'd be back.

"Gone on the booze, I'd say," she announced.

"Where d'you think he'll be?" Spike asked.

The landlady had no ideas to offer and Spike started on a round of the clubs of Soho. It was six o'clock before he found Len leaning on a bar with his hat on the back of his head. He was wearing his long yellow overcoat. He nodded to Spike and gave him a drink.

"Where you been?"

"Looking for you." Spike was cross. Len patted his shoulder. "Well, all's well that ends well."

"We've got to do this job to-morrow."

"Got to?"

"I've told Rivers we'd do it."

"What's he offering?"

"Two hundred apiece but it may come to more. It depends on what he gets for the stuff."

"Who's buying it?"

"Izzy Hyams."

"Damn' dago. Got to use a pick to get money out of him."

"You won't have a lot to do. Drive the car, that's all. I'll do the sticking up."

"What about that funny-looking gink who was with us yesterday? We'll want him."

"Leave that to me."

"You'll have to get Rivers to double that two hundred."

"I'll see if I can work him up a bit."

Len wanted to go on drinking, but Spike got him into a taxi and took him to his room and put him to bed.

"Now you stop there till I fetch you in the morning. Don't forget you've got to drive a car to-morrow."

Len picked a magazine off the floor and flipped over the pages. "Leave us some 'bines, will you? I'm nearly out of them."

Spike emptied his case on to the table by the bed and then turned to the door. "Night-night."

Spike slept at Mrs. Kemp's that night, and early next morning he was up and dressed. He couldn't sleep. He had done a dozen jobs, most of them more risky than this one, and every time he had gone through the same period of sheer panic. Once he was started it would be different.

It was still quite dark as he dressed and crept down the stairs to the first-floor landing. A board creaked.

"Who's that?" It was Mrs. Kemp speaking.

"It's all right. It's only me."

He heard a match struck and then Mrs. Kemp said complainingly:

"Do you know what time it is? Only just gone six. When do you start?"

"A quarter to eight."

The springs of Mrs. Kemp's bed creaked loudly as she turned over. "You can light the fire if you like."

Spike went on down the stairs into the back room. It was icy cold and smelt of stale smoke. He raked out the dead ashes and then went in search of kindling. There were sticks in a bucket in the kitchen, but no paper.

Spike came back into the room and saw some of the rubbish Alma had pulled out from under the settee. He turned it over and selected a newspaper. There were some magazines. He picked up one and turned over the pages. It was American and filled with photographs of unpleasant men handcuffed to other unpleasant men. The cover was torn half-across and Spike pulled it off.

He put the magazine on the table, laid the fire and lit it. It burned sulkily and it was some time before the coals caught and there was enough heat to boil a kettle.

When Alma came down she found Spike sitting with his feet on the fender reading the magazine.

"Oh, you did give me a start. I didn't know there was any one here."

Spike grinned. "Only me, doing the good fairy act." He folded the magazine and put it in an inside pocket. It would do later on to pass the time if he had to wait.

Alma smoothed the tablecloth and put the chairs straight. "Do you always get up early?"

"Sometimes."

"Because if you do, I won't. I hate getting up before it's properly light."

Mrs. Kemp came creaking along the passage. She looked at Alma and Spike, yawned and went into the kitchen. "How many eggs for you, Spike?" she called out.

"I'm not hungry. I'll just have some toast."

"You'll have eggs. Two," Mrs. Kemp replied. "You like 'em soft, don't you?"

"Yes. Three minutes."

"You've got to do what you're told in this house," Spike whispered to Alma, who nodded. She knew that already. "Come and get the plates and things."

Spike was still standing by the fire-place when Alma came back. She looked up at him shyly. "What's the matter? You're looking funny."

"I'm O.K."

"I wouldn't get up so early to-morrow if I was you."

"I don't mean to. I'm going to lie in bed and read the paper. Will you bring me my breakfast up?"

"I don't mind, but what about her?"

"She won't make any trouble. I'm her favourite child."

"Since when?"

"Quite a long time."

Alma had set out the plates and was turning to go to the kitchen when Spike caught her by the arm.

"Just a minute. I want to ask you something." He kicked the door shut. "You used to live at a place called Crowley, didn't you?"

"Yes. Why?"

"I'm going down there some time to look up a pal."

"Oh, who's that? I know every one in the village."

"You wouldn't know him. He hasn't been there long. You know that road that goes up the hill from the Green?"

"Of course. I lived there for years. What about it?"

"Where does it go to?"

"Only to a farm. There's a friend of mine works there."

"What's he like?"

Alma laughed. "He's not like you, anyway. He's shorter a bit, but awfully strong."

"Does any one else use that road?"

"You mean to the farm?"

Spike nodded.

"No, it stops there, but there's a path goes on down to Ewhurst."

A sharp kick from Mrs. Kemp sent the door swinging open. "Breakfast ready." She glanced at the table. "And you haven't got the knives or anything, Alma. Get a move on." She put down the plates she was carrying and walked out into the passage.

Spike heard her shout up the stairs. "Joe! Come on, you lazy blighter. Breakfast!"

Before she returned he said to Alma: "Wish me luck." She said: "Why?" without looking up from laying the table.

"Oh, nothing, but I want a bit of luck."

"What is the matter with you?"

Spike ignored the question. "Which is my egg?"

Alma picked one off the plate. "Here's one with a cross on it. Is that it?"

"I expect so." Spike put it in an egg-cup and cracked the top. He was going to speak to Alma again when Mrs. Kemp came in.

She looked at the clock. "What time are you off?"

"In half an hour."

She sat down in front of the fire.

"Aren't you going to have something?" Alma asked.

"Not now. I may later." Mrs. Kemp sighed deeply and stared at the coals.

"Come on and tuck in. Don't bother about her," Spike whispered. "She gets like that sometimes."

Joe came in a few minutes later, bleary eyed, yawning, with his thin hair streaked across his forehead. He looked at the eggs sourly. "Damn' fine breakfast. What about a rasher of bacon?"

Mrs. Kemp looked at him, but did not speak. He subsided on a chair grumbling under his breath.

Spike pushed his plate away.

"I'm through."

Mrs. Kemp turned her head. "Oh, no, you're not. Two eggs, I said. And fill up his cup, Alma."

When he had finished his second egg, Spike took out a cigarette. "Well, it's about time I was beating it." He struck a match and got up.

Mrs. Kemp heaved herself to her feet.

"I hope it goes all right." The anxiety in her tone made Alma look up, surprised. "You'll be careful of yourself, won't you?"

Spike grinned through a cloud of smoke. "I'll be all right. I haven't struck a dud yet."

Mrs. Kemp sighed windily and patted his shoulder. "You're taking his car, aren't you?"

"Yes." Spike took his cigarette from his mouth and bent over and kissed Mrs. Kemp on the cheek. "Well, so long, be good." He went out through the kitchen. Mrs. Kemp watched him walk up the path to the gate in the wall, then she went back into the room.

"You'd better go, too. Mr. Rivers wants you to mind the shop for him to-day," she said to Alma.

"What about the washing up?"

"I'll manage that. You run along."

Mr. Rivers was waiting for Spike in the yard. "Are you all set?"

Spike nodded.

"Got everything?"

Spike grinned and patted his hip pocket. "How's the bus? All filled up?"

"Yes, and running fine."

Spike opened the off-side door and slid into the driving seat. He started the engine and revved her up. "Seems O.K."

Rivers shut the door and said: "You better have a quid in case of accidents."

Spike took the note.

"How d'you feel?" Rivers asked.

"Fine. Have you seen anything of Leith?"

"Not since the night you were here. You don't want to worry about him."

"I'm not worrying. He's a goof."

"I'm not so sure of that."

"Well, I'll be moving. I'm picking Barney up at the other side of bridge. He ought to be there by now."

Alma saw Spike drive out of the yard. She waved to him but he did not see her.

Barney, like Spike, was up early. He crept through the tiny room where Mr. and Mrs. Tibbett were sleeping noisily, opened the door and let down the steps.

Captain came out from under the caravan grinning. "Eh, but you're a lucky old devil. If you get your chow you don't mind what happens." Barney followed a track which led from the settlement to the canal bank. There was not much light, but enough to enable him to find what he was looking for, a few bits of wood.

He took them back to the caravan and split a supply of kindling with a chopper which was hanging on a nail inside the door. That was Barney's job when he stayed with the Tibbetts.

"And now, Captain, what about a house for Fanny?" Captain wasn't interested. "I've got to fix her up. She's going to have a family, and if she ain't got a proper place to live in, God knows what'll happen to all the little Fannies and Georges."

Barney took a knife from his pocket and started to work away at a piece of box wood, and all the time his mind was running on the job. In a couple of hours' time he'd be on the road. He'd give a lot to be out of it. Spike was a dangerous man to be mixed up with. Not that he'd let you down, but you never knew what chances he'd take.

Barney's acquaintance with crime had been small. He had played safe so far, but now he was in for it. He was scared of assisting Spike, but he was more frightened of Rivers; he couldn't have said why exactly.

He put down the wood and crept up the steps of the caravan to look at the clock ticking away on a shelf over the stove. Seven o'clock, and he hadn't got Fanny's house finished.

Mr. Tibbett rolled over on his back and opened one eye. "What the hell are you after?"

"Nails. Got any?"

"Have a look in that drawer." Mr. Tibbett pointed to the end of his bunk. "Well, now I'm awake I suppose I might as well get up." He folded the blankets and laid them in a pile.

"What d'you want nails for?"

"Fanny. I'm making her a house. She's going to have a family."

Mr. Tibbett said something about that blooming mouse and reached for his coat. In doing so he knocked over a stool. Mrs. Tibbett sat up.

"Barney! Get out! The idea!"

Barney retreated down the steps with the drawer of nails and oddments. Mrs. Tibbett slammed the door behind him.

"You shut out too?" Captain seemed to say. Barney rubbed his ears. Captain sat back on his haunches and stretched his head and throat. Then he yawned and suddenly began to scratch.

Barney had finished Fanny's house when Mrs. Tibbett called out that breakfast was ready. She had shed her curl papers and was in a better temper.

"Weren't you comfortable?" she asked Barney.

"Yes, I was all right." He told her about Fanny. "I've got to be out all day and I don't want nothing to happen to her afore I get back."

"Where you going?"

"Down the Cut."

Mrs. Tibbett gave him a shrewd glance as she poured out the tea. "There's something on your mind. What is it?"

"No, there ain't," Barney replied almost fiercely.

Mrs. Tibbett did not press the question, but when Barney had gone she said to her husband that Barney was acting queer.

"No different to his usual. He's never been quite right ever since I've known him."

"Well, anyway, you see if I'm not correct. He'll be telling us about it later on, for if there's one thing Barney can't do, it is to keep anything under his hat for long."

Mr. Tibbett drew at his pipe. "You let him alone."

"I'm going along to see Mrs. Benson when I've cleared up."

"What for?"

"You heard what Barney said about Spike last night. I mean to find if it's true that he's working for Mr. Rivers."

"You want to keep out of that crowd. There's that Mrs. Kemp and her blackguard of a husband."

"Are you finished?" Mrs. Tibbett had no intention of being drawn into an argument about the Kemps or Mr. Rivers. She was going to see Mrs. Benson and that's all there was to it.

Barney waited at the canal bridge for ten minutes before Spike came along in Mr. Rivers's car. Spike leaned across the back of his seat and opened the rear door. "Hop in there. Feeling O.K.?"

Barney forced a grin but did not reply.

Spike didn't speak again until he stopped to pick up Len who came out of a doorway as the car drew up at the curb. He was wearing his long yellow coat. His purple felt was pulled over his eyes. He got in through the off-side door and took the wheel.

"Got a cosh?" Spike asked.

Len nodded. "But don't forget it's you that's doing the stick-up."

"Yes, but you know how it is. Things don't always work out the way you want 'em to."

Len followed the same route he had taken with Mr. Rivers and stopped the car a few yards short of the cutting into the gravel pit. "Barney," Spike said, "you get up on that hill. The one with the tree on it. When you see the van wave a handkerchief. Have you got one?"

Barney produced a grimy rag.

"That'll do." Spike looked at his watch. "We've got twenty minutes if he's on time, but you'd better get up there right away."

Spike watched Barney as he trudged through the dead bracken. "Keep an eye on him, Len." He took the magazine from his pocket and began to read. Now that the job was under way his nervousness had gone.

Ten minutes passed. Len sat hunched up in his seat pulling at his cigarette, trying to still the shaking of his hand. Spike looked up from his page. "You got the jitters? Have a pull at this."

"I'm all right."

"Go on." Spike put a flat bottle of brandy into Len's hand. "Do you feel better?"

"I tell you I'm all right."

Spike looked up the hill to the point where Barney was standing dwarfed by the tall blue-black pine. Then he went on with his reading. Len crushed out the butt of his cigarette and lit another. As he threw away the match he saw Barney's arm rise and wave once. "He's coming."

Spike tossed the magazine into the back of the car and eased the catch of the door. "As soon as I get him out, take the van into the pit. Got that?"

"O.K."

Spike took off his hat and slipped a black stocking mask over his face. Len did the same, and then grasped the door top till his knuckles showed white.

"He's taking the hell of a time," Spike muttered, and even as he spoke he heard a car coming down the slope. He opened the door and put one foot on the running-board, tense like a runner waiting for the word to go.

The van swung round the corner and slowed suddenly. Spike shot from his seat and was abreast of the van as it stopped.

Will Dorset slipped the gear lever into neutral and turned to find a revolver a foot from his face.

"Step out, chum."

Will froze in surprise. Seconds passed before he realized what had happened.

"Get out quick," Spike snapped.

There was a scuffle in the seat alongside Will. Spike saw a man struggling with the catch of the door. "Sit tight, you," but the man was out of the car before Spike could shift his aim. He heard feet running and saw Len out of the corner of his eye. He opened the off-side door with his left hand.

Will got out stiffly. "Turn round. Put your hands behind your back." Will felt cold steel lock round his wrists. "Now get back." Spike guided him into the seat. "On to the other side." Will wriggled across the cushions.

Spike slipped into the driving seat and drove the van along the rutted track into the gravel pit, stopped the van and felt in his pockets for a hank of twine. He bound Will's ankles quickly and was about to run back to the road when Len arrived, panting.

"All right. I've fixed him," he jerked out.

"Fine." Spike's eyes were shining. "Better tie him up. Take this." He gave Len a length of twine. "I'll get the car."

He ran back to the road. Barney was still at his post.

All right, so far. He drove the saloon into the pit, got out and forced open the rear doors of the van.

The skins were baled in hessian, and piled almost to the roof, with three or four loose pelts on top. There was a cold drizzle falling, but Spike was sweating before Len returned.

"How is he?"

Len grinned. "He's stiff, but not too stiff, if you know what I mean."

"Good work. Give us a hand, and pack 'em down tight. We haven't all that room."

When the transfer was complete, Spike lit a cigarette. "We'll have a couple of minutes' breather, and then for the road." He waved his hand twice to Barney. "Don't want to leave him stuck up there like a blooming statue."

Barney came running down. He looked at the car and then at Spike.

"Where do I go? On the grid?"

"You'll have to walk. Come on, Len, let's go." Spike got into the car and Len joined him. He handed Barney his mask. "Here, get rid of this somewhere. And this." He held out a revolver.

Barney stepped back. "Like hell I will. You can look after that yourself."

Spike half-opened the door as though to force the gun on Barney.

"For God's sake let's get away," Len urged, and pulled Spike back.

"Maybe you're right," Spike said.

Len reversed the car down the track on to the road. He looked anxiously ahead as they came to the village green. There was a man wearing blue goggles breaking stones, two or three children playing with a ball, and a man in a cottage garden digging. The man at the stone heap went on with his work, the children didn't appear to notice them, but the man in the garden looked up from his work. "Look the other way," Spike ordered sharply, and raised his right hand to his face. "We don't want to take any chances."

A mile farther on Len said, "I think I'll take the road over the hill." Spike nodded. He was played out after the excitement of the hold-up. He slid down in his seat, content to leave the route to Len.

Len drove on, never relaxing for one instant. It was only a matter of time before some one found the van. With luck, that wouldn't happen for hours yet, not until it was discovered that Will Dorset hadn't arrived at his destination, and a search was made. Possibly they wouldn't find him till the next morning.

Len slowed to a crawl at the cross-roads at the farm. The road was clear. He changed to second, and then to third, and set the car at the hilly, rutted track at full throttle. Speed eased the tension, and as he let her out down the other side to the Leatherhead Road he forgot the dangers which might be lying in wait.

At the next cross-roads he had to stop to let a stream of traffic go by. The short delay made him curse. Spike looked up.

"What's the matter?"

"Nothing." Spike looked out of the window, back up the road. It ran straight as a ruled line. There wasn't a car in sight. Len was chewing a dead cigarette.

"Want a light?"

Len shook his head and let in the clutch. They were off again. The needle climbed steadily up. Forty. Forty-five. Fifty-five.

"Running all right, isn't she?"

"Yes. I bet Rivers has never knocked this out of her."

The road was good and fairly clear. They made good time to Esher. A quarter of a mile farther on Len turned left to Hampton Court.

At half-past eleven he drew up outside Hyams's shop. "I'll go in and tell him we're here," Spike said.

He came back a minute later. Izzy was by his side. "What for you stop here? Go round to the back." He looked nervously up and down the street. "I told Mr. Rivers."

"Well, where the hell is the back?" Spike struck a match and lit his cigarette.

"The first on the left, and it is the second door. Don't wait here."

Spike looked at him insolently. "What the hell's biting you?"

Izzy went back into the shop and Len drove round to the back door. It was opened, and a girl came out. "Will you bring the goods in here, please?"

Spike looked at Len and smiled with one half of his mouth. "They want us to do the whole blooming job. All right, let's get busy."

They carried the bales into the back shop where Izzy was shifting cases. He told the girl to get back to her work and then said to Spike, "Put them in that corner and please be quick!"

When Len had brought in the last lot, Izzy tried to push him out of the door.

"Just a minute." Spike took Izzy by the arm and forced him back. He kicked the door shut. "Open up one of them," he ordered Len, who cut the string sewing of one of the bales. Then he laid out the skins on the top of a case, and ran his fingers through the thick black fur. The brush was white-tipped, and the silver hairs were thick down the centre line.

"Is that a good fur?" he asked Izzy.

"Yes, yes, quite good. Not the best quality, of course, but it is good."

Spike took the knife from Len and slit another bale.

"Are these any better?"

Izzy picked one out. "Now, that is a very good skin. You see the guard hairs?" He laid his hand on the long, lustrous black hairs on the back of the skin between the forelegs. "That is one of the ways of telling the quality." He blew into the hairs so that they parted. "It is all right."

"Then you can make it up as a tie, and make a good job of it."

Izzy raised his two hands in protest.

"But how can I do that? It belongs to Mr. Rivers. Perhaps I will buy it from him. I do not know. But I cannot give it to you."

"Ever heard of Socky Smith?"

"Socky Smith?" Izzy repeated slowly. "No, I do not think so."

"Him that laid out a split cold, and swung for it."

"A split?"

"A detective, then. Killed him."

"I do not understand."

"I used to work with Socky." There was something in Spike's eyes which made further explanation unnecessary.

"I will make up the skin for you."

"That's fine. Give me a pencil and paper and I'll tell you where to send it."

Spike wrote an address. "When'll it be ready?"

"Well, we are very busy, just now. Shall we say next week, Monday?"

"To-morrow'll suit me better."

Izzy was about to protest but changed his mind. The sooner this unpleasant man was out of his shop, the safer it would be for him. "Certainly. To-morrow I will have it ready."

Spike was half-way across the pavement when Izzy called him back. He was holding a bag in his hands.

"There are no furs in this. Look!"

It was a haversack stuffed full of clothes.

"I don't know anything about it."

"You brought it in with the rest of the goods. Please take it away again."

"Oh, all right. Give it to me."

Spike walked to the car and threw the kitbag on to the back seat. "Do you know anything about that, Len?"

"No. Never seen it before."

"Well, it doesn't matter. We'll dump it at Rivers's place."

They drove to Rivers's shop, garaged the car in the back yard, and walked into the shop. Alma was standing by the street door. She looked round, startled.

"Oh, you did give me a fright."

Spike smiled. "Not scared of me, are you? Where's the guv'nor?"

"He's gone out. I don't know where."

"Expecting him back soon?"

"He didn't say when he'd be back."

"Where's Joe?"

"I don't know. I haven't seen him since this morning. I think he went out with the barrow."

"This is a fine welcome home, I must say." He took Len aside. "No good your waiting, come round to Napier Terrace to-night. I'll see Rivers before that and get our cut."

"Right. If you want me, I'll be at my place."

Spike watched Len board a bus. Then he came back into the shop. Alma had taken a brass Buddha from a shelf and was polishing it.

"You working for Rivers?"

"Yes."

"Like him?"

"I think so."

"What are you doing to-night?"

"Helping Mrs. Kemp cook the supper, washing up, and after that, bed."

Spike's mouth twisted in a grin. "Sounds exciting. What about coming with me and hitting it up?"

"If Mrs. Kemp doesn't mind. I'd like to."

"Then that's—"

"Oh, no, I can't," she interrupted. "I've got a—I mean, there's some one coming to see me, and I can't put him off."

"Why not? I've got money to burn. We could do a theatre, maybe, and supper after."

"I'm awfully sorry, but I can't. I'd have loved to any other night, but my friend is only going to be in London for the day. I couldn't disappoint him."

"Where does he come from?"

"The place I used to live at, Crowley. Down in the country. He's driving up with a lot of furs."

"Crowley? Furs?" Spike froze.

"What's the matter?"

"Nothing, but I wouldn't bother about your pal."

"But I must."

"If he doesn't turn up, will you come with me?"

"Yes, of course. But there isn't a chance of that. If Will says he'll do a thing, nothing'll stop him. I'm meeting him in Town this evening."

"Something might stop him."

"I rather wish something would," Alma said.

"Well, I'll be round for supper, and if he's not there, we'll go out together."

Spike left the shop and took a tube to Piccadilly Circus. He bought two circle seats for a revue. He was fairly certain that Will Dorset would not keep his appointment that night.

CHAPTER SEVEN

THE FRONT of Larry's café was a boarded shop window plastered with advertisements. There was a door with a catch which sometimes worked, and a notice, painted in leaning letters, "Coffee Bar."

Three steep steps led down to the shop, which was dark and smelt of cheese and paraffin. Larry had broken off negotiations with the electric light and gas companies, and relied on candles and the daylight which filtered through a dirty pane of glass for illumination.

There was nothing worth seeing. A few broken chairs, two benches against the walls, and a long deal table covered with American cloth, torn and stained.

A curtain hid an oil stove tended by Larry's mother. On it she cooked mysterious bits of meat, bought late at night, when the butchers were selling off cheap. The sweepings of greengrocers' shops provided the stew with a certain interest, for one could never be quite sure if an odd lump which looked like a piece of wood was a badly cooked carrot, turnip, or merely a piece of wood.

When Spike came down the steps Larry was sitting on a stool tilted back against the wall. A greasy mark showed where his head rested.

"What cheer, Larry. How she go?"

Larry's long, lugubrious face, not unlike that of a depressed cab horse, was turned slowly towards him.

"Len's been down. He told me to tell you he's coming back."

Spike nodded and went behind the curtain to warm his hands at the stove, which was showing a red, sooty eye. Ma was sitting crouched over it gutting a rabbit into a bucket. She was a little more cheerful than her son.

"It's good to see you again, Spike. And you look as if you'd had a lucky day."

"Yes. Not so bad."

"I knew," the old woman quavered. "I knew. And Len was with you, too."

Spike's face hardened. "Has he been talking?"

Ma gave a cracked laugh. "I don't need people to tell me things. It's second sight. That's what it is." She turned the rabbit inside out. "There was a time I made good money telling people their fortunes. Some of 'em didn't like it, though."

Spike, impatient of the old woman's maunderings, called out to Larry. "I want a drink."

"Well, you know where it is. Help yourself."

Spike took a black bottle from a shelf and poured out a cloudy liquid into a tin mug. It looked harmless, but it stung Spike's throat. Some people called it "Fight your mother brandy" with good reason, for if taken in any quantity it made even a rabbit quarrelsome. How it was concocted was Larry's secret.

Spike left the "kitchen" and sat on a chair at the long table. "Ever heard of a bloke called Hyams?" he asked Larry.

"Izzy Hyams or Ikey Hyams? I know 'em both."

"Izzy."

Larry scratched the stubble on his jaw and looked at the ceiling. "He's a wop. Why?"

"I want to know."

"Been selling him stuff?"

"No."

"Then don't start. Better chuck it in the ditch. Save a lot of talk and you wouldn't be much worse off."

"Do the splits know him?"

"I wouldn't be surprised if they did, but I think he's kept clear of them up to now."

"He's sending a parcel here for me. I want you to keep it till I come in again."

"Who's bringing it?"

"I dunno."

"I don't want no strangers round here. You know that."

"He'll post it, most likely. Have you got any beer? This stuff of yours is fierce as hell."

Larry let his chair come down on its four legs and stalked to a corner of the room.

Spike took the bottle he produced and filled his mug. "You want to keep that stuff a bit longer. It would be all right then."

"Got cleaned out last night. That was the trouble," Larry explained. As he spoke the street door opened and Len came in, the skirts of his coat trailing on the steps. He had a sheaf of papers in his hand.

Ma poked her head round the curtain.

"Hullo, Len. Stopping for supper?"

"I don't mind if I do. What's on?"

"Rabbit stew. It won't be ready for a bit, though."

"I ain't in a hurry." Len put the papers on the table. A late *News*, *Star* and a *Standard*. "They haven't got anything in about it."

"What ha' you two been up to? Knocking off?"

"Stick-up," said Spike. He had meant to keep his mouth shut, but his vanity got the better of his caution. "And I'll bet we got the splits guessing this time. They won't have any strings on us."

"Go on thinking that and one of these days one of 'em'll be asking you to take a little walk. 'Just as far as the station,'" Larry said in an affected voice. "'We won't keep you long. A matter of form.' And before you know what's happening you're stuck in a row of blokes and a half-baked clerk picks you out as the man what laid him out. As like as not they show him your photo afore he starts, so's there won't be no mistake."

"I've never been inside."

"Then you've got a chance," Larry conceded. "But all the same, I'd lie up for a spell, if I was you."

"Like hell I will. I'm going to have a night out. I've got a new girl."

He got up and fetched the bottle.

"What about you, Len?"

"Thanks."

Spike laced his mug of beer and took a deep draught. "It's better this way."

By six he was feeling fine. Len was lying on the floor snoring. Rabbit stew had ceased to have any attraction for him.

"I'll be moving," Spike said. "Don't forget about that parcel. I'll be in for it to-morrow night." He gave Larry three shillings, and stumbled up the steps into the street. It was raining. He swore, and felt in his trouser pocket. Only five bob left, but enough for a taxi, and he'd get all he wanted from Rivers.

"Thirteen hundred pounds." That was to be his share. "Thirteen hundred pounds." He kept repeating the words over and over again. And even if he had to give Len four hundred he'd net another nine hundred. He'd go abroad. He'd take Alma with him. He might even marry her. Give her a hundred to buy dresses with. Spike was feeling generous. The taxi carried him northwards, away from the lights of the West End through mean little streets to the canal bridge.

He got out of the cab unsteadily, and gave the driver two half-crowns. "Stinking night, ain't it, chum?" He walked down the path to Napier Terrace. Supper would be ready at Mrs. Kemp's, but what the hell did he care about her supper! A mouldy bloater. He was going to feed at a restaurant. With Alma.

He stopped at the gate of No. 3. He'd like to see her face when that man of hers didn't turn up. "Wonder what she'd say if I told her where he is now?" Footsteps came down the cinder path behind him. It was Joe.

"Hullo. Spike. Ain't you coming in? The old woman's expecting you."

"Got to see Rivers first. I'm going round there now. I'll be along later."

CHAPTER EIGHT

BARNEY WAITED until the car had driven out of the gravel pit and had disappeared down the road in the direction of the village. Thank God they were gone! He listened for a minute or two, and climbed up the bank. There was no one in sight.

It would be better not to go through the village. Over the hills would be safer. He knew a track which led to Poynings. There was a bus ran from there to Snailsham. He turned up the collar of his coat and set off through the bracken and heather. If he stepped out he'd be in Town by tea-time.

Then he saw something white in a ditch. He stopped. Two boots, toes up. Barney felt his stomach turn. It was a man on his back. He took a step forward cautiously. The man didn't move. His eyes were open, staring upwards at the leaden clouds.

"Hi!" Barney edged forward and bent down, his hands brushing the dripping heather till they touched the man. He lay quite still. Barney gripped the man's shoulder and shook it. His head fell suddenly to one side.

Dead! The realization came swift and overpowering. Stumbling and falling, Barney ran wildly away from it. His legs were trembling, and he was breathing hard when at last he stopped. Rain was beginning to fall. Gentle and cooling. He wiped his face and leaned against a birch sapling.

Spike was a devil. What was the good of knocking the bloke out cold? Once the police got going there'd be only one end to this business. He took two gulping breaths and went on. Leith Hill, with its wooded slopes, gave him a line, and soon he came to a path. He followed it for a mile to a fork where a signpost said, "To the village."

He plunged on down a narrow path to the village of Poynings. He'd been there before, and knew that the bus started from the village shop. It was standing in the road now, but there was no sign of the driver. Barney stepped off the road, and stood behind a hedge. He could still see the bus.

Ten minutes passed, and then a man came out of the shop. He was wearing a peaked cap and a long dust coat. He stood on the footpath chatting with a woman. Then he walked round the front of the bus and got into the driving seat.

Barney came out from the shelter of the hedge and walked quickly across the green. The driver saw him coming, and leaned over and opened the door.

"Where d'you want to go?"

"Snailsham."

"Sevenpence."

Barney took his ticket and sat at the back of the bus. He went by electric train from Snailsham to Waterloo, and walked from there to Mr. Tibbett's caravan. With his last penny he bought an evening paper, and read the headlines. Nothing there. Nor in the Stop Press.

Mr. Tibbett was out mending one of his merry-go-rounds when Barney reached the settlement. Mrs. Tibbett was knitting. She dropped her hands on her lap when she saw Barney.

"What in the wide world have you been up to?"

Barney tried to grin, but failed. He was tired and very frightened. "Why?"

Mrs. Tibbett pointed to a square of looking-glass. "Take a look at yourself."

Barney twisted sideways. "I am a blooming sight, ain't I?"

His face was streaked with dirt. His collar was pulp, and the knot of his tie had disappeared.

"There's some water in the pitcher. Better have a wash, or people'll be thinking things."

"What's that?" His voice was harsh and strained.

"What I say." Mrs. Tibbett had taken up her knitting. She counted a row of stitches. "If you was to meet a policeman he might want to know what you'd been up to. Now, don't stand there staring at me like that. Go and clean yourself, and I'll make you a nice cup of tea. Roger'll be in any time now and he'll be wanting some, too." Mrs. Tibbett lit the oil stove and put a kettle on the burner.

Barney took off his coat, collar, and tie, and washed his face and neck. It made him feel better. Then he combed his hair and put on a scarf. It was more comfortable than the collar, which Mr. Rivers had told him to wear. Rivers! He was at the back of all this trouble.

"How's Fanny?"

"She's all right. I was wondering when you was going to ask."

"And George?"

"He's in that drawer right alongside your hand. He hasn't had any supper yet."

Barney opened the drawer and put in his hand gently. He felt the tickle of George's tiny feet. "Hungry, are you?" he muttered. "We'll soon fix that."

"There's some bread and milk I put out in a saucer. It's in the pantry."

Barney put George down to his meal, and looked round for Fanny's box. He lifted the lid carefully. "She's made her nest, all right. I won't worry her." He dropped a piece of bread into the box and shut and fastened the lid.

Mr. Tibbett came in as the tea was being made, and he and Barney played a rubber of cribbage. Barney won tuppence and told the old man he was losing his dash. Mr. Tibbett replied that he'd play another game; double stakes.

"Not now," Barney replied. "I'm going round to see a pal."

"After supper, then."

Barney agreed and got up to go. "Come on, George. You'll be company." He put the mouse in his pocket and left the caravan.

Mr. Rivers was in. Barney could tell by the light in the top window. He knocked on the door and Rivers came down and let him in.

"Hullo. It's you, is it?" He appeared to be disappointed. "I thought it was Spike." When he had shut the door and locked it, he asked: "Well, how did it go?"

"I'll tell you when we get upstairs."

Rivers pulled down the blinds and drew the curtains as soon as he got into the room. Barney sat down on the arm of a chair.

"Let's have it."

"Spike got the stuff."

"No trouble?"

"He killed the man." Barney spoke the words so calmly that at first Rivers did not grasp their meaning. Then he went quite white, took a short, unsteady pace backwards, and clutched at the mantelpiece.

"Killed!"

Barney nodded slowly twice.

"Spike?"

"I think it was him. I didn't see it happen, but I found the bloke what copped it. He was stiff, all right."

"What did you see?"

"The van come along. I saw that. It stopped. Only the top of it was showing then. I heard a fellow running. As he came into sight he fell, and there was one of 'em on top of him. He pulled him away into the heather."

"Who did?"

"I dunno. I wasn't near enough to see, but it must have been Spike."

"Why?"

"Len's not a killer."

"Spike had a gun. Did you hear a shot?"

"No. There wasn't a gun fired while I was there."

"You were up on the hill?"

"That's right." Barney wasn't feeling so bad now that he had told his story. "I came down and saw Spike. He had the skins in the car. They drove away soon after that."

Mr. Rivers didn't say anything for two or three minutes. Then he filled a pipe and, when it was going, went over to the sideboard and poured out two drinks. He gave one to Barney.

"What are you going to do, Mr. Rivers?"

Rivers returned to his position in front of the fire and took a sip at his drink before he said, "I'm not thinking of doing anything. Why?"

"They used your car on the job."

"You're thinking of your own skin."

"I'm going to clear out."

"That's your business."

"I want some dough."

"How much?"

"A tenner."

"I haven't got that on me. Come back in the morning."

"I'll be out of it before then."

Mr. Rivers took out a wallet and produced three one-pound notes. "That's cleaned me out."

Barney stuffed the money into his pocket, finished his drink, and walked to the door.

"So long."

Spike took the back way to the yard behind Rivers's shop. He got there half an hour after Barney had left and found the door unlocked. Rivers was standing just inside.

"That you, Spike?"

"Yes. Let me past."

"Get out, and keep out."

Rivers put out a hand to the door and tried to shut it. Spike put his foot on the sill. "What the hell are you playing at?" Spike lowered his shoulder and heaved. Rivers fell back. "Have you gone off your blinking rocker, or what?"

Spike took a grip of Rivers's shirt below his throat and pushed him against the wall. "Go on, speak, you rat. Send me out on a job. I risk my blooming neck. Pull it off, and then you tell me to get out." He loosened his grip and shut the door. "Go on up. I'll follow."

Spike swaggered into the room and threw his hat on a chair and stripped off his raincoat.

"Give us a drink and let's hear your trouble."

"I thought Leith might be round this way to-night. I don't want him to find you here."

"If he comes I can get out the way I did before, through the shop."

"All the same, I don't like it."

Larry's home-made brandy had made Spike aggressive. "I don't give a toss what you like. It's what I like that counts. I'm the bloke that's done the work while you sit tight and snug and get the wind up over a poop like Leith; and look at that job I pulled off to-day. Clean as a whistle."

"Clean be damned."

"It was. What the hell do you know about it?"

"Barney's been here. He's only just gone. He's clearing out."

"What the blazes for?"

Rivers pulled a chair round and sat down facing Spike.

"You know, all right. And for the same reason I don't want you here."

"So it wasn't Leith. I thought you were lying."

"I'm not going to have a murderer in my place."

"Murderer?" As Spike breathed the word he gripped the arms of his chair and pulled himself to his feet. "Murderer! Have you gone right off your blooming onion or are you trying to be funny?"

Rivers got up and put a chair between Spike and himself. "That man in the van. He's dead."

For a split second the yellow streak showed. Spike felt his legs go dead and his stomach rise. Then he took hold of himself. A laugh came, shaky and uncertain. Dead!

"Damn' funny, ain't it?" Rivers snapped. "Go on. Laugh all you want if it helps."

Spike got up and steadied himself on the back of a chair. Rivers watched him.

"That's got you thinking. Dead! He's dead!"

"Shut up, blast you!" Spike pulled at his cigarette. It had gone out and tasted bad. He spat it out and felt in his pocket for his case. When his lungs were filled with smoke he had regained his nerve.

"Who told you?"

"Barney."

"He's a blinking liar, and the next time I see him he'll be wishing he was born dumb."

"Barney wasn't lying. He found the man in a ditch. Stiff. He said he saw you chase him up the road. Then he fell."

"Dead!" Spike brushed a hand across his face. He was looking blankly at the wall. "That was Len," he muttered. "I didn't do it." He turned his head slowly and focused his eyes on Rivers. "What else did he say?"

"Nothing. You've cooked it properly, the two of you. It doesn't matter which of you did it."

"The furs are at Izzy V's."

"What do I care about that? I can't handle them. You know as well as I do what the splits are like when there's been a killing. They don't let up."

"Maybe they won't find the bloke. There's nothing in the papers."

"They'll find him, all right."

"Oh, for God's sake shut up! You give me the dry heaves with your croaking. Give me a drink."

"Help yourself, and then get out."

Spike went to the sideboard and half-filled a glass with whisky. "I'll get out when I'm ready." He took a gulp of the spirit. "The splits haven't got anything on me. And what the hell is there for you to worry about? I got away, and you've got the stuff; or rather, Izzy has."

"That's not the same thing as me having it. If he talks, there'll—"

"Why should he?"

"If the police find he's got the stuff, he'll spill everything."

"He doesn't know anything."

"He knows you and Len did the job."

"I'll go and see Izzy to-morrow and put the fear of God into him."

"Like hell you will! You'll keep under cover. If there's anything to be done about Izzy, I'll do it."

"Maybe you're right. But I want some cash. I'm cleaned right out."

Rivers felt in his pocket, took out a dirty, crumpled note, and tossed it towards Spike. It fell on the floor.

"What's the idea?"

"What d'you mean?"

"I want my share. Cut three ways was what we fixed. And I'll take Len's lot, too."

Rivers laughed.

"Two thousand six hundred quid's what I want."

"You've got a hope."

Spike's lips tightened on his cigarette.

"Two thousand six hundred," Spike repeated.

"You'll be lucky if you get a pony. And you'll have to wait for that until I can unload the skins."

"A pony! Now, just wait a minute. A bargain's a bargain. And two-thirds of four thousand is the figure."

"It was," said Rivers. "But only for a clean job. You've messed it up."

"I've messed it! You mean, Len has."

"It's all the same," Rivers snapped. He was getting very red. "You told me he'd be O.K."

Spike put down his glass and took three unsteady strides across the room. Rivers was too angry to be frightened. He stood still.

"You're going to pay me what you promised. If you don't I'll take it. And if I have to do that it'll cost you something for the trouble."

"If you do that I'll—" Rivers stopped short.

"Go on. Tell me what you'll do." Spike's pale blue eyes were cold and his voice was deadly calm. Mr. Rivers began to realize his danger. He tried to smile.

"Now then, Spike. There's no need to get all worked up. I'll give you some dough. I can't give it you all because I haven't got it, but I could manage a tenner." Rivers spoke quickly. He had raised a suspicion in Spike's mind that was not to be easily stilled with mere words. "A tenner," he repeated. "And I'll get the rest for you when I see Izzy."

"You've got it without going to that dago. And what was it you were going to do?" Spike put up his hand. "All right. Don't tell me. I'll guess. You were going to call up your old friend, Mr. Leith. Oh, I forgot, he's coming up here to-night. I suppose you've been on to him already."

"He's not coming here. I swear that."

"God! You twist all ways. You told me to keep out because you were expecting him."

"I wasn't."

"I see what your game is. You'll wait till there's a reward out. And tip off the splits to me and Len, and then when everything's over you'll cash in on the skins." Spike took a pace backwards. "Well, it's not going to work out that way." Blood rose to his head. "You double-faced twister, I'll—"

Rivers was on his feet in one jump. He was really frightened now. "Easy on, Spike. There's no need to get excited."

"You skunk!" Spike looked round the room. At the rugs. At the pictures. At the cabinet filled with china.

Money! It all spelled money and here was this double-crossing swine telling him he'd have to wait. And then not get his proper share!

His gaze fell on the laughing boy. His arm shot out. There was a crash and tinkle of falling glass on the polished floor as he flung the figure with all his strength at an etching on the wall.

Anger overcame Rivers's terror. He flung himself on Spike. "Would you? You swine."

Spike's hand went to his hip pocket. There was a flash of steel. Rivers saw the open razor blade and opened his mouth to scream. Spike put a hand over Rivers's face and forced his head back. The razor flashed again and Rivers crumpled and fell with a horrible choking cough. Blood spattered the boards and then flowed in a steady stream.

Seconds passed before the red mists of blind rage faded from Spike's brain and he saw clearly. The room was different now. Everything was different. Unreal. His eyes focused on the smashed picture, on the china fragments at his feet. The head of the laughing boy was looking up at him, still laughing, mocking. He tried to grind it with his foot but it would not break. He kicked it aside.

A purple stream was oozing slowly across the floor and soaking into a Persian rug. He saw Rivers with one arm outstretched, fingers straight, dead white against the crimson of a rug.

"Now try and squeak." Spike lurched to the sideboard and finished the contents of his glass. He filled it up again and took another drink.

"The little swine," he mumbled. "Going to do a double-cross, was he?" Then he remembered that Leith might be outside. He ran down the stairs and bolted the door leading to the yard and stood listening. There was no sound. He went back up the stairs. Money! There must be a cash-box somewhere, or a safe. He looked in a cupboard in a corner of the room. That was no good. It was full of old papers and books.

The sideboard contained only cutlery and glass. He went on to the landing and down the stairs to the shop and through it to a small room at the back. It had been used as an office, for there was a desk littered with papers, two or three files, a typewriter, and a stack of drawers.

There was no money in that office. There wasn't even a book of stamps.

Spike went to the street door, unlocked it and slid back the bottom bolt. He tried the top one; it worked easily. If necessary he could get out that way quickly. But the money. Money! money! He must have money. The bedroom at the back. He hadn't looked there.

The body was lying on the floor. He stood staring at it for a moment. "You got what you asked for." Then he went into the bedroom at the back and again drew blank. He opened drawers wildly and threw their contents about the floor. Shirts, ties, socks. His fuddled brain had but one aim in view. Money. Maybe there was some in Rivers's pockets. Not much, probably, but a pound or two was a damn sight better than nothing.

Rivers's wallet had three notes in it. One ten-shilling and two pounds. Then blind rage seized Spike. Two pounds ten! He seized a chair and flung it across the floor. It fell with a crash. The noise made him realize the danger of his position. Any one passing, who heard the noise, might come to see what it was about; a policeman on patrol, or Leith.

He switched out the light and parted the curtain of the window overlooking the yard. The rain had stopped and the light of a pale crescent of a moon was sufficient to show that there was no one about.

He stood undecided what to do. Another drink and then he'd go along to the Kemps. Alma would be waiting for him, expecting to be taken out. Well, why the hell shouldn't he? He had two pounds ten and tickets for the show and it wasn't gone seven. Plenty time.

He walked quickly along the back street, passed the back door of No. 3 and turned right to the canal path. It was dark and deserted and no one saw or heard the razor as it fell into the water.

Joe opened the front door in answer to Spike's knock. "Hullo. You've been a hell of a long time. We waited supper half an hour, but—"

Spike brushed past him and went into the back room. Mrs. Kemp was sitting in a chair picking her teeth with a match. Alma was gathering up the dishes. She smiled when she saw him. "I thought you'd never come," she said.

Spike jerked his head. "I won't be a minute," and went into the kitchen and turned on a tap.

Mrs. Kemp took the match from her mouth and got up. "You stop there," she said to Alma and joined Spike, who was washing his hands at the sink. "What's up?"

Spike kept his head down as he answered. "Nothing. Why?"

Mrs. Kemp put a red pudgy hand on the draining board. "Where you been?"

"Having a walk round."

She gave a wheezy sigh. "Well, I don't know. You always was a dumb one."

Spike dried his hands on a roller towel.

"The bloke didn't turn up, did he?"

"You mean Alma's young man?"

"Yes."

"No. Not a sign of him. But I don't think she's caring much. What did you do to him?"

"Tied him up."

"Then how could he have come here?"

"Someone might have found him and cut him loose."

"He hasn't come here." Mrs. Kemp laughed. "He don't know this address."

"Then that's all right. Tell Alma to get her things on."

"You're going to stop here. What the hell's the good of going out and getting picked up?"

"No blooming split's going to put his hands on me. It was a clean job. The stuff's at Izzy's and the car's in Rivers's yard. They can't pin it on me."

"No good asking for trouble."

"Look here, Ma, you know as well as me that if I lie up they'll think I did it and never stop looking till they find me. I'd sooner get it over right away than wait here. Anyway, there's nothing in the papers."

"I know that."

Mrs. Kemp poured some coffee essence into a cup. "You better have this afore you go. You've been drinking. Try and steady yourself up a bit, and don't go telling Alma what you've been up to."

"Do you think I'm a blinking fool?"

"Sometimes you are and sometimes you're not. Drink doesn't help. Not the stuff you've been having."

The door opened and Alma came in with a tray. Mrs. Kemp took it from her. "I'll wash up. You go and dress. Spike's taking you out and don't be late back. I'll be sitting up."

CHAPTER NINE

ALMA PUT her arm in Spike's as they left the house and turned up the path to the bridge. He pressed it close to his side. "Feeling like a binge?"

Alma laughed. "I've had supper. I didn't think you were going to turn up."

"I said I would, didn't I?"

"Yes, I know, but—"

They went by Underground to Piccadilly Circus. Spike looked at his watch as they neared the top of the escalator. "Only ten minutes before the show. If you don't mind we'll feed afterwards."

Alma slipped her hand into his pocket. "Of course I don't mind. I'm going to love to-night. I've never been to a theatre in London before; only a movie with my aunt and that doesn't count."

Spike fell asleep soon after they got into their seats in the circle but Alma was too thrilled to notice. When the lights went up at the interval she said: "I'm loving this. Aren't you?"

Spike woke up and yawned. "Not bad."

"I say, you are a fine one to take a girl out. Do you always go to sleep at a theatre?"

Spike grinned and felt for his cigarette-case. He put a cigarette in his mouth and was fumbling for a match when a man in the aisle leaned across. "Here you are." He held out a lighter. Spike sucked in the smoke.

Leith shut the lighter and straightened himself. "Having a night off? So am I."

Spike stared at him. "What do you want?"

"Nothing. I told you. I'm off duty."

Spike's set expression relaxed. "Meet my friend."

Leith shook hands with Alma. "Are you enjoying the show?"

"Oh, I think it's ever so nice."

They talked awkwardly for a minute or two and then Leith said: "I didn't catch your name, Miss—"

"Robinson."

"Yes, of course. Well, good night. Pleased to have met you."

Alma turned to Spike. "Who's that? He's rather nice."

"Friend of mine."

"Well, I don't think you were very friendly."

After the show Spike changed his mind about going to a fashionable restaurant. "Do you mind if we go somewhere quiet? I've got a bit of a head."

"Oh, I am sorry. No, of course I don't mind. But why not go straight home? I've had a lovely evening."

But Spike negatived that idea. He wanted a drink. They went to the café in Old Compton Street where he had found Len the night before. It was quite a small place with only a double row of tables the length of the room. At the far end there was a bar where two or three men were talking and drinking. There was a notice which said: "Domino Club. Members Only."

Spike ordered smoked salmon sandwiches, a pilsener for himself and a cup of coffee for Alma. She looked at the crude flamboyant drawings on the wall. "I say, I've never been in a place like this before. It is fun."

But Spike was unable to respond. He couldn't get Leith out of his mind. Was it a mere chance that he had been at the theatre or—? But if he'd known anything he wouldn't have behaved so casually. Nosey devil, wanting to know Alma's name, but that was just like Leith.

He drank his beer abstractedly and pushed the plate of sandwiches to Alma. "You go ahead. I'm not hungry." Alma bit into the fresh white bread. "Ooh, this is good. What is it?"

"Smoked salmon."

"I must remember that. Perhaps Mrs. Kemp would like some."

"A bloater's more her mark," Spike replied and got up. "Excuse me a minute." He walked up to the bar. One of the men turned his head.

"Hullo, Spike."

"Have you seen Len?"

"No. Not to-night. He was in here yesterday. I thought you and him had teamed up."

Spike ordered a double whisky. "If you see him tell him to look me up."

"Sure I will. Where'll you be?"

"He knows. Tell him, that's all."

Spike took his glass back to his table. He sat down and stared at a vase of paper flowers.

"You're not looking well," Alma said. "Let's go home. I've finished."

Spike roused himself. "Righto. I don't feel too well. You're a good sort, Alma. Most girls would have kicked up a shine at jacking up early."

"Early! I usually go to bed at ten."

They took a taxi to the canal bridge, and walked in silence down the path to Napier Terrace. Mrs. Kemp opened the door.

"You're back early. I thought as how you was going to make a night of it."

Spike pushed past her without a word. Mrs. Kemp caught sight of his face and put an arm round Alma's shoulders. "You go on up to your room, deary. I'll come and see you in a minute." She locked the door, put on the chain and shot both bolts. She didn't like the way Spike looked. There was trouble about.

She found him in the back room standing by the fire waiting for her.

"What's you done with her?" he asked.

"Sent her to bed. What's up?"

"Nothing."

Mrs. Kemp didn't say anything for a minute, then she went into the back kitchen. "We'll have some tea. Put the kettle on," she called out and came back with two cups, a teapot and a jug of milk on a tray. "You were round seeing Mr. Rivers, weren't you? How did you get on?"

"I wasn't there."

"You wasn't? Then I must have dreamed that Joe said that was where you was before supper."

"Yes, I know I told him I was going but I changed my mind."

"What about your money?"

"That can wait. I'm not in a hurry."

"You not in a hurry for money?" Mrs. Kemp laughed. "I like that. What about the ten bob I lent you last Saturday fortnight?"

"I forgot about that."

"Well, I haven't. Not by a blooming long chalk." Mrs. Kemp stirred her tea and then drank noisily. It was rather hot. "You haven't told me how you got on to-day."

"Oh, for God's sake stop talking!"

Mrs. Kemp sat quite still for a moment. Then she reached across the table and grasped Spike's wrist. "Go on, tell us about it, son. You'll feel better if you do."

Spike half-turned in his chair and said quickly: "It's Rivers. I killed him. And there's blood. Buckets of it all over the floor." He tried to laugh.

"You—killed—Rivers!" Mrs. Kemp stared at him with fallen jaw and goggling eyes.

"Yes. I meant to get his money. They say he's got hundreds tucked away somewhere in that place of his. I couldn't find a cent of it. There was two and a half thick 'uns I got out of his wallet. That was all."

Mrs. Kemp took a gulp of tea and choked on it. When she recovered she said: "What are you going to do?"

"I dunno. I've only got a quid left."

"Let's have a look at you." She came round the table and turned back the cuff of one sleeve. She unbuttoned his coat, looked at the front. There was no blood on his shirt. "Razor?"

Spike nodded.

"I thought it would be that. What have you done with it?"

"Chucked it in the cut. I'm all clear."

"That's what they all think and then something goes wrong. Some one slips in a word that sets the wheels working and once they start there won't be no stopping till they gets you."

"Trying to put the wind up me?" Spike smiled feebly. "Well, there's Joe. If any one asks him anything he's as like as not to say the wrong thing. I could tell him what to say but he'd forget it in half a tick and tell the truth. I've never known a man like him before."

"But he doesn't know anything."

"He knows you were going to see Rivers to-night."

"I can say I didn't go."

"Where'll you say you was, then?"

"At the Green Man."

"Who's going to speak for you if you wasn't there?"

"I can get plenty of blokes who'd be glad to do it."

"Spike! Sometimes I thinks you're clever. And sometimes I thinks you're barmy and then there's other times I knows you're off your blinking rocker. And this is one of them times."

"You've got an idea. Come on, out with it."

"We've got to get the corp out of the way. We'll make out he's gone on a holiday. I can manage that. No one'll miss him. He ain't never had no real friends, nor relations neither, who'll make a fuss. If we leaves him where he is the gas man'll find him when he goes to read the meter or some kid'll climb up and look through the windows and chuck a fit."

"Let them find him. I don't care."

"Now listen, Spike. You looked for money in the shop, didn't you?"

"Yes. All over the place. There's nothing there."

"You were in a hurry. That was your trouble. I knows, never mind how but I does, that Rivers had a wad stowed away."

"I've heard the same thing."

"He never used a bank and I'll wager if I had a day on my own with a screw-driver I'll find his dough. But it's not going to be with no blinking corp lying around. We've got to shift it to-night."

"Where to?"

"Into one of them there barges lying in right abreast the front gate. We can roll him up in a bit of sacking or something. Put him on the barrow. It won't take two minutes by the back way, and it's only a matter of yards from the front door to the cut."

"It's a hell of a risk to take."

"Not if we're careful. We'll wait till the flatty goes by. He usually passes round about one. They leaves a pint out for him at the back of the Green Man, so it's not often he's late. When he's gone by we'll nip round and have an hour clear. Not that we'll want all that time."

"I wouldn't do it for a thousand quid. Walk through the streets in the middle of the night with a stiff 'un on a barrow! It's you that's barmy."

"Wait a minute, son. There's a shorter way, and it's safer. Through old Hicks's yard. There's a lock on the gates but we can soon knock 'em off."

"Hicks's yard? Where's that?"

"Right opposite our back gate, and it runs through behind that block of garages and comes out near the back of Rivers's place."

Spike sat up in his chair. "That sounds more like it. Can you get me a screw-driver?"

Mrs. Kemp pulled herself up slowly. "I think I can. Anything else?"

"I could do with a fine bradawl or a bit of wire."

"What sort of wire? Stiff?"

"Fairly."

"Have some more tea. I won't be long."

Spike listened to Mrs. Kemp scratching about in the kitchen. He went over her plan in his mind. Certainly it was the only way of getting the money—if it was there. But—Hell! It must be there. He'd go right away for a long spell. To the Continent. He knew a man who'd fix him up with a passport for a tenner.

"Will this do?" Mrs. Kemp returned with a coil of wire and a short screw-driver. The handle of it was split.

Spike took the wire and worked the end between his fingers. "Yes. That's all right." He slipped the screw-driver in his pocket. "Which way does the flatty come?"

"Along the canal path. I'll go and watch for him from the front room."

Spike had nearly finished his cigarette before he heard Mrs. Kemp come creaking along the passage.

"He's gone by. And in a hurry too. I expect he's thirsty."

"Does he come back this way?"

"No."

"Then I'll nip out and see what I can do on the yard gate."

Mrs. Kemp let him out through the back door.

"D'you want a light?"

"No, I can manage." Spike ran lightly up the path to the gate in the wall, opened it and stood listening. He looked up and down the alley-way. All clear. He reached the yard gate in three strides and felt for the lock. It was a common type but rusty. He bent half an inch of the wire, put it in the keyhole and worked it round until it took against the tumbler. Then he gripped the wire with a pair of pliers, and with a twist of his wrist the lock snapped back.

He opened the gate and shut it behind him. There was room enough between the uprights to reach through and put the padlock back on its staple and jam it with a rubber wedge, in case a policeman came along and tried it. It was an old dodge.

At the far end of the yard opposite the back of Rivers's shop, Spike found that there was a wicket gate in the big double doors, locked and bolted on the inside. The lock was easier to work than the other for it was apparently in daily use. He eased it back with the wire and tried the bolts. They were free and worked without noise.

Mrs. Kemp heard his footsteps as Spike came down the path to the back door and was waiting for him. "How did you get on?"

"It's all clear through Hicks's place. Are you ready?"

"I will be in half a tick." She took a shawl off a nail and put it over her head. Then she looked into the back room. "The fire'll be all right till we come back. Do you want to take anything?"

"No. I am all set."

"Come on then. Let's get on with it."

Neither spoke until they got inside Rivers's yard. Then Mrs. Kemp asked if Spike had the key of the door.

"Yes, but we'd better get that barrow out and clear these boxes out of the way."

When everything was clear Spike unlocked the door and took a torch from his pocket. "Better not switch on the lights."

Mrs. Kemp followed him up and stood wheezing and panting on the top step.

"Stop there while I cover him up." Spike picked up a rug from the floor and rolled it round the body. He opened a window, cut out the sash cord and tied it round the body. Then he looked over his shoulder. "Are you still there?"

Mrs. Kemp took an uncertain step forward.

"Yes. What next?"

"Take this end and we'll get him to the top of the stairs."

Mrs. Kemp walked backwards awkwardly. He was a weight and no mistake.

"Hold it there till I get round." Spike went down three steps and pulled the body towards him. It slid fairly easily over the treads but took some holding.

Mrs. Kemp came down slowly, putting her full weight on each foot. "Shall I get the barrow?"

"Yes. But have a look round first."

She went out into the yard and Spike waited. He was breathing heavily and feeling sick. It was that last lot of whisky. He should have kept off it.

"All clear." Mrs. Kemp maneuvered the barrow up to the door.

"Right. Take your end and when I say the word, lift! That's got it. Wait here a minute."

Spike ran across the yard and opened the door of Rivers's car. He took out a haversack and carried it over to the barrow. "We've got to get rid of this at the same time."

When they got into Hicks's yard and had bolted the wicket gate behind them, Spike began to feel better. He felt for a cigarette but changed his mind. Get the job finished first.

The track through the yard was soft mud; it was heavy pushing, but the wheels made hardly any sound. At the next gate they stopped and Spike listened for a minute or two before he took the wedge out of the lock.

"We'll have to carry him across," he whispered. "The barrow won't go through into your place."

"I'm ready."

It was an awkward lift to get the body off the barrow, and as they lifted it over the edge on to the wheel the string lashing began to give way. Mrs. Kemp shifted her grip and felt something wet and sticky on her hands. Her nerve began to go. She wanted to scream; to run away; to get away from it. Nicely tied up with nothing showing she had been able to shut out the reality. But the blood! It was all over her hands. She made an instinctive movement to wipe them on her overall but stopped herself in time.

"I'm through."

Spike held the body with one hand and took a step to her side. "For God's sake hold up! We're nearly there." He pressed her hand in his.

Mrs. Kemp shivered and then pulled herself together with an effort. She smiled feebly. "Sorry, son. But it got me all of a heap. I'm all right now."

Spike put his head through the gate. There was no one in sight. He ran across to the back gate of No. 3 and unlocked it.

Half-walking, half-running, Mrs. Kemp and Spike carried the body into the back kitchen and dropped it on the floor.

Mrs. Kemp collapsed on a chair and wiped her face with a dish-cloth she picked off the table.

"You wait there," Spike said. "I'm going to take the wheels off the barrow and put it in the garden."

As soon as he had gone, Mrs. Kemp left the body in sole possession of the kitchen and went into the back room. She raked out the ashes of the fire and poked it into a blaze. She didn't know when she'd felt so bad before, and it wasn't the first time in her life she'd handled a corpse. She laid out her own brother and her sister May's first husband. It was the blood that had done it.

It had been her idea, too. Spike would have left him where he was. She wished now she'd never suggested it, and then again she was glad. Once they'd got it in a barge and out of here, it'd be all right.

She started up at the sound of the back door shutting, and sat upright, very still, till she heard Spike call out softly.

"Everything's okey-poke. Have you got a pair of scissors?"

"Yes, I think so." She got up and ran her fingers along a shelf where she kept her mending things. "I've found 'em."

"All right. Give them here."

She heard him snipping away at cloth.

"What are you doing?"

"Removing all evidence of identification. In other words I'm making as sure as I can that when some one does find him, they won't know who he is or where he comes from." Spike came into the back room a few minutes later with a handful of cloth slips and threw them on the fire.

"That's finished that. Now I'm going to get his teeth out. They're false. That's another thing they can trace a guy by, his teeth."

Mrs. Kemp stared at him. "You're not human, Spike. Playing about with a corpse as if it was a tailor's dummy or something. When you was a kid you was all right." Spike went back into the kitchen while Mrs. Kemp was talking.

In a minute or two he was back carrying the haversack. "We've got to get rid of this." He pulled out the wad of clothes it contained and put it on the fire.

The coals which had barely consumed the cuttings from Rivers's suit were no longer red.

Mrs. Kemp got up and reached under the settee and brought out a handful of paper. "This may do the trick. The coals are out and there isn't a stick in the place." The paper charred and curled into a sulky flame.

"That's no good." Spike took up the haversack and put the clothes back into it. "We'll chuck it in the barge."

"It's the only way to get rid of it," Mrs. Kemp said. "All right. Let's get on with the job. Open the doors and then come and give me a hand."

They had almost reached the front door when a door opened on the first-floor landing. Mrs. Kemp let Rivers's feet fall and ran heavily up the stairs. It was Alma.

She said: "Oh, it's you, is it? Is there anything wrong?"

"No, of course not. You get back to bed."

"I thought it was burglars or something. I'm sure I heard a man in the back garden."

"That was me, deary. I was putting out the dustbin."

"Well, what was that noise downstairs?"

"It was only me and Spike. We've been sitting up having a chat. Now you get along to your bed."

Alma went reluctantly. She knew that Mrs. Kemp was lying but what was the use of arguing at that time of night?

Mrs. Kemp joined Spike in the hall.

She told him what Alma had said. "Don't you think we'd better do something about her door? But there isn't a key to it and we don't want her to come out and—"

"Take this." Spike took a small wedge from his pocket. "Go up and wish her happy dreams and slip this in the jamb."

While Mrs. Kemp was gone he went out into the front garden. The only light showing was on the bridge a couple of hundred yards away. The canal path was in complete darkness overshadowed by the gaunt warehouse opposite. He walked to the railings and looked over. There were three empty barges alongside. The railings weren't high. It was a good idea of Ma's. He'd never have thought of it himself.

She was waiting for him as he tiptoed back up the path. "I've fixed her. What about it?"

"All ready. And let's do it quick. When we get to the fence, stop. Swing it twice and then lift and over."

Hours seemed to have passed from the time when Spike let go his grip and the body fell, until he heard the dull reverberations of the barge as the body fell against the steel side and slid down. The haversack followed it.

Mrs. Kemp took him by the arm. "Come on back, for God's sake. We've finished. That's the last of Mr. Rivers."

The lid of the kettle was dancing a jig when they got into the back room.

"We'll have a toddy. Reach me down the bottle. Funny to think that I always kept this for him and now—" Her voice trailed away.

"What's going to happen when they find him? Right alongside the front door."

"That barge'll be shifted before it's light. The tug comes about five or soon after."

"Where does it take it to?"

"I dunno. Down the river somewhere, to a coal hulk. You'll be all right. They'll never trace him back here." Mrs. Kemp put two lumps of sugar in each glass, a good tot of whisky, and filled them up with boiling water.

"I was thinking of Alma and that boy friend of hers. What if he comes here?"

"He won't." Mrs. Kemp chuckled. "I made sure of that. I tore the address off the letter before I sent it. I wasn't taking any chances seeing as it was you that was doing the job."

"He'll try to find her."

"He can try."

Spike and Mrs. Kemp were tired when they went up to bed, stepping softly past Alma's door. But neither could sleep. There was no remorse in Spike's heart for what he had done, and little fear. He had the murderer's feeling of omnipotence which sometimes attends them even up to the time of trial, the appeal and to the last day. They can't die. They can't. . . . Like people in an earthquake who believe that whatever happens they will not be harmed, murderers believe that something will occur to save them. But Spike had, deep down in his being, a doubt. If they found the body before the barge was moved!

He lay on his back on his bed, fully dressed, smoking a chain of cigarettes. He stubbed them out on the floor. His body was tired but his brain was active. He thought of Alma. She was a good kid. If he could string her along she'd stick to him.

A girl sometimes could be more use than a man. Than Len for instance. Len! He'd have to do something about him. If the splits got a hold of him and handled him a certain way, he'd talk and if Len talked—Hell! He'd have to go along to Larry's in the morning and see him. Put the fear of God into him and make him lie up for a spell.

Maybe the man Len slugged wouldn't be found. At least, not for a time. That would give him time to think what to do. Time to search Rivers's rooms and get the dough that must be there.

Spike was dozing when the milkman woke him. The candle had burned down to a guttering blue flame. He lit a match. Ten past five. The tug would be there at five, Ma had said it would.

His legs were stiff and cold as he swung them to the floor. He rubbed some feeling into them and stood up and yawned. Later on he'd have a good sleep but now he had to make sure about that damn' barge. Some one was moving about below on the first-floor landing. He could hear the creak of a board and the sound of breathing.

"That you, Spike?"

He crept down the stairs keeping close to the wall. The black bulk of Mrs. Kemp showed dimly. "Yes," he whispered. "What are you doing?"

"Same as you. Come on."

Spike followed Mrs. Kemp down to the hall and into the front parlour. He bumped into a table and knocked over a photograph frame. Mrs. Kemp stretched out a hand to guide him.

They stood at the uncurtained window.

"Is it still there?" Spike whispered.

"Look!" Three men came along the path, climbed the railings and disappeared. "Them's the blokes what steers the barges. One on each. It'll be all right. You wait."

Spike waited. Mrs. Kemp sat on the arm of a plush uphol-stered chair. "Shouldn't be long now," she said as Spike lit his third cigarette. Five minutes passed and then he heard a slow cough-cough coming from the direction of the tunnel. It was the tug. It came nearer. Spike heard the swish of her wash as she turned. The tinkle of a bell. The engine slowed. Some one shouted: "Catch hold." The engine went astern, slowly at first and then gathering speed. The bell sounded again. The rush of water subsided. A man ran along the deck of the barge. "All fast." Again the bell. The engine began to pick up, became fainter and finally died away. Mrs. Kemp got up and sighed. It was still dark outside.

"What did I tell you?"

"I'm going to sleep now," Spike said.

"And me. Don't make a noise going up. When you wake, sing out and I'll bring you your breakfast up."

"That'll be dinner-time. I'm played out."

CHAPTER TEN

A GYPSY found Will Dorset. He had been up before dawn ranging the common for sticks, which would cut up into clothes pegs, and came to the edge of the gravel pit as dawn was breaking. He saw the van.

At first it didn't strike him as odd that it should be there, and he was turning away when his questing eyes saw a black blot on the clay of the track leading in from the road.

Puzzled, the gypsy dropped down into the pit to investigate. What he had seen from above was a black fox skin. He picked it up with acquisitive fingers and looked round. Some birds in a stunted oak broke suddenly into a chatter and, a moment later, as suddenly were silent.

In the silence which followed, the gypsy heard a man breathing heavily; a man asleep, in the van. He looked at the fur in his hands, and then thrust it under a clump of heather. It would be all right there till he could collect it.

He stared at the side of the van and spelled out the words "North Down Fox Farm." That was the place just up the road. Funny the van standing here, not half a mile from home. The driver was drunk most likely. But that was none of his business.

Curiosity, however, drew the gypsy to the front of the van. He saw Will Dorset sitting in the driving seat with his head thrown back and mouth wide open. "Sleeping it off," he muttered. "Lucky for him the slop didn't find him. Drunk in charge. They jail you for that."

Will Dorset opened his eyes. Like a wild animal disturbed, the gypsy was out of sight at the first danger sign. Will called out: "Hi! Wait a minute," in a weak voice.

The gypsy halted, rigid, five paces away.

"Help!"

The gypsy came cautiously back.

"What's up, mate?"

"Get a policeman and tell him to bring a handcuff key."

"A what?"

"A key for handcuffs. I've been held up."

"Held up?" The gypsy was not a quick thinker.

"Go and get a policeman," Will said slowly and deliberately. "Get a policeman. I'll give you half a crown if he's here in twenty minutes."

The gypsy said: "Yes, I understand. I'll go." He took a side-glance at the heather clump where he had hidden the fur and then ran down the road.

Police-Constable Wilkins hated gypsies as badly as they hated him. At no time did he dislike them more than at six-thirty on a winter's morning following a turn of night duty.

But the gypsy was insistent. There was a man in a van in a gravel pit.

"What's the matter with him?" Wilkins asked.

"He said he'd been held up."

The words dispelled the sleepy distrust in the policeman's brain. "It ain't the Fox Farm van, is it?"

"That's right. North Down Fox Farm. It's writ on the side of it."

"You stop there. I'll be down in half a tick."

"The bloke said you was to bring a handcuff key."

Wilkins stared at the gypsy for a moment. "It's like that, is it? All right, you start back. I'll come on my bike."

As soon as his hands and legs were free, Will slipped from his seat and tried to stand. The policeman caught him as he fell.

"Take it easy, chum. Feeling bad?"

"Rotten. I'll be all right in a minute." Will sat on the running board and rubbed his numbed legs. Wilkins gave him a cigarette.

"We got word last night you hadn't got to London. What happened?"

"Two blokes held me up, soon after I'd started. Tied me up. That's all there is to it."

Wilkins looked over the seat into the body of the van. "You had a load on board, hadn't you?"

"Yes. They lifted the lot."

"What sort of a car did they have?"

"A saloon. I didn't notice much about it."

"Did you get the number?"

Will shook his head.

"We'd better get back," Wilkins said. "I'll put a call through right away. Can you drive?"

Will clutched at the top of the door and pulled himself to his feet. "Yes, I think so." He reached over and pressed the button of the self-starter. It whirred and whined but the engine didn't fire.

"She's cold. And so am I. Like blinking lumps of ice my legs are." He climbed awkwardly into the driving seat, pulled out the choke and worked the starter again. The engine fired, irregularly at first and then, with many coughs and one shattering backfire, it broke into a steady rhythmic beat.

He drove out of the gravel pit and turned right-handed up the hill to the farm. There was no one in the yard. He got out and walked to a door and beat on it.

He told his story to Captain Harding's cook, to Captain Harding himself, and then waited in the kitchen, drinking tea, until Wilkins arrived with a sergeant of police and he told it all over again.

Police-Constable Wilkins wrote it all down laboriously in a very small note-book. The gypsy added his quota. An inspector came on a bicycle, and later a portly superintendent in an Austin Seven which fitted him like a glove.

The superintendent, the inspector and the sergeant talked it over while Wilkins kept a close watch on the gypsy, who by now was feeling acutely uncomfortable. Policemen gave him gooseflesh.

Two constables on motorcycles were sent to search the roads around Crowley. Every man in the district was called out and told to look for two men, one about five foot six, wearing a dark suit and a felt hat, and the other, height six feet, young appearance. At that hour of the morning there were apparently no men in felt hats abroad, and negative reports came in with depressing regularity.

The superintendent called up the chief constable and suggested that Scotland Yard should be informed and asked to assist. The chief constable agreed wholeheartedly, put through the request and had an early and a tepid bath.

The superintendent, with the aid of a constable who said he could write shorthand, questioned every person in the village of Crowley. It was a long job and the results were disappointing.

No one remembered having seen any mysterious visitors in the village during the previous two or three days, and only one man had seen a saloon car drive past the green at about the time of the robbery.

This man, who ought to have been tending his employer's garden, had stolen an hour to attend to his own front plot. Naturally he denied that he had been near the village during working hours.

Two children, however, had seen him, and he was forced to admit to the superintendent that he had been in his own garden and had seen a car pass down the road.

The time he reckoned as being a couple of hours before the pub opened, and ten minutes after the bus had left for Guildford.

"Put down ten-ten," the superintendent ordered his amateur stenographer. "Now then, my man, what sort of a car was it you saw?"

"There was two men in it, and one of 'em was wearing a lightish sort of coat. Yellow, I'd say it was. It caught my eye as the car went by."

"What was the car like? Was it open or shut?"

The gardener thought hard. "It was what they call a saloon, but I didn't hardly notice it; it was the man who was driving that caught my eye."

"Was that the one who was wearing the yellow coat?"

"That's right."

"Would you know him if you saw him again?"

"No, I didn't see his face. He was holding his hand up."

And that was all the superintendent could get out of the gardener.

Two men in a saloon car, colour and number unknown. The driver wearing a yellow coat.

A pile of reports based on the questioning of strangers in the district were bundled together and sent up to Scotland Yard.

At seven-thirty Chief Inspector Thompson was informed by the duty officer of what had happened. He gave orders for a radio call to be sent out, dressed hurriedly and took a tram to Scotland Yard. The fact that he was able to get a workman's ticket gave him a certain melancholy satisfaction.

Detective-Sergeant Perry was waiting for him.

"What's all the flap?" Thompson sat down at his desk. "It's only a van been knocked off, isn't it?"

"Yes, but it had a lot of furs in it worth somewhere near three thousand pounds."

"Oh, furs! Do you think it might be Lynch's crowd did it?"

"Maybe." Perry gave Thompson a paper. "That tells you all about it."

"If you've read it, tell it me in words of one syllable."

"There was a stick-up. Two men in it. They wore masks. One of them had a gun."

"Lynch never carried a gun in his life."

"The driver of the car gave a man a lift. He picked him up a few minutes before the hold-up."

"What had he got to say?"

"They didn't find him."

"Have we got a description?"

"Nothing that's any good. Short, sandy-haired. Looking for a job."

"There's quite a few like him. Got any idea as to who pulled the job?"

"Hilton's been out checking up."

"Has he done any good?"

"Cardy wasn't at home."

"This business isn't down his street. Who else?"

"Mick Swarty."

"It wasn't Mick."

"Spike Morgan was away all day, but he was seen at a club in Old Compton Street round about midnight."

"Spike? I don't seem to know him."

"He used to work with the Borough race gang, but he's shifted up north. Camden Town, Hilton said."

"Put a call through to pick him up, and then check over the receivers. We'll pay them all a visit."

Mrs. Kemp was almost tearful in her entreaties to Spike to stay at home on Saturday morning. "What's the sense in taking a risk? You're all right here."

"They've got nothing on me."

"Not yet they haven't, but don't forget Len. He talks too much when he's got a load aboard."

"That's who I'm going to see. I expect he's at Larry's, sleeping off last night's jag."

Spike didn't reach Larry's that morning. As he was waiting for a bus, Leith came up to him.

"'Morning, Spike. You're out early."

"That ain't a crime, is it?"

"No. It's a virtue. Where were you last night?"

Spike hesitated for an instant before he replied: "At Larry's. Why?"

"Sleep there?"

"Yes."

"You've got a funny taste. The last time I was there the smell nearly turned me up. It's a lousy hole."

"That's where I was, anyway. At Larry's."

"What were you doing before you went there?"

"Knocking round. I can't remember."

Spike decided to give the bus a miss and take a tube. He started to walk away. "So long."

Leith fell into step beside him. "I'm going your way," he said. Spike made no reply.

At Fenner Street the traffic was thick and Spike leaned against a lamp-post waiting for a chance to cross the road. "When did you go to Larry's?"

"Eleven o'clock. I stopped there most of the day."

"Your memory's improving. Had time to think things up?"

Spike gave Leith a side-glance and then looked down in the gutter. He sucked at his cigarette. It burned his lip. He dropped it into a puddle.

"What are you getting at?"

"Some one pulled the hell of a fine job last night. Haven't you heard about it?"

"No."

"And I thought you got all the news at Larry's. The place must have changed since last week."

Leith took a short pace forward and ran his hands over Spike.

"Drew a blank that time," Spike sneered. "I suppose you thought I had a gun. Well, I don't carry one and I never have."

"Then you have got some sense."

"And I was at Larry's all day yesterday."

"You said that before. It doesn't mean any more than it did the first time. I think we'll take a walk."

"All right. I don't care, but you're wasting your time."

"I'm paid for that. Come on."

At the police station Spike nodded to the sergeant in charge and sat on a wooden bench. It wasn't the first time he'd been brought in for questioning. They'd never got anything out of him before, and they weren't going to this time.

Leith spoke to the sergeant who got off his high stool and walked over to Spike.

"Stand up." Spike got up slowly. "You say you were at Larry's all day yesterday?"

"That's right. I'll write it down if you like and then you won't have to ask me again."

"Who was there?"

"Quite a crowd. There always is."

"Give me a name or two so's I can check up."

"Larry'll speak for me."

"I bet he will," was Leith's dry comment. "He'd say anything."

"There was Benny Hart and Tiger Smith."

"That all?"

"All I took notice of."

Leith tried a bluff. "You were seen driving a car yesterday."

"That's a lie." There was too much vehemence in the denial for it to be convincing. Leith looked at the sergeant and then turned back to Spike.

"There's no need to get excited. Nothing wrong in driving a car if you haven't pinched it and you've got a licence."

"I've got a licence. Here you are." Spike took a wallet from his pocket and pulled out a small red book. "And it's clean."

Leith almost smiled. "That must be a great comfort to you."

The sergeant glanced at the licence and handed it back. "Where were you going in that car?"

"I wasn't going anywhere. I mean I wasn't driving a car yesterday. How could I? I was at Larry's."

"Maybe it was some one else." The sergeant shuffled through a pile of papers, selected one and ran his eye over it. "I'm afraid you'll have to stop with us for a bit. There's a few things we may have to ask you later on."

Spike stiffened. "What's the charge?"

"Detained on suspicion of having been concerned in the theft of a quantity of furs." The sergeant dipped his pen in the ink and wrote in a ledger. Then he blotted the words, looked up and caught the jailer's eye. "Number seven."

Spike stepped forward and gripped the desk. "Furs! I don't know nothing about them. You've no right to keep me here. I've told you where I was yesterday. Ain't that enough? And I've got witnesses to say—"

Leith took him by one arm. "Time enough to go into that later."

The jailer stepped up on his other side. "Come on, mate."

They ran him down a passage to the cells.

"Give us your boots."

Spike sat on the narrow plank bed and pulled at his laces.

"Anything you want?" Leith asked.

"I could do with a pint."

"Can't manage that. Against the rules. Anything else?"

"Go to hell!"

Leith left the jailer to lock up and went back to the charge room.

"Well, what d'you think?"

The sergeant rubbed his chin. "I have my doubts. It may be as he says that he hadn't anything to do with yesterday's job, but I don't know."

"If it wasn't that, it was something else. He was lying."

"It's a habit with blokes of his sort. He couldn't tell the truth if he wanted to."

"Thompson's on the job, isn't he?"

The sergeant nodded. "He's death to a quiet life."

"Yes, I know that. If I'd had any sense, I wouldn't have brought Spike in. Have you got a pencil?"

"There's one sticking out of your pocket."

"I'll need a dozen before long. Thompson loves reports. 'On the night of the fifth inst. I was keeping observation.' That's how I always start. It's a polite way for saying, 'When I was standing outside a public house in the perishing cold with both feet dead.' And it's a funny thing, but I always seem to have to be near a pub."

The sergeant gave him a pencil and grinned. "You should never have gone plain clothes. Look at me. Regular hours. I keeps warm and dry."

Leith sat down and took a paper off the sergeant's desk. "Well. I'm going to keep warm and dry till Thompson turns up. And improve my mind at the same time." He turned to the sports page, and started reading an article entitled, "Best for Harringay to-night."

When Thompson got the report about Spike, he left Perry to organize a search of pawnshops and fences likely to deal in furs, and went himself to the police station where Spike was detained.

Leith greeted him suspiciously.

"Well, where is he?" Thompson snapped.

The sergeant gave an order to the jailer. "I don't think he's the man we want," he said to Thompson. "But there's something he's keeping back, and I thought it better you should see him."

Spike appeared in his stocking soles. He looked at Thompson and then dropped his eyes.

The sergeant opened a door. "Perhaps you'd like to see him in here, sir. More private."

"Yes. Bring him in." Thompson sat on a chair at a table. "Morgan's your name, is it?"

"That's right."

"Sit down. Have a fag." Thompson waited a minute, and then asked, "Where were you yesterday?"

"Ask the sergeant. I've told him all I'm going to say."

"I want you to tell me."

"I'm not talking."

"That won't do you any good."

"Talking won't, neither."

"Oh, then you have been up to something. Come on, Morgan. Spill it."

"There ain't nothing to tell. I've got witnesses to say I was at Larry's bar all day yesterday."

Thompson did his best, but Spike became dumb. When he had been taken back to his cell, Thompson saw the sergeant. "You'd better let him go, but put some one on to trailing him, and let me have full reports of where he goes and what he does."

A faint groan came from Leith. Reports! He fingered the pencil the sergeant had given him. It was nicely pointed, and had plenty of lead in it.

"Where's your D.I.?" Thompson asked.

"I'm expecting him in any time now, sir," the sergeant replied.

"All right. Tell him about Morgan, and ask him to put a good man on to him."

When Thompson had gone, the sergeant grinned. "A good man, he said. That's you, Leith. And I hope Morgan's fond of pubs."

When Perry saw Thompson's expression, he said, "Not so good?"

"No. Drew a blank, that time. I told 'em to let him go—on a string."

"I see. Spike's just the sort of man who would pull a job like this."

"I've been thinking that, too. He's got a rotten alibi. He said he was at Larry's."

Perry laughed. "I'd like to see Larry in the box. I wonder what a jury would think of him?"

"No one will ever know what a jury thinks about anything. They're weird and wonderful. I put up a case once that was cast iron. Not a hole in it. Judge summed up dead against the prisoner, and the jury, bless their hearts, let the blighter off. That was Benny Hart. He's still going strong. But he'll fall one of these days, and when he does you'll hear the bump all over Town."

Mrs. Kemp watched Spike go, and then went into the house and shut the door. Joe was standing in the passage with his coat on and his cap on his head.

"Where are you off to?" she asked.

"To Rivers's place. I'm waiting for Alma. She's going to mind the shop."

"Mr. Rivers has gone away."

"Gone! He never said nothing to me about it. When I saw him yesterday evening he told me to come round at the usual time. We was going to the Lower Marsh."

"He's gone away. He doesn't know when he'll be back. Tell Alma she needn't bother to go round." Mrs. Kemp took a shawl from a chair and wrapped it round her shoulders. "I'm going out."

She went to Rivers's yard by a roundabout route. The yard gate was as she had left it on the previous night. The door to the top room was shut. She looked up at the window and then walked back to the gate. There was no one about.

Her heart was thumping as she unlocked the door and slipped in. She bolted it behind her, and went up the stairs. The room smelt bad with stale smoke, and she was about to draw back the curtains and open the window. Better not. Don't want anybody to know I'm here.

She forced herself to look at the place where Rivers had lain, and was relieved not to see him there.

The boards were stained black where the rug had been. Another rug was ruckled back. She pulled it straight. Glass from the shattered picture was strewn over the floor.

She went on to the landing and found a brush and a mop and pail in a cupboard. She filled the pail at a tap downstairs, and went back to the top room. The blood took a bit of moving for it had soaked into the wooden floor, but after half an hour's work she was satisfied she had cleaned it all up. The water in the pail had turned a murky brown and she emptied it out in the sink before she set to with the broom to sweep up the glass.

There wasn't a dustpan, and in the manner familiar to her she pushed the debris under a cabinet in a corner of the room. The room was beginning to look a bit better now, if it wasn't for that rug that Spike had put round the corpse. It had left a gap. She pushed back the sofa and chairs against the wall and rearranged the other rugs so that the space was partly covered.

Then she sat down for a breather, and saw the smashed picture. Better get that out of the way. She got up with a sigh and many creaks, carried it down to the shop, and put it on a shelf with the broken side to the wall.

It was lucky for Spike he'd got her to clear up after him. If any one had seen the room as it was before she had started on it, they'd have thought things. Told the police, most likely, and then where'd they have been?

Spike! He was a devil. Always had been. Hardly human, was what his own father used to say when he saw him torturing a stray cat. He'd leathered him for it, but it hadn't done no good.

Mrs. Kemp felt very blue, and when she was that way there was but one remedy. She went to seek it at the Green Man at the canal bridge.

"Mild and Burton, if you please, Fred, and let's have it right up to the top this time. I'm thirsty."

Her purse, which had many divisions but few coins, yielded two ha'pennies.

Fred looked at the coins laid out on the counter and kept a firm hold of the glass he had filled.

An easy, ingratiating smile came over Mrs. Kemp's face. "Well, just fancy that, now. I could a' sworn I'd got another tuppence somewhere." She felt optimistically in the pocket of her overall. "That's no good." She turned her purse upside down. Some dust fell out. Also a button, a shoe lace, and a peppermint.

Mrs. Benson, who was standing at the bar, sniffed, and winked at Fred. He preserved a wooden stare. Threepence was what he wanted for the half can.

Mrs. Kemp fawned on Mrs. Benson. She hated to do it, but the call of beer was strong within her. "You haven't tuppence you could let me have till to-night, have you?"

Surprisingly Mrs. Benson produced a sixpenny bit. "Here you are."

"But I was only wanting tuppence. I'll get you change."

"You hang on to the tanner. That's what I'm lending you. If it was tuppence you might forget. A tanner's different."

"Well, I'm sure that's real nice of you, Mrs. Benson, ain't it, Fred?"

Fred sucked a back tooth and nodded. Mrs. Kemp returned her ha'pennies to her purse and gave him the sixpence. Before he had turned to bang the cash register the mild and Burton was well on its way to a good home.

"Your old man's home to-day, I see," observed Mrs. Benson, with the gracious condescension of a creditor.

Mrs. Kemp stopped in mid-swallow to say, "Yes, the bloke he works for has hopped it."

"Really, now." The loan of the sixpence had paved the way for the question Mrs. Benson was burning to ask. She had seen the shutters up on Rivers's shop. "And is he going to be away for long, may I ask?"

"A week or two," replied Mrs. Kemp. "He said he wasn't sure when he'd be back."

Fred put down the paper he had started to read. "Mr. Rivers gone away? That's funny. I've been here two years, and he's never missed coming in here of a night-time. He was in yesterday about six and never said nothing about going away. In fact, now I comes to think of it, he said that him and Joe was going to try the Lower Marsh this morning."

"He's gone, all right." Mrs. Kemp finished her drink. "Give me the same again."

"Did he say where he was going?" Mrs. Benson asked.

"No, he didn't. His business is his own, and if he likes to go off for a day or two I wouldn't ask him about it. He'd bite my head off if I so much as took the liberty."

"But you knows him well, Mrs. Kemp. He was having supper with you the other night, wasn't he?"

"Yes, he did look in."

"I saw him going up to your door. You had a lot of company that night, didn't you?"

Mrs. Kemp decided that the conversation had gone far enough. She finished her second glass of beer. "Well, I must be going now. I've got my shopping to do yet."

Mrs. Benson was going to say that a penny wouldn't go far, but Mrs. Kemp was out of the bar with the door swinging behind her before she could utter the words.

Mrs. Kemp passed Rivers's shop on her way home, and saw a bottle of milk and a paper on the step. She hadn't thought of that. If the police were to see a lot of milk bottles, they might think things and start asking questions. She picked up the milk and the paper and thrust them under her shawl. She hadn't been seen. She hurried down the alley-way to the street at the back and home by the door in the back garden wall.

Alma was dusting the mantelpiece. "What have you got there? Milk?"

"That's right, deary. And a paper. I thought you might be wearying."

"I'm all right. But what d'you want with more milk? There's a jug in the kitchen not touched hardly."

Mrs. Kemp was too finished a liar to lie unnecessarily. "Well, as a matter of fact, it's Mr. Rivers's, but seeing as how he's gone away and won't want it, I thought we could make use of it." She added, as an afterthought, "Of course, I'll pay him for it."

Alma had grasped the state of the finances in the Kemp household sufficiently well to doubt the last statement.

"And as he's going to be away for some time, I thought it'd be as well if we was to put a sort of a notice on his door. What did you do with that pen and ink?"

"On the dresser." Alma put them on the table. "And here's the paper."

Mrs. Kemp thought, "No it won't do to use that paper. They might trace it back here." She said aloud, "Wait a minute," and went into the kitchen. Part of the lining of a drawer supplied her with her needs. It wasn't too clean. She gave Alma the pen. "Here, you write it, if you don't mind."

"What d'you want me to say?"

Mrs. Kemp frowned. "Now how would you put it? You see, we want to stop people leaving things."

Alma looked blank. "I dunno exactly."

"How about 'Gone away. Back soon'?" After a moment's thought Mrs. Kemp said, "No, that's not right. Sounds as if he'd gone to his lunch."

"When will he be back?"

"I don't know. Weeks, maybe."

"Why not say, 'Nothing wanted. Back in a week's time'?"

"That'll do. Now you write it."

Alma dipped her pen in the ink and started. "This paper ain't no good. Look! The ink runs all over the place. It's more like blotting paper."

"Print it, then." Mrs. Kemp gathered up the sheets of note-paper, and put them back in their box.

The result was not pretty, but it was legible. "That'll do fine," said Mrs. Kemp, when Alma had finished. She took the paper and held it in front of the fire until it steamed and began to curl. "Where's Joe?"

"Out. He didn't say where he was going."

"Then you stop here. I won't be long." Mrs. Kemp rummaged in a drawer and found a drawing pin. She put it in her pocket, and went out.

The wood of Rivers's shop door was hard, and the drawing pin bent and fell to the ground as Mrs. Kemp tried to push it in. She picked it up, but its useful life had ended. She knew what she'd do. She folded the paper and walked up the street to a sweet shop which had a post office sign outside.

The woman behind the counter was weighing out half an ounce of barley-sugar drops. She looked up as the door bell rang. "'Morning, Mrs. Kemp. I won't keep you a minute." She poured the sweets into a twisted paper cone and gave it to a very small boy who regretfully handed over a ha'penny in exchange.

"Sorry to trouble you," Mrs. Kemp said. "But all I'm wanting is a bit of stamp paper. I wonder if you could oblige. A small bit'd do."

"Certainly. It's no trouble at all." The postmistress took a flat book of stamps from a drawer. She laid it on the counter and put her elbows on it preparatory to a good, long, gossiping talk. But Mrs. Kemp was unnaturally silent. All she wanted was the stamp paper, and to get the job finished.

When she got it she hurried to Rivers's shop and stuck up the notice, and then, having but one penny in her purse, she went back to Napier Terrace. Joe was lounging in the doorway smoking.

"What time's dinner?"

"There ain't going to be no dinner," Mrs. Kemp snapped. "Not unless you can find something to buy it with. We're broke."

Joe smoked on equably. Then he took his pipe out of his mouth to ask, "What was going on last night?"

"Where d'you mean?"

"Here."

"Why?"

"Alma's been asking."

"Where is she?"

"In the back room. And you might tell her to stop all this cleaning up. She fair gives me the jitters."

"I'll talk to her."

Joe went on smoking.

Mrs. Kemp took off her shawl as she pounded down the passage. She'd got to put a stop to this talk of Alma's. Once word went round, people would start asking questions, and that there Nosey Leith would be making trouble. Wanting to know this and that.

When Alma saw her, she said, "Oh, Mrs. Kemp, about last night. I've been meaning to ask you—"

"Well." The aggressive tone made Alma stop her dusting. "What did you want to ask?"

"Oh, it's nothing."

"Let's have it."

"I was just wondering what was going on last night. I heard you walking about. You and Spike. It sounded as if you were carrying something."

Mrs. Kemp laughed. "What time was it?"

"Late. Near one o'clock."

"What d'you think we'd be doing shifting things at that time of night?"

"I don't know, I'm sure, but it sounded like that."

"You were asleep, and dreamed it."

"Perhaps I did," Alma conceded.

Mrs. Kemp thawed. "Then forget it, and don't you go saying things to anybody outside."

"Of course I won't. Why should I?"

"Well, don't, that's all. Put the kettle on, and we'll have a nice cup of tea. And you can lay off that cleaning and dusting. If you want something to do, I'll give you some mending."

Joe came down the passage from the front door. "Where's Spike gone?" he asked.

"I don't know. He ought to be back any time now." Mrs. Kemp's mouth broadened in a smile. "And I expect he'll be wanting to take you out, Alma."

"I don't know that I want to go."

"Of course you do. Don't be silly," and Alma knew that if Spike did ask her she would have to go with him. Mrs. Kemp would see to that.

CHAPTER ELEVEN

SPIKE LEFT the police station relieved at his dismissal, but yet uneasy in his mind. He hadn't liked the look of Thompson. He would have to watch his step from now on, and see that Len did, too. Curse Len! Once the splits found the body of the man in the ditch, things would begin to hum. Still, they hadn't anything on him, and if he kept his trap shut he'd be safe.

He found Len at Larry's. He was sitting at the long table playing whisky poker. Spike watched him for a few minutes, and then touched him on the arm.

Len threw down his hand and said, "You can count me out this round." He turned to Spike. "What's up?"

"Nothing much. Come over here." Spike pulled up a chair to a table in a far corner of the room. "Where've you been?"

"Since when?"

"Last night."

"Here, mostly. I've been for a walk round a couple of times."

"Any one stop you?"

"You mean the splits?"

Spike nodded. "Leith, for instance."

"No. I haven't seen him."

"That's something. They picked me up."

Fear came to Len. His jaw dropped an inch. "What happened?"

Spike gave a short laugh. "Usual stuff. Where was I yesterday? What was I doing? You know."

"What did you say?"

"Said I'd been here. It was the only place I could think of."

"Who was it asked you that? Leith?"

"He started it. And then Thompson had a go."

"Thompson? Who's he?"

"A big shot from the Yard. You don't want to try any funny stuff with him. He's hot."

"They haven't found out anything, have they?"

"If they had, I wouldn't be here. Brixton'd have been my address till further notice." Spike called to Larry. "Give us a spot of that fire water of yours."

Larry slid off his stool and produced a bottle and glasses. "This stuff's all right." There was a knock at the street door. Larry padded across the room and up the steps. He was back in a minute with a paper parcel in his hand. "Know any one of the name of Jones?"

"That's me," Spike replied, and stretched out his hand. Larry grinned and gave him the parcel. "I thought somehow as it might be you."

Spike worked off the string and unfolded the paper. "What'd you think of that?" He laid a black fox tie across his arm.

Larry ran his fingers through the fur. "Not so bad," he said, and went back to his stool.

"If you showed that guy the Crown Jewels he'd say the same. He's born that way. Who's it for?"

"That kid at Mrs. Kemp's. She's the goods."

But Len wasn't interested in Alma. He was more concerned with his own safety. "What d'you think about clearing out?"

"Don't you worry. Once get on the run and you can't stop. Town's safest, in the end." Spike held his glass up to the light. "Dammit, Larry's been putting meth. in this. Taste it?"

"It's the usual muck. I suppose you've seen Rivers?"

"Yes, I saw him. Last night."

"Did you get the dough?"

"Not yet."

"Hell! Why not? I thought he always anted up. I'm on my bones."

Spike was staring into a dark corner of the room. Len took a pouch from his pocket and began to roll a cigarette. "What's the matter with you?" He touched Spike on the arm.

Spike turned his head slowly towards him. "Nothing. What were you saying?"

"Why didn't Rivers pay up?"

"He hasn't got the cash from Izzy. But you needn't sweat. We'll have it in a couple of days. Perhaps sooner than that."

A man came into the shop and went up to Larry. They whispered together for a minute or two. Then Larry came over to Spike's table. "Leith's hanging round. He's on the corner now."

Spike ground out the stub of his cigarette in a saucer. He didn't look up. "All right. Thanks for the tip."

"You knew Leith was there," Len said. "And something's been happening you haven't told me about."

Spike blew out a thin stream of smoke. "Windy?"

"No. I'm not windy."

"I didn't know Leith was outside, but I thought he might be. He doesn't count, anyway."

"Why did you think he'd be there?" Len was cooling down.

"Haven't I just told you he picked me up? You're getting rattled."

Len splashed some more drink into his glass.

"Now, go easy on that stuff. You'll want a clear head from now on, and before you leave here work out an alibi for yesterday. If you're asked about it, don't bring it out too pat. Act stupid. And don't say more than you have to, to make it sound right."

"I've a pal in the Borough. I can say I was with him." Len picked up a paper. "We went to Hurst Park and didn't get back till late."

"That'll do. Now, about to-night. I want you to give me a hand."

"A job?"

"Yes, a break. As soft as kiss your hand. All you'll have to do is to keep a look-out."

"Whereabouts?"

"Camden Town way."

"Shop?"

"No, a house. I've got the keys, and the bloke'll be away for the night."

"What about Leith?"

"We'll slip him, all right."

Spike waited until it was dark, and then said to Larry, "We're off. Give us the cellar key."

Larry got up. "I'll come with you." He lit an oil lamp and opened a trap in the floor. An earthy, damp smell came up on a current of cold air. Larry sat on the edge of the trap and felt for the rungs of a ladder. He climbed down slowly. Spike and Len followed.

"Keep close behind me," Larry said. "There's a lot of junk down here." There was a squeak and a scuffle. "Rats. The place is rotten with 'em since that house at the back was pulled down."

Len shivered. He, who feared no man when he was at the wheel of a car, was scared of rats.

Larry gave Spike the lamp to hold while he took down a shutter and opened a window. They climbed through on to a space surrounded by three roofless walls and covered with heaps of broken bricks, planks and joists. A hoarding had been erected in place of the fourth wall, which had faced on Ely Street.

Larry prised back two loose boards and poked his head through.

"It's all clear," he whispered. "Slip through quick."

"Wait a minute," Spike said, and took Len by the arm. "You've got to leave that coat of yours here."

Len protested, but Spike overrode his objections. "Stow it away somewhere," Spike ordered Larry, and led Len into the street.

They kept together as far as the first corner, and there separated. Forty minutes later they met at the canal bridge, and walked quickly along the crowded pavement to the alley-way leading to the back of Rivers's shop.

Spike opened the gate. "You go over in that corner and get up on one of these cases so as you can see the street. Have you got a flash?"

"Yes."

"That's good. I'll be working on the first floor." Spike pointed to the windows. "If any one comes along, show your light, and keep it burning."

Spike, who had called in at Napier Terrace for the key, opened the door and ran up the stairs to the top room. The fact that he had killed a man in that room meant nothing to him. He had no nerves and no imagination.

He pulled down the blinds and drew the curtains. For two hours he worked; quartering the rooms, tapping the walls, and trying the boards. At last he gave up and rejoined Len in the yard. "Have you seen any one?"

"No. Did you get the stuff?"

"No. It wasn't there. And yet it must be, curse it! I've half a mind to go back and have another go." Spike stood undecided, fingering his cigarette-case.

Len said, "It's damn' cold. Let's beat it."

"All right."

"Is there anywhere else we can try?"

"Yes, but I've done enough for to-night. Besides, there's a dog loose there and he's a devil." Spike was thinking of Mr. Tibbett in his caravan, and Captain. He was as scared of Captain as Len was scared of rats.

"Well, what are we going to do for a doss?"

"I know where we can go."

They went to Mrs. Kemp's, who looked a question at Spike when she opened the door. He shook his head and muttered, "No luck." Then he pulled Len forward. "This is a pal of mine. Do you think you can fix him with a bed?"

"Yes, if he doesn't mind sharing a room. Come on in."

A wireless was blaring in the backroom as they entered. Joe didn't hear the door open, and jumped up when he saw Spike, who laughed at his startled expression. He introduced Len. Alma, who had been washing up, came in from the kitchen.

"We've been wondering what had happened to you," she said with a smile, and shook hands with Len. "Pleased to meet you."

Spike produced the black fox skin and stretched it out on the table. "I've been getting that for you. D'you like it?"

Alma looked at the fur and then up at Spike. "For me? D'you mean you're giving it me?"

"That's right. Try it on."

Mrs. Kemp put it round Alma's neck. "Well, now, isn't that nice? Handsome, I calls it. And it doesn't half suit you, deary. Don't it, Joe?"

Joe, who had had bread and dripping for supper, grumbled, "Waste of money, I calls it." He fiddled with a knob on the wireless set. A lady singing throatily faded out, and a man's voice announced, "Missing from his home since six o'clock on Friday—" Joe turned the knob again, and brought in a dance band. He picked up his paper and began to read.

The eulogy of the black fox fur continued.

"I never thought I'd ever have one like this," Alma was saying. "And it's the real thing. I know, because when I went up to the farm to see Will, he showed me the ones there. But there wasn't any as good as this. It's so long. And look at the thickness of it. Thank you, Spike."

The man who could kill and forget was confused, and mumbled something no one could hear.

Thompson had an early lunch after he had interviewed Spike and, as he was eating, he went over in his mind the facts of the case. He didn't like that business of the other man in the van. It looked as if the robbery had been a put-up job.

He met Perry outside his room when he got back to the Yard.

"I think we ought to see that man Dorset."

"We've got his statement."

"Yes, I know. But I'd like to know what he looks like. I have an idea he might be in it. Working in with a gang."

"The local people gave him a good character."

"Money has made many a good man go wrong. In this case there wouldn't have been much risk from his point of view. Let himself be tied up. That's all there is to it."

"It certainly was timed nicely," Perry said. "I wonder how they knew when he was leaving the farm, and the fact that there were all these furs in the van?"

"That's just it. If Dorset didn't put 'em wise, who did? That's the end we've got to work from, if we're going to get anywhere."

"Shall we get them to send Dorset here?"

Thompson thought for a minute, and then got up and walked to the window. "No. I'll go to Crowley. You'd better stop here and watch this end. We might get a report in that'll need following up."

Thompson went to Snailsham by train, and was met by the local inspector, who drove him to the fox farm. On the way the inspector said:

"I haven't told Dorset about your coming here."

"Good. What's your opinion of him?"

"A thoroughly reliable man. A bit slow, but I should say dead honest."

"I wonder if I'm a damn' fool," Thompson muttered to himself. When he saw Will he was still more doubtful.

The inspector drove up the hill past the gravel pit. He pointed it out, and Thompson said, "We'll stop there on the way back. I want to have a look at the place."

The entrance to the fox farm was through a gate in a twelve-foot wire fence. That, the inspector explained, was the guard fence. If any fox escaped from its run it couldn't get any farther.

A hundred yards on they stopped outside a wooden hut where a man was chopping food on a bench.

"Captain Harding about?" the inspector asked.

Will put down his chopper. "No, he's gone up to London to see about the insurance."

"Well, it doesn't matter. It's you I want to see."

Will looked at five empty buckets waiting to be filled. "It's getting on for feeding time," he said.

"I won't keep you long. This is Mr. Thompson."

Will wiped his right hand on a cloth and shook hands. "You're the man who drove the van, are you?" Thompson said.

"That's right."

"Would you know the fellow who held you up if you saw him again?"

"I'm afraid not, sir. You see, when he first came up he had a mask on. Later on, after he'd put them handcuffs on me, he took it off, and I got my head round far enough to catch a glimpse of him, but he was a little way away then, talking to the other man."

"Did you see his face?"

"No, sir. He had his back to me."

Thompson made Will describe the clothes of the two men and checked what he said with his original statement. There were one or two minor discrepancies, but nothing that mattered or threw doubt on Will's story.

"Did you tell any one you were going up to London on that day?"

"Did I tell anybody?" Will pushed his cap back and scratched his head. He looked to the sky for inspiration. "There was Mrs. Sims," he said at last. "I lodges with her."

"What did you say to her?"

"Just that I was going to London and not to wait supper for me. She made me up some sandwiches to eat on the road."

"How long was it going to take you to do the journey?"

"An hour and a half, I reckoned."

"And what time did you start?"

"A quarter past ten, sir."

"Then why was Mrs. Sims not to wait supper for you?" Will grinned feebly. "That was on account of my girl, sir. She lives in London, and I was to have met her after I'd delivered my load. She was going to show me round, like, and we were to have supper at some friends of hers, where she's staying."

"Who is this girl? Where does she live?"

"Robinson is her name, sir. Alma Robinson. But as to where she lives, I can't say."

"Where were you going to meet her?"

Will took a letter from his pocket and smoothed it out on the bench. His forefinger traced three lines, and then he said, "At Hornsey Rise Tube Station."

"Hornsey Rise Tube Station?" Thompson was surprised. "Let me have a look."

Will kept his finger on the place. "There it is, writ clear enough."

"Do you mind if I read the rest?"

"No, sir. I don't mind. There's nothing there that I wouldn't like my old mother to see."

Thompson picked up the letter and walked to the door of the shed to get a better light. When he had finished reading it, he turned it over and held it up to the light. There was no sign of any erasures. At the top of the sheet he saw the words "North-West One" written in full, and a ragged edge above where part of it had been torn off.

"Have you got the envelope this came in?" he asked Will, who made a search of his pockets and produced it, crumpled and dirty.

The postmark was clear. "Camden Town. 9th Nov. 7.30 p.m."

"I'll take both the letter and the envelope, if you've no objection," Thompson said.

Will looked puzzled. He took a knife up from the bench and tapped on the rim of a feeding dish. "Why do you want this letter?" he asked in a low voice. "There's nothing wrong with Alma, is there?"

"Not that I know of, but all the same I'd like to have a talk with her. I gathered from what you said that she knew that you were taking a lot of skins up to Town yesterday?"

"Yes, she knew that, but—"

"And it's possible she might have told some one else?"

"She might have," Will admitted.

"You don't know her address?"

"No, sir."

Thompson raised his eyebrows.

"How long has she been in London?"

"Only since Monday. You see, sir, Alma used to live in Crowley with her old aunt, but she died last week. An uncle of Alma's came down and arranged all about the funeral and everything, and when I met her on Monday she told me he was going to have her in London to stay with him."

"Did you see the uncle?"

"Only in the distance. He was a stockily-built little man, and the thing I noticed about him was his hat. It was black with a wide brim."

"Was his name the same as Miss Robinson's?"

"It may have been, I don't know, sir. She called him Uncle Barney."

"When you met Miss Robinson on Monday, did you ask her where she was going to stay in London?"

"Yes, but she didn't know. Her uncle was going to meet her at Waterloo. She said she'd write when she was fixed up and arrange where we was to meet on the Friday. That was yesterday."

"And the letter you've just given me was the only one you received from her?"

"That's right, sir. I got it on the Thursday at dinnertime."

"Did you tell any one else besides Mrs. Sims and this girl that you were going to London yesterday?"

"I may have mentioned it to the fellows in the pub. I expect most of the village knew I was going."

"Now about this man you gave a lift to. Where did you pick him up?"

"I saw him walking ahead of me when I got to Prettyman's Corner. He was carrying a sort of a kitbag and looked respectable enough, so I stopped. He said he was going to Snailsham and I told him I'd take him there as it was on my road."

"I think you told the inspector that he was short and sandy-haired. Was there anything else you noticed about him? What was he wearing?"

Will was vague. He thought the man had on a dark suit. It may have been blue, or brown. He couldn't be sure. He hadn't got a hat; he was sure of that.

"I suppose you talked together?"

"No, sir. You see, the road was narrow and there was some nasty bends and I had to watch my driving. And then again it wasn't many minutes after I'd taken him aboard when I saw the car stopped by the opening to the gravel pit. I drew up and a bloke come up with a black mask right over his face, made out of a stocking I would say it was."

"We found it," the inspector interposed. "It's in my office if you'd like to see it."

Thompson nodded. "Thanks, but I don't think it'll tell me anything. Now, Dorset, what happened to the sandy-haired man when you were held up?"

"He vamoosed, sir."

"He got out of the van?"

"Yes. I heard him go. The man who had the revolver called out to another bloke and he ran to the near side. I didn't see no more of him till we was in the gravel pit."

"You mean you saw the sandy-haired man again?"

"No, sir. Just the two who was doing the hold-up."

"Yes, I understand. Well, I think that's all I want to know."

Thompson left Will to get on with his work and drove with the inspector to the gravel pit. The rough track was scored deep with the marks of tyres.

"We've taken a few casts," the inspector said. "The saloon car had Dunlop Forts all round. One tire was worn down and had a cut in it, but it's impossible to tell which, as there was a lot of turning."

"What do you think about it yourself?"

"We haven't come to any definite conclusion. The superintendent is inclined to the view that Dorset's account is probably fairly accurate." The inspector spoke slowly and was obviously repeating the words of his superior. "Did you make any casts of footprints?"

"No, sir. Everything was fair mucked up before me and the superintendent got here. There was the gypsy who found the van and Dorset and Police-Constable Wilkins walking about. Then again there's a lot of gravel about as you can see for yourself."

Thompson nodded. He walked round the pit until he came to a spot where there were marks on the bank. A tuft of heather had been uprooted; a branch of a birch sapling was broken off, leaving a white scar on the bole. There were similar marks at two other places.

Thompson climbed up the bank and searched through the bracken but was unable to find any track which he could follow.

The dead bracken had been trampled down, but it soon gave way to heather as he went on up the hill.

He stopped by a stunted oak and lit a cigarette. "It was a well-worked job," he said to the inspector. "What was the value of the haul?"

The inspector smiled. "Well, Captain Harding puts it at four thousand pounds, but I dunno."

"What d'you mean?"

"That's what I'd call the insurance price," the inspector replied. "Of course, I know that he gets up to twenty-five for one skin, but there's plenty he has to sell off cheap for a matter of four or five pounds."

"How many skins were there?"

"Three hundred and sixty-nine."

Thompson took a folded paper from his overcoat pocket. "The average sale prices last week seem to have been in the region of fourteen pounds. I don't think Harding is much out in his figures. Well, I'll be getting back to Town. If anything turns up, ring through at once."

"The whole thing's dead at this end," the inspector replied. "We've completed our investigations."

"Yes, I know." Thompson buttoned up his coat and got back into the car. "Still, you never know. It's funny sometimes how people start remembering things days after they've told you all they know."

Thompson went by electric train to Waterloo and walked across Hungerford Bridge to Scotland Yard. He found Perry checking a pile of reports.

"Anything interesting?" he asked.

Perry shook his head. "No. Nothing. What about Crowley?"

"I saw Dorset. He seemed a decent sort of chap, but look at this." Thompson tossed Alma's letter on to the desk. Perry read it.

"Something's been torn off."

"Yes. Looks as though it was the address." Thompson studied a street map pinned on one wall. "North-West One. That's the Camden Town district."

"Leith picked up Spike Morgan in Fenner Street," Perry said and joined Thompson. "That's north of the Canal."

"I'm beginning to wish we'd held on to Spike."

"He'll be more use on a string. Leith's tailing him."

"What's Leith like?"

Perry smiled. "One of the old brigade, but a damn' good worker. Spike'll have a job shaking him."

"Have you heard from Leith yet?"

"No. But I told him to report if he got on to anything interesting. Clark's backing him up."

"Good. Then I'm going home, and when you finish, leave word that if anything turns up I'm to be informed at once."

Thompson caught a tram which took him to his house in Streatham. A smell of cooking greeted him as he opened the front door. His wife called to him from the kitchen.

"Supper won't be long. You won't have to go out again, will you?"

"I hope not. Why?"

"I've asked the Smiths round. I thought we might play a little bridge. They said they'd teach me contract and I do so want to learn."

But the lesson in contract bridge was cut short at nine o'clock. Thompson was dummy and had turned on the wireless to listen to the news. With half his mind on his partner's play, he listened to the weather forecast and two police messages. They were of no interest, but the next announcement made him forget the fortunes of his partner and turn on the wireless louder. "Missing from his home since six o'clock on Friday morning, John Brook, aged thirty-two. Sandy hair. Fresh complexion. Five foot two inches in height. Last seen wearing a blue serge suit. No cap. Believed to be carrying a haversack. This man, who left Cranleigh at six o'clock on Friday morning to walk to Snailsham, did not reach his destination. Any person who saw this man should communicate with the nearest police station or Scotland Yard. Whitehall one two, one two."

Thompson wrote down as much of the message as he could remember and walked over to his wife whose hand was hovering over the cards on the table.

"I'm sorry, dear, but I've got to go out."

"The Ace or the Queen. Now which shall I play?" Mrs. Thompson said under her breath. She tried vainly to remember what Mr. Smith had called. "Oh, do be quiet, Jim."

Thompson waited until she had made her decision. Mr. Smith put his King on the Queen. Mrs. Thompson gave a cry of distress. "Now that was all your fault, Jim, interrupting me when I was thinking. I can't get another trick."

Thompson said again that he had to leave then.

"And just when I was really getting into it. Surely you needn't go to-night?"

But her husband was firm in his resolve. He apologized to the Smiths and then went into the hall and rang up the Information Room at Scotland Yard. He learned that John Brook lived in North Street, Snailsham. The name of the house was Wincanton, next door to a baker's.

He rang up Perry. "Sorry to drag you out but I've got a line that may help us on that fur robbery. I'll be along with the car in a quarter of an hour."

They drove to Snailsham and found Brook's house without difficulty.

Through a curtainless window Thompson looked into a tiny lamplit room. A grey-haired woman was sitting by the fire, her head bent over a book. Perry looked for a bell push, found none and knocked on the door.

The woman got up and ran to open the door.

"Excuse me, but are you Mrs. Brook?" Thompson asked.

"Yes." The woman was expectant, eager.

"I am a police officer and I have called in connection with the disappearance of John Brook of this address."

"Yes, yes. He's my son. Have you found him?"

Thompson shook his head slowly and the hope died from Mrs. Brook's tired eyes.

"Do you mind if we come in for a minute or two?"

"No, of course not." Mrs. Brook backed into the passage and stood by the door of the sitting-room. Then she went to shut the front door and came back slowly. Thompson was standing with his back to the fire with his hat in his hand.

"I understand, Mrs. Brook, that your son has been missing only one day. That is from early yesterday morning."

"Yes." Mrs. Brook's voice was without expression.

"Isn't it rather early to send out a broadcast?"

"Yes, that's what every one says, but they don't understand. You see, John had the promise of a job here in Snailsham starting this morning, and he isn't the man to turn that down. I had his tea waiting for him and—"

"He was coming from Cranleigh. Is that correct?" Thompson interrupted.

"Yes. He'd been down seeing his aunty and she said he'd started off early to walk here. I waited and waited and then I went to the police."

"Does he live here as a rule?"

"Yes, always. He had a steady job at the brickmaking up to last Saturday, and then what with the bad weather and one thing and another he was stood off. He come into the house and put his money on the table and said: 'Mother, I'm finished with bricks from now on. Mr. Scarlett's offered me a job and I'm going to take it.'"

"Does he go up to London much?"

"Hardly ever. After his work he has his tea and then he goes down to the club for a game of billiards. He's always in his bed by half-past nine."

Thompson, who had been looking at a photograph on the piano, pointed to it and asked: "Is that your son?"

Mrs. Brook blinked back a tear. "Yes, that's him." Thompson got up and looked at the photograph under the light. "When was it taken?"

"Just a month ago."

"Do you mind if we borrow it? It might help."

"The police at the station have got one."

"I'll let you have it back."

"I'm sure you're welcome if it'll be any help." Thompson slipped the photograph out of its frame and put it in his pocket. "I don't think I need bother you any more." He held out his hand and Mrs. Brook clasped it in both of hers.

"You will let me know as soon as you hear anything, won't you?"

"Of course. And don't worry too much. I expect everything'll turn out all right."

In the car Thompson gave Perry the photograph and asked: "What d'you think of him?"

Perry held it down under the dash light.

"He doesn't look like a fellow that would go off the rails."

"That's my idea, too."

Perry switched out the light and sat back in his seat. "Are you going to look up Dorset?"

"Yes, and I hope to blazes we won't be too late." Thompson's expression was grim.

Will Dorset, aroused from his bed, studied the photograph for a full minute. Then he said: "Yes. That's the man that was with me in the van. His hair grew that way. Back on his head and parted in the middle."

"Get your clothes on. I want you to come down the road with us."

"What for?"

"We're going to look for something. Get a move on." Will, frightened by Thompson's tone, pulled on his trousers and picked up his coat.

Thompson got into the driving seat of the car and drove to the entrance of the gravel pit, where he stopped the car. "This is where we get out." He took a torch from his pocket and started to walk back up the hill. "You were held up about here, weren't you?"

"Near that bush, yes," Will replied.

"And the sandy-haired man ran back up the hill?"

"He must have done. If he'd gone the other way I'd have seen him."

Thompson switched on his light. "You take the other side," he ordered Perry. "And look out for any marks on the road. It's soft enough."

They made their way slowly up the hill. When they had covered about a hundred yards, Perry stopped and called out: "Come and look at this."

A ditch ran down off the bank. Where it joined the road the soil was black and soft. "Something's happened here."

"Yes." Thompson bent forward and traced long scoring marks which led away from the road. Bracken and briars hung over from either side. He forced them aside until he saw two upturned feet. He knelt and flashed his light over the man lying there. Perry joined him. "He's dead," he whispered.

"Yes. No doubt of that." Thompson felt the rigid legs. "Take the car to the village and get an ambulance and tell the local police. I expected something like this."

The body of John Brook was taken to the mortuary where the inspector was waiting with the police surgeon. "How d'you think it happened?" he asked.

"They hit him just a bit too hard," Thompson replied. "The swine!"

The doctor opened his bag. "I suppose you'll want a report as soon as possible?"

"Yes. We'll wait. Come on, Perry, we'll take a walk." The long street of the country town was deserted and the shop windows blank. "About as cheerful as that morgue," Thompson commented. "Hell! It'll be a long time before I get the look on that bloke's face out of my mind."

They walked on for a few yards and then Perry asked: "What's the next move? We'll have to get busy."

"Pull in Spike Morgan and every other rat who might have done it." Thompson stopped at a call box and got through to the Yard. "Information Room, please. Detective-Inspector Thompson speaking. About that Crowley job. Any report from Leith yet?" He listened for a minute or two and then said savagely: "Curse the man! Who's on night duty? . . . Put me through to him." He waited and then said: "That you, Hilton? Leith's mucked things up. Get every man you can on the job and pull in Spike Morgan. . . . No, I don't know where he is." He slammed the receiver back on the rest and rejoined Perry.

"What's up?" Perry asked.

"Leith's lost Spike—that's just the sort of thing that would happen. Damn and blast!"

"But we haven't got anything on Spike."

"He's in it. I'd bet a month's pay on that, and when we get him I'll make him talk."

They walked to the end of the street and back to the mortuary. The door was open and, in the shaft of light pouring from the doorway, the doctor was standing talking to the inspector. When he saw Thompson he said: "I've done all I can. Fractured skull. He must have been dead at least twenty-four hours."

"What was it done with?"

"Anything hard and heavy."

"Thanks, doctor. Sorry you were dragged out at this hour of the morning."

The doctor picked up his bag. "Then I'll be off to bed." He switched off the light and locked the mortuary door.

Thompson smoked his cigarette for several minutes. Then he threw it away. "We'll go back and see if we can find what that man was killed with. Maybe it'll tell us something."

The search continued until the light of day came greyly over the moorland, but without result.

Thompson left the inspector and got into his car. He was silent all the way up to Town. He was thinking of Mrs. Brook.

CHAPTER TWELVE

WHEN BARNEY LEFT Rivers in the top room he couldn't make up his mind where to go. He had been present at the hold-up. A man had been killed and though it might be some time before the body was discovered it would be found sooner or later.

It wouldn't be any good stopping with the Tibbetts down at the settlement; the rozzers wouldn't be long in trailing him there. He had the three pounds which Rivers had given him and half a handful of coppers. He crumpled the notes in his hand as he slouched along at a swift, shambling gait.

Three pounds would take him a few hundred miles away by train, but Barney wasn't used to trains.

He got on to a bus and took a ticket all the way. It was eleven o'clock before the bus reached its turning point on the borders of Epping Forest. There was a shelter where two or three people were waiting. He stood back in the shadows and saw them come out and board the bus. The conductor talked with the driver, smoked a cigarette and then turned out the lights in the shelter and locked the door.

Barney walked up the road. A car passed him, its swift blaze of headlights throwing the trunks of the trees and bare branches into eerie silhouettes. A lorry came rumbling along, its dim oil lights jerking and quivering. Barney stepped into the road and raised his hand. The lorry drew up. "What about a lift?"

The driver, hunched over his wheel, nodded. "Jump up."

They jolted on into the black pit ahead. Barney felt in his pocket for George. His fingers felt in every corner. George had gone.

"Hell!"

"What's the matter?" The driver, dozing over his wheel, gave Barney a glance and then turned his attention to the road ahead.

"Nothing," said Barney and put his left hand in the other pocket. George wasn't there. "Going far?" he asked the driver.

"Norfolk. Want to go all the way? You can if you like."

Norfolk was a foreign country to Barney. He'd never been there before. No. Norfolk was no place for him. "I want to get down."

"I'll be stopping soon."

Barney was cold and numb when the lorry drew up by a shed at the side of the road. It was open-fronted and there was a counter covered with American cloth; shelves with bottles of sauce, pies and cakes studded with currants and sprinkled with shredded coco-nut.

A man who was sitting on an upturned box reading a paper, got up wearily.

"Hullo, Bert." He reached for a mug and filled it from a tin pot on an oil-burner.

Barney wanted to get away from the light cast by the hurricane lamp but hunger held him.

"Coffee and pie," he said. "How much?"

"Fourpence ha'penny."

Barney counted out the coppers.

The coffee was burning hot and very sweet. The pie was pork and tasted good.

The keeper of the stall sat down and laid his paper on the counter. "Filled up your coupon yet?"

The driver said he hadn't and entered into earnest talk about the chances of football teams Barney had never heard of. Another lorry drew up. Barney finished his pie and drew back with his mug in his hand. He was feeling better now that he had some food and drink on board.

The driver talked on. Others joined him and he forgot about Barney when he made a move. "Have to be getting along," he said and walked into the darkness. Barney watched him clamber into his seat, heard him rev up his engine; heard the lorry pick up and move off. He edged back to the counter and put down his mug. Then he set off to tramp northward.

The country was all right in the summer, when he could sleep out under a hedge, in a barn or on a hayrick, but it was too damn' cold now for that sort of thing.

He slouched along for a couple of miles and then he saw ahead a cottage standing back from the road. There was a crudely painted notice on the gate. "Teas. Bed and Breakfast." He stood staring at it, jingling the coppers in his pocket.

Then he walked on up the road for half a mile. A wind was springing up from the south-west, whipping over the low hedge and bending back the brim of his black felt hat.

Barney clutched at the crown and strode on. The road was grey-white between the grass verges and easy to follow if it wasn't for these damn' cars. A blaze of headlights dazzled him. He took a step to the side, stumbled, and fell full length into the ditch.

The water was icy cold and he swore loudly with a satisfying fervour as he crawled back on to the grass. His trousers were soaked through. He'd lost his hat. When he found it after a minute's groping he changed his mind about making the great out-of-doors his bedroom for the night. It was too cold and wet even if it did cost nothing.

He went back to the cottage. A woman answered his knock. She was wearing a mackintosh which trailed on the floor. Her hair hung in greasy, grey wisps.

She looked at him with a dead-fish gaze.

"Got a bed?" Barney asked.

"A bed," she repeated.

Barney wiped his face with his sleeve. "Let's in. It's wet out here."

The woman opened the door wider and he slipped into the passage. "There is a bed you can have." She forced the door shut against the wind. "In here."

The lamp she was carrying burned steadily in the still air of the room. Long shadows ran up the walls. She put the lamp on a table.

"This is all we've got. Will it do you?" She shook up the cushions on a settee and stood back.

"That's all I want." Barney took off his coat. "You go to bed. I'll be all right."

"It's a bob for the doss."

Barney produced a pound note. "I can pay all right."

Her eyes widened, and she said apologetically: "There's some come here and tries to bounce me. That's why I spoke. You don't mind, do you?"

Barney grinned. "We've all got to live."

She retreated to the door. "I'll leave you the light. Mind you dowse it afore you turns in."

Barney watched the door close. Damn' fool he was to show that money! He folded the notes and put them into the lining of his hat. Wouldn't do to have them pinched. He felt the cushions of the settee and lay down. He was soon asleep.

He woke early on the Sunday morning and breakfasted with the woman. Her hair was drawn back into a tight "bun" and she was wearing a waisted blouse and skirt.

"Where you making for?" she asked when Barney had demolished four rashers of thick bacon.

He finished his coffee and said: "North."

"Why don't you stop here till Monday and get a lift? There'll be two or three along early."

"I might." Lying soft had made Barney lazy. Crowley seemed very far away. The sight of the man in the ditch flashed into his mind but he shut it out. "Give us some more of that coffee." He reached over to the sugar bowl and helped himself liberally. "Lonely up here, ain't it?"

The woman nodded. "Yes, but there's a living to be got and that's all that matters."

Barney looked out of the window at a field of rotting cabbage stumps. Water lay in puddles; beyond, a ragged hedge and a clump of trees bare of leaves bent to the wind. He shivered and felt in his pocket for his tobacco pouch.

He spent the whole of that Sunday pigging about helping the woman; carrying coals, cleaning out pots and frying pans, peeling potatoes. He walked to a farm a mile away for milk.

At six o'clock a lorry came in. The driver brought a Sunday paper which he gave to Barney; smoked and drank and ate and went on his way. When he was gone Barney dried the dishes which the woman washed, and then sat down to read the paper.

The words "Startling find at Crowley" caught his eye. He read on quickly, skipping the unimportant phrases. They'd found the man in the ditch. "Believed to have been the victim of foul play."

"The police are without a clue." Barney was alarmed at first and then comforted. There was nothing that could tie him up with that crime. He hadn't had anything to do with it. It was Spike Morgan.

"Anything interesting?" the woman asked.

"No. Usual tripe." Barney got up. "I think I'll take a walk up the road." He paid what he owed and left the cottage.

Half an hour later he was southward bound on a lorry which was light and shook every bone in his body. There were lots of places in the Smoke where he could lie up and no questions asked. He'd been a fool to try the country. Anywhere he went he'd be a stranger. Better to get back into the warm obscurity of London.

The dawn light of Monday morning found Barney on the northern outskirts of London. Fields had given way to embryo building estates; melancholy little houses with gardens adorned with builders' rubble heaps and concrete garages. Buses either hadn't started running or hadn't penetrated thus far. A public house with the shutters up and garbage cans out completed Barney's dejection.

He trudged on until he came to a shop which sold breakfasts to workmen with lazy wives. Barney drank coffee and ate a plate of bacon and eggs. As he was finishing he saw the welcome sight of a red bus.

It stopped and discharged two passengers. Then it turned and drew up to the kerb near the shop. Barney paid for his meal with one of the pound notes which Rivers had given him. The man behind the counter grumbled and went into a room at the back for change. "Eighteen and three pence." He counted out the coins. Barney picked them up and boarded the bus.

The Tibbetts' caravan was lightless and silent when Barney came down the path between the high board fences. Captain dragged himself out of his bed in a sugar box. He thrust his warm muzzle into Barney's cold hand and wagged his whip of a tail.

"They're all asleep, the lazy blighters," he said. "But don't bother about them. Let's go for a walk." He ate a mouthful of broad-leaved, rank grass and ran on towards the canal.

Barney looked at the caravan. There was a bed there for him but Mr. Tibbett would be cross if he were waked at that hour.

"All right, you old scoundrel. I'll come."

The tall warehouse opposite Napier Terrace stood up gaunt and blind-eyed against the lightening sky. A rat hopped into a hole in an ash-heap. Barney climbed over a broken fence on to the towpath and sat on a stone. He filled a clay pipe and lit it. It tasted good in the keen morning air. He'd been a fool to think of running away. He was all right here, and besides they hadn't got nothing on him.

Captain rooted about among the rubbish heaps and came back to Barney, sitting at his feet and pressing his warm body close to his legs.

"You're all right, you old sinner. You've got nothing to worry about."

Captain yawned and began to search feverishly for something.

There came the steady beat of an engine from the direction of the tunnel. A squat tug came out of the black circle. Behind her were three steel lighters loaded down with coal. Barney heard the faint ting of an engine-room telegraph and the tug turned sharply to port into the bay opposite Napier Terrace. A man on the first barge ran forward and hauled in his tow rope, as it slackened and was cast off from the tug.

"Damn' awful job, lightering," thought Barney, as he sat hunched up with his hands clasped round his knees. "They must have started early and now there's the job of unloading."

Captain, tired of his hunt after an elusive flea, sank down with a grunt and laid his long muzzle between his forepaws. Lighters and tugs and coal did not interest him.

Barney waited while the lighters were maneuvered alongside the wharf. Then he got up and walked back to the settlement. A thin line of smoke from the Tibbetts' caravan told him that Mrs. Tibbett was up and about. He climbed the steps and knocked on the door. Mrs. Tibbett, in a dressing-gown and curl papers, greeted him.

"Well, you are a funny one and no mistake. First you goes off all day and then you stops out all night. Fanny's had her family."

"Have you got George?"

"No."

"I can't find him."

"Then that looks like he's lost."

Barney fed Fanny who poked a quivery pink nose out of her sleeping quarters. Then he looked for George. There are many hiding places even in a small caravan but George was in none of them.

"You'd think you'd lost something valuable," grumbled Mr. Tibbett. "'Stead of a ruddy mouse!"

After breakfast Barney lay down and had two hours' sleep. The sun was well up when he woke. Mr. Tibbett was hammering away outside.

"Will you keep this for me?" he asked Mrs. Tibbett, and gave her two one-pound notes.

"Seems that a night out has done you a bit of good," she said. "I'll put 'em with our own little lot." She took a cocoa tin from a cupboard and stuffed the notes into it.

Barney showed interest. "You don't mean to say you keeps all your cash in there?"

"It's all right." Mrs. Tibbett put the lid on the tin and returned it to its hiding-place. "It's safe as a bank as long as we're here or Captain's around. Safer, I reckon."

"Well, I don't know. Seems to me a Savings Bank would be better."

Mrs. Tibbett went on with her work of tidying and dusting and polishing. Barney talked with Mr. Tibbett who was never happy without a hammer or a saw in his hand. There was some warmth in the sun and it was pleasant to watch some one else working, but Barney tired of it when he had finished his pipe. He wandered down to the canal. Captain watched him go. That sort of a walk didn't lead to anything, he decided; he stayed and watched Mr. Tibbett.

The unloading of the barges was well under way when Barney reached the tow path. One had been emptied and was lying at right angles to the wharf. A grab on the end of a crane wire dipped into a barge. "Heave up!" A winch engine rattled and the grab rose slowly. A thin stream of coal dust poured down from it.

"Don't seem to be working too well," Barney muttered, and then he saw it! A long black bolster held at one end in the lips of the grab. A man shouted an order. The winch stopped. Barney was interested. He got up and walked to the water's edge.

"Caught something this time all right," he thought to himself.

A man stuck his head out of the crane-house. "Shall I drop it in the drink? We don't want it, do we?"

A man came along the wharf with a hitcher in his hand. "Swing her in here," he ordered.

The crane creaked and whined as it turned a half-circle.

"Lower away. Hold her there."

The man with the hitcher knocked back the catch and the bolster fell in a cloud of coal dust. He signed to the winch man to heave up and poked about in the heap which the grab had dropped.

A minute or two later Barney saw the man drop his hitcher and run along the wharf to the office. He came out a few minutes later and stood smoking a cigarette.

The crane driver, leaning on the sill of his cabin window, asked:

"What is it, boss?"

Barney couldn't hear the reply. Two men who had been trimming coal in the barge came up on deck to see what had happened. They jumped ashore and walked over to the heap. Barney saw them talk to the man with the hitcher and then draw back. Ten minutes passed. Barney heard a car come down the street outside the coal yard and draw up. A man in a raincoat came through the gate followed by two policemen.

Thompson was reading through a pile of reports when a messenger summoned him to the room of his chief, Superintendent Chivers.

"Good morning, Thompson. How are you getting on with the Crowley job?"

"I'm afraid we're up against it. Can't find a trace of the furs."

The superintendent bent down and groped under his desk. "Take a look at this." He pulled out a bulging haversack grimed with coal dust.

"Where did it come from?" Thompson asked.

"Out of a coal barge on the Regent's Canal. There was also a body tied up in a rug." Chivers emptied the haversack and held it up so that Thompson could read the name "J. Brook" written with an indelible pencil on the inside canvas flap.

"Brook," Thompson muttered. "That's the man who was killed down at Crowley. Whereabouts was the barge when this was found?"

"Napier Wharf, Camden Town."

Thompson showed the superintendent the letter which Will Dorset had received from Alma. "North-West One. That's the same district and my guess is that the address was torn off after the girl finished the letter, possibly by some one else."

"I think you'd better go up to the wharf and have a look round."

Thompson put the clothes back into the haversack. "I suppose we'd better have this identified formally by Mrs. Brook?"

"Yes. Will you see to that?"

Thompson turned over the haversack to Perry and then drove to Napier Wharf. He spent an hour in conference with the officer in charge and then returned to the Yard. "How did you get on?" Perry asked.

"I've seen a few deaders in my time but that poor blighter in the barge was worse than any I've seen."

"Messed about?"

"He'd had eighty tons of coal on top of him. Even when they'd got him cleaned up he didn't look exactly cheerful."

"I suppose he went there for a doss and no one saw him before they started loading."

"His throat was cut."

Perry dropped his pencil. "Another murder!"

"Looks like it. And if he hadn't been trussed up in a rug I don't suppose we'd have known it was a man."

"Have you found out who he is?" Perry asked.

"No. The tabs on his clothing were cut out." Thompson lit a cigarette. "The rug that was round him was a Persian, and worth about twenty quid. That's what the D.D.I. thought, anyway."

"Anything else?"

"No."

"Leith is coming in at two o'clock."

Thompson looked at a clock on the mantelpiece. "I want a word with him. I suppose you haven't heard anything about Spike Morgan?"

"No. Mackay and Clark are after him as well as Leith. They know what he looks like."

Thompson lay back in his chair and puffed out clouds of smoke to the ceiling. Perry went on with his work of checking reports.

A quarter of an hour later a call came through to say that Leith had arrived.

"Tell him to come straight up," Thompson said, and when Leith came warily into the room he glared at him.

"Well, you've messed things up all right."

Leith fingered his cap and looked at the floor.

"What happened?" Thompson continued.

"There's a back way out of Larry's. A building at the back has been pulled down which I didn't know about until after Spike had slipped me."

"Perhaps it isn't your fault. Anyway, come and have a look at this." Thompson unfolded a large scale map of North London. He made a cross in pencil on the position of the coal yard opposite Napier Terrace. "A barge came in there to unload. There was a body in her. It's a murder case."

Leith sucked his teeth and waited for Thompson to go on.

"The barge was emptied at this same yard on Friday, and was taken away at about five o'clock next morning and towed to Black wall Reach."

Leith coughed and shuffled his feet. He felt that some intelligent comment was expected of him, but he couldn't think of anything to say.

Thompson got up and began to walk up and down in front of the window. "Somewhere between the coal yard and the wharf in Blackwall Reach this man was put into the barge. It's possible, but not probable, that he got in himself and was then killed."

Leith nodded. He still couldn't think of anything to say.

"You know the Canal, I suppose?"

"Bits of it," Leith agreed cautiously.

"You've seen lighters being towed up and down?"

"Dozens of times," Leith replied.

"What distance are they from the sides of the canal?"

"A matter of four or five feet."

"So it wouldn't be difficult to drop anything into a passing lighter."

"Into an empty one?"

"Yes, of course."

"When it was under way?"

Thompson nodded impatiently.

Leith thought for a minute. The brisk tick of the clock emphasized the passing of time. Hurry, hurry, hurry, it seemed to say. There's no time to be lost. But Leith was thinking. He didn't hear the clock. He saw in his mind a big, empty lighter moving slowly in train of others of its kind down a dirty canal.

"Each one of these lighters have a man at the tiller to keep it clear of the sides. There's a lot of turns and narrow bits under the bridges, and they take a bit of handling."

"Yes, I see what you mean. The man steering would be looking ahead and would see if anything was dropped on board."

Leith agreed that that would be so.

"But there might be a time when he was not keeping a look-out ahead."

A smile twitched at the corners of Leith's mouth. "They wouldn't hold their jobs long if they didn't keep their eyes on their work. Steering in a canal's trickier work than you'd think. Hit the bank and you stand to do a tidy bit of damage. How many were there in the tow?"

"Four. The lighter we're talking about was the second."

"If the body was chucked aboard, it must have been seen and heard. These lighters are made of steel and boom like a drum if you so much as graze a wall."

Thompson looked at Perry. "We'll have to start from the coal yard and work down to the Regent's Canal basin."

"Did the tug stop anywhere?" Perry asked.

"Not until she got into the basin. The dock-master says that the body couldn't have been thrown in there."

"What about the loading wharf at Blackwall Reach?"

"There were men about there all the time. They didn't see anything." Thompson sat down in front of the fire and kicked a coal into a blaze. "It's the Persian rug that's bothering me. Have you got any ideas, Leith?"

"Persian rug?"

"Yes. One was wrapped round the body."

"That's not the sort of thing you'd expect to find in Camden Town."

"No. Rag mats are more usual there, I should think." Thompson turned in his chair and took a folder from the table. "Here's the latest edition of the Missing Persons list. See if there's any one in it from your manor."

Leith ran his finger slowly down the names. When he came to the end he gave the list back to Thompson. "No one I know there," he said.

"Any chance of tracing the rug?" Perry asked.

"There wasn't any label on it and it's in a terrible state. Almost black. When the lab people have had a go at it we'll have it cleaned and get the Press to run a photograph of it."

"What about the body?"

"Hilton's made out some sort of a description. It's at the printer's now. The doctor puts the age of the man at about forty. Brown hair, greying at the sides. The face was crushed in. No teeth."

Thompson looked up at Leith. "You'd better get back on the job. Trace the movements of the lighters from the time they arrived laden at the Napier Wharf on Thursday until they returned from Blackwall Reach this morning."

Leith left the room much quicker than he had entered it. He felt like a schoolboy released from a very dull lesson. Once he was out on the embankment he could breathe freely. It didn't matter that the clouds hung low; that the wind smelled of rain; that there was no knowing when he'd get home. He was on his own. There was no one to ask him awkward questions or invite his opinion on things he didn't understand. He knew what he had to do and knew that he could do it.

At Waterloo Bridge he got on to a north-bound tram which ground its way through the Kingsway tunnel, the walls flinging back the sound of the wheels in a screeching, clattering din. Out into the open again. Grey skies. Grey walls. Rain beating on the windows in slanting, gleaming spears. Who would be a policeman! Two years to go for pension and then he'd finish with all this. Two years! It seemed a hell of a long time.

"Cable Street," the chanting voice of the conductor broke in on his thoughts. Leith clattered down the steep stairs on his heels and jumped off as the tram started with a jerk.

Napier Wharf. Now, what was his best way? He stood for a minute or two on the edge of the pavement while a trickle of rain ran down inside his collar. Napier Wharf. Why, it must be about here somewhere. He asked a newsboy.

"You goes down there and turns left and when you comes to the gas-works you bears left-handed—"

"Yes, I know. Thanks." Leith bought a paper. Another trickle of rain found a way inside his shirt. "Left-handed at the gas-works." Yes, he remembered now. He had been this way before.

The gate of Napier Wharf stood wide open and a road of cobbles and mud and coal-dust led straight to the wharf.

A barge was alongside. Overhead swung a grab.

"You'll get smothered if you stops there." A man in dungarees and a bowler hat came out of a shed. Leith side-stepped to safety as the grab released its load.

"What are you after?"

"The foreman."

"That's me."

"I'm a police officer."

"Thought we'd finished with your crowd. They've taken the corpse, and Gawd, wasn't he in a mess! Have you found out who he is?"

"No, they haven't got him cleaned up yet." Leith unbuttoned his raincoat and took out a packet of cigarettes. The foreman took one.

"One of my blokes says his throat was cut, right across."

Leith nodded. "Something like that. Which barge was he in?"

"The *Ipswich*." The foreman went to a window and pointed. "There she is, laying third bottom out."

"I want to know where he could have got aboard, or been put aboard, I should say."

"There's lots of places that could have been done," the foreman replied. "She was lying on the other side after we emptied her Friday."

"Friday night?"

"Yes, and then the tug took her down the cut."

"What time was that?"

"Five o'clock Saturday morning."

"What's the name of the tug?"

"*Sandpiper*. She ought to be along any time now."

"It's a straight run to the Regent basin, isn't it?" Leith asked.

"Usually it is," the foreman replied, and went about his business, leaving Leith to enjoy the doubtful comforts of the hut alone. The view of Napier Terrace soon palled and he braved the rain and the coal-dust to find that the *Sandpiper* had arrived. Her skipper, an animated oilskin with a sou'wester on top, protested that he had already told the police all he knew.

Leith explained that all he wanted was a passage on one of the barges.

"You want to go on a barge?" squeaked the oilskin. "All right, you can if you like. Which one?"

"I don't mind."

"Then jump on board. If we get away now we'll save the tide at the basin."

Leith walked round to the *Ipswich* accompanied by the foreman, who explained his presence to the lighterman in charge.

"There ain't no cabin, mister."

Leith said that that didn't worry him and sat on a bollard.

In point of fact he would have welcomed the shelter of any cabin however small, but duty called and he cursed his conscience as he sat cold, wet and miserable. Twice the tug stopped to let another tow go by. High walls pressed in on either side; bridges; tunnels, black as night with a tiny pin point of light ahead.

"Enjoying yourself, mister?" The lighterman leaned on the long tiller.

"Like hell," said Leith.

"You're trying to find out where that corp was put aboard, ain't you?"

"Yes. What d'you think?"

The lighterman spat over the side. "It wasn't done along this stretch. Nor in the basin. Nor on the river."

"That leaves the coal-yard."

"Ay. There or when she was tied up on the opposite side near them houses."

"Napier Terrace?"

"That's where I mean."

"I told my chief the same but he sent me along to make sure."

"We're not coming back to-night after we've loaded. You'll have to walk home. The buses don't run down that way."

There was a half-hour to wait at the Regent Canal basin until high tide. Then the gates were opened and a river tug took charge. The wind was blowing off the south shore, slapping the waves against the steel sides of the lighter and lifting little drifts of spray over the deck. Leith felt very glad that he wasn't a sailor.

When the loading wharf was reached he sprang for the ladder and climbed up. It was just like those blokes at the Yard to send one out on a job like this. He'd known all the time what the result would be.

The lighterman had been quite correct. There were no buses. The streets were narrow and all the same. When he asked the way children said "Garn" and laughed shrilly and went to collect their friends to jeer at the foreigner.

Leith was not in a good temper by the time he sighted the welcome lights of a broad street with trams and buses. As he sat on the back seat of a bus he took out his notebook and wrote in it: "Expenses, fourpence."

Spike, from his bedroom window, saw Leith on the coal wharf. He drew back behind a lace curtain. Leith, with his hands thrust deep into the pocket of his raincoat, was leaning against a strut of a crane talking to a man in dungarees.

"What the hell's he after?" Spike muttered.

Len, who was lying on a bed, looked up from the paper he was reading. "What's up?" he asked.

"Leith."

Len swung his legs to the floor. "Where?"

"Across the other side."

"I can't see him."

"Alongside the crane."

"Hell! I thought you meant he was outside here." Len sat on the bed and lit a fresh cigarette. "I think I'll get back to my place."

Spike drew the curtains across the window and turned towards him. "You'll stop here."

Len stretched his arms and yawned. "Well, if you're paying I don't care." He leaned forward and took a folded newspaper from under the pillow of Spike's bed.

"Drop that!" Spike snatched it from him.

"What the hell's the matter with you?" Len stared at Spike, then he got up slowly. "You're holding something back on me. What's in that paper?"

Spike faced him, his pale blue eyes cold and without expression. "I'm boss here."

"You mean you were. The job's finished."

Spike looked at the paper and refolded it so that a headline was showing. "Read that." He thrust it into Len's hands. A minute later he said: "Well, what've you got to say now?"

"He's dead," Len mumbled. "I must have hit him too hard."

"That's what it looks like." Spike's voice was hard and even. "And if you don't do what I tell you you're going to be in a jam."

Len put his elbows on his knees and sunk his head in his hands.

"That makes you think." Spike parted the curtains and looked out. Leith had gone.

"How much cash have you got?"

Len put his hand in his pocket and produced a few coins. "Seven and ninepence ha'penny."

"I'll have to see Izzy and get him to loosen up."

"What's the matter with Rivers? He's paying us, isn't he?"

"I'll call on him, too."

"And I'm coming with you."

"Like hell you are!"

Fear was behind Len's sudden rage as he leapt to his feet. Fear that Spike would squeak. His left arm shot out. Spike side-stepped and caught him a heavy blow in the pit of the stomach. He fell sideways on the floor, doubled up, gasping for breath.

"And that's not the half of what's coming to you." Spike, with his head thrust forward, spat out the words.

The door opened, and Alma took one step into the room and then stood quite still. The look on Spike's face made her feel sick.

"What d'you want?" he asked savagely.

Alma drew back. "Dinner's ready," she said. Then she saw Len on the floor, fighting for breath.

"Get out. And tell the old woman I'll be down in a minute."

Alma walked backwards on to the landing and shut the door behind her. Then she went slowly down the stairs. As she passed Mrs. Kemp's room she saw a screw of paper on the floor just inside the door. As she picked it up a word caught her eye. She unfolded the paper with trembling fingers, and read, "3, Napier Terrace, Camden Town."

She had written the words herself. They had been part of the letter she had sent to Will. Mrs. Kemp must have torn off the address. But why? Her dislike and fear of Mrs. Kemp returned.

She must get away from this house. She would go—but where? She had only a few coppers left from the money which Barney had given her.

A door opened on the floor above and Spike came clattering down the bare wooden treads. He smiled when he saw her, and tried to put an arm around her waist. She drew back from him.

Spike assumed an expression of dismay.

"What's the matter? I thought we were good pals."

"What were you doing to Len?"

"Rough house. That was all. Come on, give me a kiss."

Alma tried to fight him off, but he only laughed and gripped her by the wrists.

"God! But you're a little tiger." His smile faded.

"Let me go."

He loosened his grasp and made a mock-polite gesture towards the stairs. "After you."

She ran past him down to the back room.

Mrs. Kemp, who was in the kitchen, came out when she heard the door burst open. Alma was crying.

"Now what's been happening?"

"It's Spike."

"I'll speak to him."

"No, please don't. It doesn't matter. I'm going away from here." Alma found her handkerchief and wiped her eyes.

"Going away! Don't be silly. Sit down and have your dinner."

Spike came into the room and avoided Mrs. Kemp's eye. He sat down at the table and poured out a cup of tea.

"You'd better go up to your room and lie down for a bit," Mrs. Kemp said to Alma. "I'll bring you up something later."

"I tell you I don't want anything. I'll go and pack." When the door had closed behind her, Mrs. Kemp tackled Spike. "I told you to keep off that girl."

He looked up and grinned. "She's got a temper; but I like 'em that way."

"What did you do to her?"

"Asked her for a kiss."

"And now she says she's going away."

"You've got to stop her."

"And if I can't?"

"You've got to. Lock her up in her room. We can't have her going to that boy friend of hers at Crowley. If she does the splits'll get hold of her, and then where the devil will we be? She heard us taking Rivers out to the canal."

"She didn't see anything. Still, I suppose you're right. I'll lock her up in her room." Mrs. Kemp poured some tea from her cup into a saucer, and drank it noisily. "I never seem to finish clearing up after you."

"I couldn't help it," Spike said sulkily.

"That's what you always say." Mrs. Kemp got up and walked to the door and down the passage. She locked the front door and put the key in her pocket. Then she locked the door of the front sitting-room.

Alma was bending over her trunk when Mrs. Kemp came into her room. She looked up and asked, "What d'you want?"

Mrs. Kemp moved a dress off the bed and sat down. "You can't go away like this," she said, and smiled ingratiatingly. "I don't know what Barney would say if you did. You see, I promised him I'd look after you." Alma went on with her packing. "I don't think he'll mind much. He hasn't been near me for days."

"He's probably busy somewhere. I expect he'll be in to-night."

"Then you can tell him I've gone back to Crowley. I'm not staying here."

"Alma, you're acting silly. All because Spike got a bit fresh, that's all. I'll see he doesn't do it again."

"I'm going away now."

Mrs. Kemp stretched out a hand and picked up Alma's purse off the dressing-table.

Alma tried to snatch it from her, but Mrs. Kemp chuckled fatly, and held it tight. "Don't seem to be much in it." She half turned, and opened the catch. "Seven-pence! That won't take you far."

"Give it me." The colour had risen to Alma's cheeks and she was breathing quickly.

"Here you are! Catch!"

"I think you're horrible. I hate you. I hate Spike. I wish I'd never come here!"

"You can take these things out of your bag. You're not going away."

"I will, if I want to."

"Oh, no, you won't." Mrs. Kemp got up and gripped Alma by the shoulders, swung her round and forced her down on a chair. "If I say you're to stop, you'll stop. Get that into your stupid little head."

Alma was rigid, frozen with fear. She didn't say anything for a minute; then she relaxed and said quietly, "All right."

"That's better. I thought you'd see sense."

Alma lay on her bed, her face buried in the pillows, trying to shut out of her mind the sight of Mrs. Kemp's face.

Mrs. Kemp herself was feeling very pleased with herself. "I've settled her hash," she said, as she walked into the back room.

"Good." Spike had finished his meal and was smoking in front of the fire. "What did you say?"

Mrs. Kemp laughed until she shook all over. "I told her where she got off. And I've got the key of the front door in my pocket, and the front room as well."

"She's in the room over this, isn't she?"

"Yes. Why?"

"If she tried to get out of the window we'd see her."

"I hadn't thought of that, but you're right. One of us'll have to be here, just in case."

"I'm going to see Izzy Hyams to-night."

"I'll stop in."

"Where's Joe?"

"Looking for a job—in the Green Man, most likely."

"Why did you marry a boob like that?"

"Company," Mrs. Kemp replied. "I was lonely, all on me own when you went off. When he was working for Rivers he was making good money, and if he wasn't so dumb he'd have made a bit more on the side."

"I had a bit of a turn up with Len."

"What about?"

"He got fresh."

"He's all right, ain't he?"

"I wouldn't trust him. He's got nerve. Plenty of it when he's in a car, but that's where he finishes. There's going to be trouble if he doesn't get his cut."

"Then you'd better make sure there isn't no trouble, or else—"

"I'll fix him." Spike picked up a paper and lit another cigarette. Len didn't worry him.

CHAPTER THIRTEEN

SPIKE LEFT Napier Terrace at six o'clock. Joe came in soon after he had gone.

"Where've you been?" Mrs. Kemp asked.

"Looking for a job. I met a bloke who said he'd fix me."

"Well, that's something—if it comes off," Mrs. Kemp sniffed. "I'm going out. Alma's in her room, and if she tries any funny stuff, stop her."

Joe was taking off his coat. He stood still, with one arm half out of its sleeve. "Funny stuff? What's the game?"

"She's wanting to clear out, but I told her she's got to stop here. Lock the door when I goes out, and keep the key in your pocket."

"What d'you want to keep her here for if she doesn't want to stay?"

"Never you mind. You do what I tells you. If she tries to get out of the window on to the shed roof you'll hear her."

"What do you want me to do then?"

"Nip out into the garden and bring her back into the house."

"But what if she won't come?"

"You've got to make her."

The call of beer was strong, otherwise Mrs. Kemp would never have trusted Joe to act as jailer. She put on her shawl, and with ninepence in coppers in her hand disappeared up the canal path. Joe locked the door behind her and pocketed the key. Then he went into the back room and shovelled coal on the fire.

He didn't like Spike, and he didn't like Mrs. Kemp, even though he was married to her. That hadn't been any of his doing. He hadn't even bought the ring, and had gone through the ceremony with the indifference of a sick sheep too spineless to help himself.

Alma was different. She made him feel awkward, and—she was different. Decent. Honest. Young. Joe sighed and stared at nothing. If only things had been different. If only he'd kept that first job. If only—What the hell was the use of it all? He turned on the wireless. There was a dance band on somewhere. He spread the evening paper across the table and turned the pages until he came to the program section. Yes. Regional. The oily strains of a waltz kept the thoughts of what might have been at bay. "We have just played—We are now going to give you a new rendering—"

The stuffy, overheated little room was hot. He forgot the days of dog-like toil pushing a barrow through streets which had no end. Rivers's bullying. His wife's nagging. "You're so easy to love. . . . So easy to idolize." He didn't take in the words, but his brain fell under the strain of the melody.

Gosh! He'd like a gramophone. And records. Stacks of 'em so's he could put on what he liked, when he liked. Mrs. Kemp had no place in that dream in the back room of No. 3 Napier Terrace.

He'd heard Tauber and Tibbett and Rudy Vallee on the wireless. Five minutes' pleasure, and they were gone. Pleasure? Heaven to Joe Kemp. "I believe in miracles." The tune had changed. One day he'd strike it lucky. The miracle would happen. "Impossible things come true. But miracles only happen to just a few."

Up in her cold room Alma heard the music faintly. She was putting on her coat. Will! She must get word to him somehow. He'd help her. She could depend on Will. She moved the candle nearer to the mirror, and bent her head. Her eyes were red and puffed. She dabbed them with a scrap of wet sponge. Drops of water ran down her cheeks like tears. She smiled at her own despair. No good sitting down under Mrs. Kemp. That fur Spike had given her would fetch something. Enough to pay her fare to Crowley, at any rate. Crowley. There was peace there. And Will! She loved Will very much at that moment, when she fastened the catch of the black fox tie.

She got up and looked round the room. She had her purse and handkerchief. It wasn't much of a drop from the window on to the roof. She opened the window. From below came the sound of a man singing. "Miracles sometimes happen. Impossible things come true."

Joe was in a state of musical intoxication when Alma dropped lightly on to the roof of the shed outside the back room. He heard no sound.

The gate in the wall at the end of the garden was locked, but Alma was determined. She climbed over the wall and dropped into the lane outside. She stood for a full minute while she regained her breath, and then ran westwards to Cable Street, and boarded a bus which took her southwards over the canal bridge. When it stopped she got out and walked on until she came to a pawnshop. A group of women were standing outside gossiping. She hesitated, and was trying to summon up courage to go into the shop when a man stopped in front of her.

"Just a minute, miss. If you don't mind."

"What d'you want?" She stared at Leith with frightened eyes.

"I'm a police officer."

"Oh?"

"That's a nice fur you're wearing." Leith put his hand on the white tip of the black fox fur. "It looks like the real thing. No fake."

"Of course it's not."

In the light of a street lamp Leith priced Alma's dress at a guinea. Her shoes at the same figure, maybe a little less, and the scrap of black cloth she called a hat at a few shillings. They didn't add up to a black fox fur tie.

"Where'd you pick this up?"

"A boy friend gave me it." Alma, alarmed at the questioning, looked for a way of escape. There was a gap in the stream of traffic.

She was half-way across the road before Leith realized what had happened. The black fox fur was in his hand, its broken chain hanging down.

He waited his chance and crossed the road. A police constable was standing on the edge of the pavement. Leith asked him if he'd seen a girl come across the road, and described her briefly. The constable said he had and pointed in the direction of a tube station. "That's where she went," he said.

Leith knew that to find her was a hopeless task, but he took a penny ticket and went down the escalator. The platform was almost empty. "When did the last train go?" he asked an official.

"Half a minute ago. There'll be another along in a minute."

Leith went back to the street level, turned into a phone box, and rang Scotland Yard.

Alma got out of the tube train at the first stop, and asked the way to a post office. She'd got sixpence left in her purse. Enough for a wire. She scribbled it out and counted the words. There was one too many. She crossed out "please" and pushed the paper under the grille.

Out in the street again, among a jostling crowd, she walked a hundred yards and then asked the way to Napier Terrace. There was nowhere else she could go.

Mrs. Kemp opened the door in answer to her knock. "That man!" was all she said, and pulled Alma into the passage. "Go up to your room." She rocked down the passage to the back room. Joe looked up sleepy-eyed from the paper he was reading.

"Who was that? Spike?" he asked.

"It was Alma."

"Alma! But she's up in her room."

"She was. She got out."

"I never heard her."

"You wouldn't. What were you doing when I was out?"

"Nothing."

"Have you been playing the wireless?"

"Yes, but not for long," Joe answered defensively.

"Spike'll have something to say to you."

"What's it got to do with him?" Joe was weakly rebellious.

"You'll see, soon enough." Mrs. Kemp walked over to the fire and raked out the dead ashes. "You can't even keep the fire going proper. You and your blinking wireless."

"The coals are out. That's all there is in the bucket." Joe spoke the words with satisfaction, forgetting for the moment that he would suffer as well as his wife.

Mrs. Kemp put one hand on her ample hip and the other on the mantelpiece and looked at Joe. "And you're what some people would call the breadwinner." She laughed and showed every one of her crooked front teeth. Joe half turned away from her and took up the paper he had read.

There was a knock on the front door. Mrs. Kemp's laugh died quickly. "It's Spike," she said under her breath, and went down the passage quickly.

Joe heard the bolt shot back and the heavy lock turn, and then Mrs. Kemp saying, "Oh, it's you, Mrs. Benson."

The door closed and Mrs. Benson came down the passage into the back room. "'Evening, Joe."

He put down his paper and smiled. He rather liked Mrs. Benson. She never bullied him.

"Come and sit down," he said. "How are you keeping?"

"Not so bad; but the weather's cruel, ain't it?"

"Yes, and no sign of a change, neither."

Mrs. Benson nodded and settled herself down in the basket chair. She smoothed down her sparse grey hair and spread her hands to the blaze.

Mrs. Kemp sat on a hard chair. There was no welcome in her eyes, and a suggestion of only a temporary occupation in her attitude. Her guest ignored the silent hint that her stay should be short, and at first chatted easily and volubly with Joe.

But Joe, after a few minutes' talk, showed signs of flagging under Mrs. Kemp's withering disapproval.

Mrs. Benson then introduced the purpose of her visit. She wanted to borrow a pinch of tea and a few lumps of sugar.

"I'm sorry, but I can't oblige you," was Mrs. Kemp's uncompromising reply. She was thinking of Alma, and willing her unwelcome guest to depart.

"Well, that is a pity," Mrs. Benson said. "Because now I'll have to trouble you to give me that sixpence you borrowed."

"I'll pay you to-morrow."

Mrs. Benson sniffed. "I was expecting it before this."

"You'll have to wait." Mrs. Kemp got up and opened the door.

"So that's how it is." Mrs. Benson looked to Joe for support, but Joe avoided her gaze. "Oh, well. I suppose I ought to be getting along." She waited, in the forlorn hope that Mrs. Kemp would relent and ask her to stay. She was disappointed.

Mrs. Kemp stood at the door ready to speed her unwelcome guest.

Mrs. Benson obeyed the unspoken summons to leave. "Good night, Joe."

"'Night."

As she slammed the front door behind Mrs. Benson, Mrs. Kemp cursed all interfering neighbours. Then she called out to Joe, who came slowly.

"I'll want you to go out to-night, and put the fur up the spout."

"What fur?"

"Alma's, of course. I'll go and get it. And stick out for a fiver."

Mrs. Kemp went up to Alma's room. "Where've you been?"

"That's none of your business, and you've no right to keep me here."

"That's as maybe. Anyway, I'm going to fix your window so as you can't open it." Mrs. Kemp looked round the room. The fox fur wasn't to be seen. She opened a cupboard door. "What've you done with that tie Spike give you?"

"I—I—I lost it."

"Lost it! Where?"

"In the street. When I was out."

"You mean you dropped it?"

"No."

"You pawned it," Mrs. Kemp accused.

"No. I'll tell you."

"Go on."

"A man stopped me. He took hold of the fur and asked me where I'd got it. I ran away. When I was on the other side of the road I found I hadn't got it. He must have it. I remember now feeling the tug and hearing the catch snap."

"That's a fiver gone down the drain. You damn' little fool!"

"He said he was a policeman."

Mrs. Kemp breathed more quickly. "A policeman!"

"He said he was, but he didn't look like one. He was wearing a dirty old mackintosh and a bowler hat."

Mrs. Kemp locked the door behind her. Then she went upstairs and knocked on the door of the top bedroom.

Len said, "Come in."

The room was thick with smoke. A candle was burning on a table at the head of one of the beds.

"Who's that?" Len raised himself on one elbow. The magazine he'd been reading fell on the floor.

"It's all right. It's only me. Did Spike say when he'd be back?"

"No. He's gone to Izzy's to raise some cash."

"I know that." Mrs. Kemp turned back the blankets on Spike's bed and started to re-make it. "There's supper downstairs."

"I'll come down." Len sat up and squashed out his cigarette in an overladen saucer.

"I've locked Alma in her room, but if you hear her trying to get out give me a call."

"O.K. What's she been up to?"

Mrs. Kemp grunted something Len couldn't hear.

"Is that the girl Spike's got a crush on?"

"He thinks he has. It won't last long."

"They found the bloke down at Crowley."

"The one you tied up?"

"No, the other." Len hesitated for a moment, and then said, "The stiff."

"God! Do you mean to say Spike—He never said anything to me about it." Mrs. Kemp stood still, with a pillow in her hands.

"Don't tell him I told you."

"All right." Mrs. Kemp dropped the pillow and pulled a blanket over it. He hadn't told her. He hadn't trusted her. She swung round suddenly on Len. "You're lying!" Her black eyes were closed to mere slits. Len shrunk back against the head of the bed.

"It's gospel truth. Spike slugged him and hid him in a ditch. We never thought he'd be found. But he was."

"But the paper said the bloke in the van was alive."

"There was two of them."

Mrs. Kemp finished making Spike's bed. Then she emptied the saucer of cigarette stubs and ash out of the window. "Come and get your supper."

They went down to the back room where Joe was crouched forward over the dead fire.

"Here, you. Get busy. There's some kindling in the coal box. Spike'll want something hot when he comes in."

Mrs. Kemp waited until Joe had carried out her orders, and then went into the front room. She pressed her face to the cold panes. "I wonder if he's all right," she muttered.

Mrs. Benson, when she was so summarily dismissed from No. 3 Napier Terrace, turned along the canal path towards the bridge. Her old man would be back soon, and tea she must have, and sugar.

Of course, there was Mrs. Tibbett. She'd oblige her for certain sure, as she'd often done before. The only thing was the dark path to the settlement. Mrs. Benson was possessed of a fear that one day she would be robbed, but what of she never stopped to think. Her purse, like Mrs. Kemp's, was more often empty than full.

Still, there it was. She hadn't got any tea; but though her need was great, she hesitated at the corner of the street which led from the bright lights and noisy life to the deadly quiet of the lane. At the end of it Captain would be lying in wait.

"Drat the dog!" she said aloud, which was the nearest she had ever got to swearing. "And drat that there Mrs. Kemp."

Annoyance overcame her fear of Captain and, before she quite realized it, she was walking very quickly down the path to the Tibbetts' caravan. Then she slackened her pace and approached the caravan nervously. She gave a little scream as Captain came out and sniffed at her ankles. "Good dog. Good dog," she said, and reached down a hand to give him a placatory pat. "Mrs. Tibbett! Mrs. Tibbett!"

The top half of the door opened, and Mr. Tibbett's brown bear face appeared over it. He called back to his wife, "It's Mrs. Benson," and let down the ladder.

Mrs. Benson sighed her relief when she got out of Captain's reach.

"Come along in, Mrs. Benson." Mrs. Tibbett put down her knitting and pushed her spectacles up on her nose.

"I'm sorry to bother you at this time of night, I'm sure, Mrs. Tibbett, but I just popped in to see if you could let me have some tea and sugar. I'm right out of them, and all the shops is shut."

"Of course I can. But you mustn't hurry away." Mrs. Tibbett's needles flashed again in the lamplight. "It's not often you look us up here. Have you got any news?"

"Yes, I have." Mrs. Benson leaned across the table. "It's them Kemps. There's something funny going on at their place."

"Well, I'm not surprised," Mrs. Tibbett replied. "Spike Morgan's there, so I've heard, and when he's about there's usually trouble."

"I don't know nothing about him. I don't think I've ever seen him," Mrs. Benson replied. "But did you know that Mr. Rivers had gone away?"

"Some one did say something about him, but I didn't pay any attention."

"Well, he has gone. Mrs. Kemp told me herself. I asked her where he was. She said she didn't know, but if you ask me, she knew, all right. I went in to see her not five minutes ago and she practically turned me out of the house. There's something going on in that house she don't want anybody to know about. That's what I think."

"It ain't no business of ours, anyway." Mrs. Tibbett tried to turn the conversation, but Mrs. Benson, like a dog with a bone, would not give up the subject of Mrs. Kemp. She could not forget the cavalier treatment which Mrs. Kemp had meted out to her, nor of the unpaid loan of the sixpence.

"And there's another thing. I was out on Friday night. I'd gone to me old Ma, what lives at Ilford, and I didn't get back till after midnight. There was a light in Mrs. Kemp's hall. I could see it through the fanlight over the front door. 'You're up late,' I says to myself, but I didn't think no more about it till I was up in my room getting undressed, then I heard what I took to be some one in my back garden.

"I looked out, but couldn't see nothing. Then I heard a man speaking. He was in the Kemps' garden, and there was a woman with him. 'Ho,' I says, 'what's going on there?' I listened a bit longer, but there wasn't nothing more said, and the two of 'em went in at the back door of No. 3. It seemed to me they was carrying something."

"Did you speak to Mrs. Kemp about it?" Mrs. Tibbett asked.

"Not me. She wouldn't half have bit my head off if I had."

Half an hour later Mrs. Benson departed with her tea and sugar. Mr. Tibbett escorted her past Captain and up the path to Cable Street.

Leith rang up Scotland Yard from the phone box outside the tube station where he had lost Alma, and asked for Thompson. He told him of what had happened.

"Where are you?" Thompson asked.

"Euston Road."

"Take a taxi down here."

Thompson put down the receiver and said to Perry, "That was Leith. He's coming along and bringing a black fox fur with him."

"A black fox fur! Where'd he get it?"

"Off a girl. She got away."

Leith, who grudged a bus fare, watched the clock of the taxi all the way to the Yard. At the same time he fingered a shilling, a sixpence, and three coppers, and kept a close watch on the route followed. The driver said something under his breath when Leith paid him.

"Anything the matter with you?"

The driver said "No," without conviction, and Leith walked up the steps. The constable grinned at him.

"Have you joined us for keeps?"

Leith answered something which sounded like, "The hell I have," and went up to Thompson's room. He handed over the fur and Thompson took it and held it out under the light. "What was she like?"

Leith described her. Perry said, "That's the Crowley girl."

Thompson handed a typewritten sheet to Leith. "Read that."

When he had finished, Thompson asked, "Would that description fit the girl?"

"Pretty well."

Perry took the fur and turned it over. There was a tab near the head. "Do you know any one of the name of Hyams? I. J. Hyams?"

"No. Why?"

"He made up this tie." Perry turned over the pages of a trade directory. "Yes. He's down here as a manufacturing furrier."

Thompson got up and looked at the entry. "It might be worth while giving him the once over. Get through to the records and find out if they know anything about him."

Izzy Hyams was not known at the Yard. Perry told Thompson and ordered a car. They drove to Whitechapel to find Izzy's shop closed for the night and the shutters up. Leith went in search of the police patrol, and returned with the information that Izzy lived in Harmer Street; number fifty-six. They drove on there.

Izzy was thinking of going to bed when the police car drew up at his house. He opened the door on the chain and asked, "What do you want?"

"Open up. We are police officers."

"How do I know that?" Izzy lived in a district where no risks were taken.

Thompson produced his warrant card and flashed a torch on it.

"All right." The chain was taken off and Izzy opened the door. "Please not to make a noise. Every one is in bed."

"I want to talk to you."

"Come in here, if you please." Izzy opened a door and switched on a light.

Thompson walked into the room and opened an attaché-case he had been carrying. "Ever seen that before?"

Izzy stared at the lustrous black fur. He felt it. "Very nice, yes."

"Have you seen it before?"

"I have seen hundreds like this. Some better. Some not so good."

Thompson took the fur and held it up so that Izzy could see the tab. "That's yours."

"Yes." He looked at Thompson and then at Perry. Their expressions told him nothing. "Let me see." He was frightened. "I am not sure?"

"That's your name on it," Thompson said.

"Yes, but any one could steal my labels. That would not be difficult."

"Why should they?"

Izzy spread his hands palm upwards and hunched his shoulders. "How can I say why?"

"Are you trying to tell me you didn't make up this fur?"

"I cannot remember," Izzy hedged. "But I do not think so. Mine is a big business. Every week, every day I send out hundreds like this."

"We'll take a look round your shop."

"To-morrow?"

"Now."

"But it is late. To-morrow I show you everything."

"Go and get your coat." Thompson put the fur back in his case. Izzy hesitated. "Get a move on," Thompson snapped.

Izzy, with an expressive gesture, accepted the inevitable. They drove in silence to the shop and got out on to the deserted pavement. Izzy fumbled with the keys and at last found the right one. When they were all inside Thompson asked for the stock-book and examined the entries for the last week. There was no mention of black fox skins. "Now we'll take a look round," he announced.

It was a long job, but the search was thorough and successful. Perry found the skins in a cupboard in a room over the shop.

"Where did you get these?"

Izzy had been trying to think up an explanation but fear numbed his brain.

"I don't know," he answered stupidly.

"Who brought them here?" Thompson asked.

"Two men. In a car."

"What were their names?"

"I don't know."

"What was the car?"

"A saloon. Black, I think."

"What day was it?"

Thompson, Perry and Leith had closed round Izzy. He showed signs of panic. "I don't know when it was. I can't remember."

"Sit down," Thompson ordered and pointed to a packing-case.

Izzy sat slowly. It was worse now with the three of them standing over him. He got up. His mouth was working. Perry gave him a shove and he collapsed.

"Tell us all you know. It'll ease your mind." Thompson took a packet of cigarettes from his pocket, pushed open the drawer and held it out to Izzy. Perry struck a match.

Izzy looked up at him with the wary gaze of an animal cornered; not knowing from which direction to expect the next attack.

Thompson did not give him time to think. "You saw the men who brought the furs. What were they like?"

"One was wearing a long yellow coat. They both had felt hats."

"Had you ever seen 'em before?"

"No. I swear that."

"They just brought a lot of skins and dumped them in your shop?"

"Yes."

"I suppose they wanted to be paid for 'em?"

"No. They put down the stuff here and then went away."

Thompson, who was now sitting on the edge of a chair, crossed one leg over the other and drew at his cigarette. Then he said: "You were expecting them to call?"

Izzy's resistance began to break down. "Yes, I was, but I didn't know there was anything wrong. A friend of mine, a Mr. Rivers, came into my shop three or four days ago. He asked if I wanted to buy a parcel of black fox skins. I wasn't keen and said I'd have to see them first. That's how it was."

"Why didn't you enter them up in your stock-book?"

"Because, you see, I hadn't bought them. I was going to wait till Mr. Rivers came round and we agreed on a price."

"He hasn't been here yet?"

"No."

"Where does he live?"

"I don't know."

"What's he like?"

"About my height. Stocky."

"What age of a man was he?"

Izzy thought for a moment. "About forty-five or fifty."

"Have you known him long?"

"No. I met him for the first time a month or two back."

"Did you know him as a dealer in furs?"

"I knew he was a street trader and did a lot of buying and selling."

"You didn't know him as a fur dealer?"

Again Izzy avoided answering the question directly· "I knew him as a dealer," he said.

"You told me one of the men who brought the furs was wearing a yellow coat?"

"Yes. I didn't notice much more about him. He was a young chap."

"What height?"

"Fairly tall. About six feet."

"And the other one who was with him?"

"He was shorter."

Thompson picked up Alma's fur. "Was this part of the consignment the two men brought to your shop?"

Izzy nodded.

"Why did you make it up?"

"One of the men asked me to."

"Which one?"

"Spike."

Thompson got up and stood over Izzy. "So. One of them was called Spike, eh?"

"I heard the young fellow in the yellow coat call him that."

"Who made up this tie?"

"One of my girls."

"In your shop?"

"Yes."

"What was her name?"

"Freda Klein."

"Where does she live?"

"Where does she live? How can I tell you that? There are ten—eleven girls who work for me. I cannot know their addresses."

"I want to ask her a few questions," Thompson explained.

"To-morrow you can see her. She will be at the shop at half-past seven o'clock in the morning."

"All right. We'll leave that for the time being. Now, after this fur was ready, what did you do with it?"

"I sent it where Spike told me."

"Where was that?"

"The address is in my day-book. Can I get it?" Thompson nodded and signed to Perry to follow Izzy as he went into the front shop. He came back a minute later thumbing the pages of a ledger. "I've got it. Saturday. Sent by hand to Number Thirty-six, Pelham Street." Leith touched Thompson on the arm. "That's Larry's place. Where Spike Morgan was on Saturday night."

"Right."

Perry made a note of the address.

"Have you got a telephone directory?"

"It's on the desk behind you."

Thompson turned and opened the book at the letter "R."

"Where does this man Rivers live?"

"I told you I don't know but I think it's up Camden Town way."

"I know the man," Leith said. "He calls himself a general dealer. He was up at the Old Bailey four or five years ago for receiving. He got away with it."

"Where does he live?"

"Over his shop in Cable Street. Number Twenty-nine." Thompson turned to Perry. "Was he on the list you made out?"

"No. I got his record but as he was only in a small way and there has been nothing against him recently I didn't put his name down."

Thompson dropped his cigarette and trod it out. "Leith, take this man along to the station and charge him with receiving goods, well knowing them to have been stolen. Put in a description and number of the furs."

"And what'll I do after that?"

"Go to Rivers's shop."

Leith stifled a groan. A good supper and an undisturbed night were his idea of Heaven. He snapped one half of a pair of handcuffs on to Izzy's right wrist. "Come on, you," he said.

CHAPTER FOURTEEN

THOMPSON LOCKED UP the shop and drove with Perry to Pelham Street. The driver stopped at a street lamp and spoke over his shoulder. "I can't make out the numbers, sir."

"All right. We'll find the place." Thompson got out and, after a short search, found No. 36. "Damn' funny place," he said to Perry. "Where's the door?"

Perry took a flash lamp from his pocket and played it over the bill-postered boards till he found a keyhole roughly cut in a plank. "This is it, I think."

"All right. Knock 'em up."

Perry beat with his knuckles on the door. Then he waited and listened. "I hear some one in there."

"Try again."

Larry opened the door a couple of inches and peered out. "Who's that?"

Thompson lowered his shoulder and pushed. Larry staggered on the top step and fell. The door swung open wide. "There's some steps," Perry said. "Look out."

"Put your light on 'em." Thompson descended to the shop level. Larry got up quickly and backed away. "Stand by the door," Thompson ordered Perry and, lunging forward, pinned Larry's right arm behind his back.

Perry found the key and locked the door. Then he ran his hands over Larry. "He hasn't got anything on him," he said.

Thompson loosed his hold and pushed Larry into a corner of the shop.

"You stop there." He looked round. "Can you see a switch anywhere?"

Perry played his light over the walls. "Yes, here's one." He pressed it down. Nothing happened.

Larry, from his corner, snarled. "You'll have to make do with the lights you've got."

"There's probably a lamp somewhere," Thompson said.

Perry lifted the blanket curtain which shut off the kitchen and stumbled over something on the floor.

A whining voice asked him what the hell he was after, and Perry lowered the beam of his torch. Larry's mother thrust her head, tortoise-like, out of a bundle of rags and swore fluently and horribly.

"Shut up!" Thompson said fiercely. The flow eased to an angry mumble.

Perry found an oil lamp and lit it; when the glass was warm he turned up the wick.

Thompson looked round the shop. The only occupants were Larry and the whining hag on the floor. "Come here," he said to Larry, who edged forward slowly. "There's a back way out. Where is it?"

"Find it yourself."

After he had examined the walls and found no opening, Thompson turned his attention to the floor. "There's probably a trap-door," he said to Perry, and moved a table to one side. "This looks like the thing." He pulled at a ring; a two foot square of the floor hinged back. "You keep an eye on Larry. I'll see what's down here."

Perry waited a good ten minutes before he saw Thompson's head reappear. He threw up a coat and then climbed into the shop.

"Whose is this?" He held up a long yellow overcoat.

"Find out."

Thompson put his hands in the pockets of the coat and brought out a box of matches, a half-empty packet of cigarettes and a few odd bits of papers. He examined them in the light of the oil lamp.

The old woman, now thoroughly awake, was hunched on a broken-backed chair. "You won't find nothing there, Mister Sherlock Holmes." She gave a cackling laugh. Larry swore at her.

Thompson dropped the coat on a table and turned to him. "Some one brought a parcel here on Saturday. What happened to it?"

"No one never brought no parcel here."

"It was for Spike Morgan."

Larry kept his eyes fixed on Thompson. His expression did not change at the mention of the name. "I never saw no parcel."

"Did you?" Thompson shot the question at the old woman.

"I don't know what you're talking about," she croaked.

"Bring him out to the car," Thompson said to Perry. "We'll drop him at the Gladstone Road station on the way."

Larry was locked up in a cell and Thompson drove on to Rivers's shop in Cable Street. He tried the shop door but it was locked.

Perry stepped back to the edge of the pavement and looked up at the first-floor windows.

"Leith told me that Rivers lived over the shop. Perhaps there's a side door."

"We'll try down here." Thompson walked down the alley-way a few yards. "Yes. Here we are." He took a torch from his pocket and put the light on a square of paper. "Nothing wanted. Back in a week's time," he read. "What d'you make of that?"

"Got the wind up and cleared out," Perry replied.

"Yes, I suppose that's the answer. Let's have a look round."

They walked to the yard. There were two open-fronted sheds piled high with empty packing-cases and barrels. All around was a little of paper and wood shavings. Thompson tugged at a padlock on a double door; he found a wide crack in the rough boards and shone his light through it. "There's a car in there. That's odd. You'd think he'd have taken it with him."

Perry found an iron bar. "What about easing up that staple and having a look at the inside?"

Thompson thought for a moment and then said: "All right."

Perry inserted the thin end of the bar in the hoop of the staple and heaved. "It's coming." Thompson added his weight and the staple came free from the wood. The padlock fell with a clatter on the cobble stones.

Thompson bent down and looked at the tyres of the car. "She hasn't been out to-day. They're quite dry." He put a handkerchief on the handle of one of the rear doors and turned it. "We've got to be careful. I wouldn't mind betting that this was the car used in the hold-up. Dorset's description fits." He knelt on the floor and switched on the roof light. A magazine was lying on the seat with half its cover torn off.

Perry opened the other door. "There doesn't seem to be anything else."

"What about this?" Thompson picked up a long hair. It was black with a ring of white. "That's enough for me. Don't touch anything else. We'll get Hilton along to make a proper examination." Thompson slammed the door shut. "I'm going to break into the shop."

"What about a search warrant?"

"We'll swing that. Go and get a couple of constables. We'll want them to keep guard."

Perry came back a few minutes later. "I got on to the local D.D.I. He's coming along himself and he's bringing a man to open the lock on the shop door."

"Good. We seem to be getting somewhere at last." Thompson lit his pipe and was half-through it when the D.D.I. turned up. "We're working on the Crowley job," Thompson explained. "I think the man who ran it lives here."

"You want the lock forced?"

"Yes. As quick as you like."

The lock gave little trouble and Thompson led the way up the steep flight of stairs which led to Rivers's living room. He found a set of switches and snapped them all on. He pointed to a door at one end of the room and said to Perry: "Have a look in there." Then he walked slowly round the room. He examined the array of china ornaments on the marble-topped mantelpiece below the tall pier glass, and the sideboard with its whisky decanter, soda siphon and three dirty glasses. The decanter was about a third full.

There were ashes in the grate. "Nothing here, Jennings."

"There's a picture missing. D'you see that mark on the wall?"

"Yes?" Thompson walked over to the place Jennings indicated, stared at it for a minute and then called out to Perry. "Found anything?"

Perry appeared in the doorway. "Some one's turned things upside down here. Come and have a look."

Thompson walked into Rivers's bedroom. The drawers of a dressing-table and tallboy were wide open. Some of their contents were lying on the floor.

"Looks as if he'd packed in a hurry or else he was looking for something he couldn't find."

Perry pointed to the dressing-table. "I don't think it's a case of packing. Hair brushes there and here's a razor and tube of cream."

"More like a burglary," Thompson said. "Any sign of the windows having been forced?"

Perry drew the curtains. The windows were shut tight and fastened with a catch. Perry released it and tried to pull down the upper sash. "It's jammed," he said.

"All right, don't bother about it. Give me a hand to shift the sideboard." They pulled it out from the wall and examined the floor and wainscoting. "Nothing there. Look under the chairs."

Nothing of interest was revealed when the chairs had been moved. Thompson looked round the room. "We'll have that china cabinet out of it."

Perry trod on something which cracked as he lifted his end. "Glass."

Thompson picked up a sliver of it. "It's quite thin. And look at this." He pointed to the head of the laughing boy. "Some one's been breaking up the happy home." He wrapped his handkerchief round the piece of china and put it on the round walnut table.

"It's hollow," Perry said, "and there's something in it." He pulled at a corner of paper and took out a folded banknote.

"Queer place to keep money," Thompson muttered and spread out the note. It was for one hundred pounds. "First time I've seen one of these. Are there any more?"

"Yes." Perry poked about inside the head of the laughing boy and dislodged three more notes. They were all for a hundred pounds.

Jennings gathered up the splinters of broken glass and fine pieces of china and put them on the table.

"Well, that's that," Thompson said. "We'd better have another look round and then go down to the shop."

It was Perry who found poor George, the fat brown and white mouse which Barney had lost on the Friday night. He was lying stretched out on his side. Perry picked him up by the tail. "Something's been at him. There's blood all over his head."

"That's wild mice," Jennings said. "They'll always kill a tame one if they can get at it."

"One brown mouse. Victim of foul play." Thompson grinned. "Put him down in your book, Perry. He may hang somebody. You never know."

George was laid on the walnut table.

"There's a car," Perry said and walked to the window. "It's Hilton."

"Right. We'll get him on to this room and then go to the shop."

Hilton came into the room carrying a large black case. Two men followed him with a camera tripod and reflectors.

"Plenty of work for you, Hilton," Thompson said. "I want all the finger-prints you can get. They're these glasses on the sideboard and this china figure." He pointed to the remains of the laughing boy. "After that there's a car down in the yard."

"Do you want photographs of the room?"

"Yes, you might as well. We'll put the furniture back where we found it. By the way, what d'you make of this glass?"

Hilton looked at the pieces and felt their thickness. "Looks to me as though it had come from a picture."

"There's one missing," Thompson pointed to the lighter square on the wall. "We'll have a look round and see if we can find it."

"What's happened here? Burglary?"

"I don't know. One of the windows was open."

"There aren't any signs of forcing," Perry said.

"And all the doors were locked," Thompson added. "I don't know what to make of it." He left Hilton in possession of the room and went out on to the landing with Jennings and Perry. They found the mops and cloths which Mrs. Kemp had used to clean up the bloodstained boards, and the broken picture. The door leading from the shop to the street was locked and bolted on the inside.

"We'll get Hilton to take some photographs down here," Thompson said, when their examination of the shop was completed. "Now we'll see if this picture fits that place on the wall upstairs, but even if it does, I don't see that it's going to help us much."

The picture did fit and Hilton took another photograph with it in place. "We've got some quite good prints off the glasses," he said to Thompson. "But that china figure wasn't any good." He unplugged his floodlamps and carried them down to the shop.'

Thompson sat down in an easy chair and stretched his legs. He stared at the broken picture on the wall for a minute or two and then said: "I can't figure it out at all. Have you got any ideas, Perry?"

"I should say there'd been a rough house. Some one started chucking things about."

"That might have been our friend Spike. It looks as though he and another man used Rivers's car to lift the furs. Took them to Hyams's shop. Returned the car here and then had a quarrel with Rivers."

"These rugs are Persian," Perry said.

"Well?"

"There was a Persian rug round that body that was found in the barge."

Thompson got up and tapped out his pipe on the bars of the grate. "All we've got to do now is to find Spike Morgan." The door to the yard opened and a man came up the stairs. It was Leith. "Did you have any trouble?" Thompson asked.

"No. He went quiet enough. First time inside, or so he says." Leith looked round the room. "I was in here last week. On Monday I think it was."

"Why?"

"I was on duty that night and was taking a turn along the street that runs at the back of this place. There was a fellow ahead of me walking fairly quickly. He was some way away but as far as I could make out he turned into this yard. I knew Rivers lived here and I'd often wanted to have a look round his place, so I waited a little while and then came into the yard. I fell over a box and made a noise. Rivers poked his head out the window."

"What happened then?"

"He let me in and I explained that I thought I saw some one come into his yard. He said he hadn't seen anybody, but he was lying. I'll swear that the boxes I fell over had been fixed as a booby trap, and there was a cigarette burning on that walnut table when I first came into the room. Rivers knocked it off and trod on it. He thought I hadn't seen."

"Have you any idea who the visitor was?"

"Might have been Spike. He was about his build and dressed the same way as far as I could see."

Leith looked closely at the walnut table. "Look here. You can see the burn the cigarette made. It's not very big but that's the right place. The table hasn't been moved." He picked up the head of the laughing boy. "That was all right when I was here before. It was sitting in the middle of this table."

"Are you sure about that?"

"Yes. I picked it up. Rivers told me how much it cost, but I forgot what the figure was."

"I had an idea it had been knocked off the mantelpiece. Anyway, that doesn't matter. Tell me, does Rivers have any one working for him?" Thompson asked.

"Yes. There's Joe. I don't know his other name. He lives in one of these streets by the canal."

"What work did he do?"

"Took the barrow to the markets. Rivers did most of his business there. There was a bloke used to look after the shop when Rivers was out, but he's been gone some time and the place was shut up for days at a time."

"Find out where this man Joe lives."

Leith put on his hat and turned to the door. "I don't think that'll take me long. Shall I report back here?"

"Yes, I'll wait," Thompson replied and proceeded to fill his pipe.

Spike Morgan left No. 3 Napier Terrace at six on the Monday evening. It was the busiest time of day in the Camden Town area. The shops and pavements were crowded. Spike kept away from the empty side streets and walked all the way to Piccadilly Circus. He did not want to sit in a bus or a tube where people could stare at him. There was a chance that the police might want to pick him up again, and it was possible that they had circulated his description.

The theatre crowds in Shaftesbury Avenue were good cover, and it was but a short dash up Greek Street to the café he had visited with Alma on the night of Rivers's murder.

The tables in the long room were nearly all occupied, and he walked quickly up the narrow passage between them to the bar at the far end. He kept his hat pulled well down over his face.

One of the men he had met on his previous visit was propped up in one corner, his slack fingers clasped round a tall glass, half-full. He nodded to Spike and said: "Where's the girl?"

Spike ignored the question and ordered a double brandy.

As the bartender pushed the glass across the counter, he said in a low voice: "There's been some one looking for you."

"When?"

"About an hour ago. Soon after we opened."

Spike took a pull at his drink. "A split?"

The barman nodded. "Clark."

"What did he say?"

"Just asked if I'd seen you. I said you hadn't been in for a month. He looked in at the back; made sure you weren't there and beat it."

"In a hurry, eh?"

"Looked like it. I'd lie up if I was you."

Spike bought a drink for the man in the corner and said: "I want a word with you."

The barman went in front of them, unlocked a door and switched on a light in a small room. It was ten feet square, carpeted with linoleum and furnished with half a dozen stiff-backed chairs and four glass-topped tables ringed with the marks of wet glasses. The barman lit a gas fire and left them to enjoy the amenities of the smoking room of the Domino Club.

Spike sat for a minute or two, studying his companion. He was drunk, he decided, but not too far gone to be unable to carry out the project Spike had in his mind. "Have you got anything on to-night, Timmy?"

A watery, suspicious pair of eyes met Spike's level gaze. "What do you want me to do?"

"Do you know Izzy Hyams?"

"I've heard of him," was the cautious reply.

"He's got a shop. Near Aldgate Tube."

"Well?"

"I want you to find out if he lives over his shop. If not, where he does hang out."

"Is that all?"

"Yes, and if you're back before ten o'clock, I'll give you ten bob."

Timmy stood out for a pound down. Spike would not agree to this demand. Timmy, with a pound in his pocket, would not get a hundred yards while the pubs were open. "I'll give it you when you get back."

"Ten bob down and ten bob when I finish."

"No blinking fear."

"How do I know you'll cough up?"

Spike leaned back in his chair, opened the door and called to the barman. "Here's a quid. Keep it till I ask you for it." He turned to Timmy. "Is that good enough for you?"

Timmy watched the note disappear with the anxious interest of a thirsty man.

"All right. I'll do it. What's the name of the bloke you want me to turn up?" His brain was muzzy with drink.

"Hyams. I'll write it down for you." Spike tore a strip off an evening paper and printed the words "Izzy Hyams."

Timmy was gone an hour and returned with Hyams's address. Spike called for the note and handed it over. He had five shillings left and he spent most of them on brandy before he left to call on Izzy. He was determined to lift a fiver off him whatever happened.

As he walked up Shaftesbury Avenue he kept repeating the directions Timmy had given him. "Second on the left after you pass his shop, and then the house is halfway down on the right. There's a street lamp opposite and you can't miss it."

Second on the left past the shop . . . second on the left . . . Hell! He wished he hadn't drunk so much. He'd look a damn' fool if he was run in for being tight . . . Second on the left . . .

It was a long walk to Aldgate and Spike did not reach Izzy's shop until half an hour after Thompson and Perry had left it. There was a policeman standing outside. His back was to the door and he had his coat buttoned up.

Spike thought of crossing the road, but before he could make up his mind it was too late. He walked a little quicker as he passed the policeman and turned his head to the right. As soon as he was past the urge came to run, but he forced himself to keep on walking. Second on the left . . . He was almost there. He turned left.

"The house . . . halfway down on the right."

Yes, there it was. By the lamp. He searched for a bell push, found it and pressed it three times. He could hear the bell ring. Three minutes passed, and nothing happened. He was beginning to sweat, though the night was cold. If a policeman was to come along! He rang the bell again and listened.

There was a vague shuffling inside the house, and the door opened a few inches.

A woman's voice asked: "Who's that?"

Spike put his foot in the crack. "Is Mr. Hyams in?"

"What d'you want with him?"

"Tell him I'm here about the black fox furs. He'll understand."

The woman laughed shortly. "Yes, he'll understand all right. That's what the police have took him for."

"The police!"

The woman opened the door a little farther, kicked Spike's foot out of the way and slammed the door.

"The police!" Spike swore savagely under his breath. Hell! He turned and walked quickly back the way he had come. A bus was slowing down as he got to the corner, and with only one thought in his mind he boarded it. He must get back to Napier Terrace and stay there. He'd been a fool to have come out. He went up on to the top deck and took a seat right at the front.

There were few passengers at that time of night, but he was glad to get off at the Angel to walk the last bit. If he had been spotted on the bus he wouldn't have had a dog's chance of getting away.

He walked quickly through the silent streets until he finally reached the canal bridge. A bus passed him and slowed down on the other side. A man got out. Spike stopped, and side-stepped into a doorway. It was Leith!

Leith was alone and walked on without looking round. Where the blazes was he going to? Spike followed fifty yards behind. Then he saw a policeman in uniform come out of the alley-way at the side of Rivers's shop and raise his hand in a salute.

Spike turned and ran blindly to the canal path and down in to Napier Terrace. When he had knocked and was waiting to be let in he saw that the window of the front room had a gaping hole.

His nerve began to fail him. He must get out of this. He must— And then he heard Mrs. Kemp's husky voice. "Is that you, Spike?"

He forced his way past her into the passage. "Lock that door quick, for God's sake!" When the bolts shot home he felt better.

Mrs. Kemp pawed at his shoulders. "What's happened?"

"The splits. They've taken Izzy, and they're up at Rivers's place now." He was breathing fast and his hand trembled as he felt for a cigarette. "Have you got a match?"

Mrs. Kemp shuffled down the passage to the back room. Spike followed her. She took a box of matches off the mantelpiece and gave it to him. Then she turned down the gas till it was no more than a blue pin-point.

"Where's Len?"

"In his room, but Alma's gone."

"Run away?"

"No, a man came and took her. He said his name was Dorset and that she'd sent a telegram for him to come. I tried to keep him out but he kicked in the front window. Mrs. Benson came out of her house to see what was the matter and I had to let him in. I told him Alma wasn't here but he went upstairs. Len came out of his room and tried to stop him. He got a crack on the jaw that put him out for the best part of an hour. I don't think he's feeling too good now."

"And this man Dorset took the girl?"

"Yes, I couldn't stop him on my own, and Joe wasn't no use. He hid under the bed."

"I've got to get out of this. Go and tell Len to come down."

Spike got up and felt along the wall for the cupboard and took out the bottle of whisky.

When Len appeared he had pulled himself together. He wasn't caught yet. Maybe they weren't after him. No one had seen him do the job and as long as he didn't talk, what the hell was there to worry about?

Len came into the room and felt his way to the table. "Spike?"

"I'm here. Sit down and take a swig at this." Spike leaned across and put the bottle in Len's hand. "You've had a bit of a turn up, I hear. How d'you feel?"

"Rotten. My head's still singing and I think my jaw's cracked."

"We've got to get away from here. The splits are at the shop."

"I know. The old woman told me. What about Larry's?"

"That's no blooming good. Too far. We'll try that warehouse across the canal by the coal heaps."

"Yes. That'll be all right for the night if we can get in, but what about to-morrow? There'll be people working there."

"It hasn't been used for five years and we can get in easy enough. Every window's smashed. Get the rest of your clothes on and let's get moving."

"What'll you do for food?" Mrs. Kemp asked.

"Give us what you've got."

Mrs. Kemp went into the kitchen. "There's some mince and a loaf of bread and a bit of cheese."

"That'll have to do for the meantime. You can send Joe along to-morrow with some more."

"I haven't any money left."

Spike gave her sixpence. It was all he had. "There's lots of stuff you can pop, isn't there?"

"I might raise a few bob, but when that's finished I don't know what I can do." Mrs. Kemp turned the mince out of its dish into a paper bag. "You can put the bread and cheese in your pocket."

"What about some 'bines?"

"There aren't any. Joe smokes a pipe."

"Give me his 'baccy. I've got a packet of papers." Spike got up and went up to his room. There was nothing there he wanted to take. He came downstairs with Len. Mrs. Kemp was waiting in the passage.

"Now when you gets into that place, stop there till I sends you word you can come out," Mrs. Kemp said. "I'll get you food over somehow even if I has to bust a bank to get the dough." She tried to laugh.

"I've left some bits and pieces upstairs. You'd better clear 'em out in case of accidents."

"I'll see to that. Don't you worry."

"Let's get away then."

Mrs. Kemp opened the front door and looked out. The night was very still. "It's all clear."

Spike gave her hand a quick pressure as he passed.

He stopped Len as they neared the bridge over the canal. "This is the only bad bit. Wait there." He walked

in the shadow of a house to the corner and listened. Then he took two cautious paces to the centre of the pavement; there was no one in sight at Rivers's shop. He ran back to Len. "We'll take a chance. Come on."

The passage of the bridge took no longer than a few seconds and, when they reached the other side, Spike stood behind a tram standard and looked back. "We're all right," he muttered. He walked on and turned down a side street. There was a fence on the left-hand side. "We've got to get over that." He jumped up, caught the top and clambered over. Len followed.

They were on a piece of waste land littered with heaps of bricks and rubble. Spike stopped to get his breath and was about to light a cigarette when Len caught his arm. "Wait till we get inside."

"All right. You take the right side. I'll go left. We've got to find a way to get in."

The windows on the ground floor of the warehouse were shuttered but Len found one on which the inside catch had rotted away. He swung the shutter out and found a window frame with its glass intact. That wasn't any good. He went on but every other shutter was securely fastened. At the corner of the building which abutted on the coal yard he met Len. "What luck?"

"It's no damn' good my side. What about you?"

"There's one shutter loose but there's glass behind it. It'll make a hell of a noise if we bust it."

"We've got to risk it."

Spike put his hand in his pocket and felt the paper bag of mince Mrs. Kemp had given him. He took it out and opened it. "It might work," he muttered to himself. "What the hell are you talking about?"

"Come on." Spike turned back the way Len had come and opened the loose shutter. "Hold it back out of the way," he ordered, and plastered a handful of the sticky meat on a pane of the window. When he had covered as much of it as he could, he ran a glass cutter round the outside of the prepared surface. Then he took off his hat, put his hand inside it and gave a quick blow on the centre of the glass.

It fell inside the warehouse making little noise and leaving a clean-cut hole.

"That's good enough." Spike put in his arm, released a catch and lifted the sash. He climbed in. Len followed and drew the shutter to behind him.

"We'll have to tie that shutter up somehow."

"Yes. There's sure to be a bit of rope knocking about somewhere inside."

The floor of the warehouse was clear except for a pile of rotting sacks in one corner. Len struck a match and said to Spike: "Have a look through them."

Len started back as a rat scampered across the floor. Spike swore at him. "Get a move on before I burn my blinking fingers."

Len picked up a sack gingerly and found a length of binding twine. He held it up. "Will that be long enough?"

Spike dropped the match. "We'll try it." He took it from Len and walked over to the shutter. "It'll do for the time being but it won't stand any strain. Now let's have a look up top."

They went up to the top floor. It was lighter there for the windows were unshuttered and there were only a few pieces of jagged glass in their frames. Spike looked down on the canal, to the houses in Napier Terrace and across to the back of Rivers's shop. The yard was in shadow, but there was a light in the windows of the top room.

"There're still there," he said.

"Where?"

"Rivers's place."

"I didn't know he lived in these parts."

"He used to," Spike replied. "The splits are giving it the once over."

"If they catch Rivers, will he talk?"

"They won't get him." Spike spoke with conviction. "How the hell do you know?"

"I know. That's good enough. We've nothing to be scared of from anything Rivers'll say."

"But even if he has cleared out, they'll get him sooner or later."

"Oh, for God's sake shut up that damn' croaking. Rivers is out of this. We've got enough to worry about without him."

"I don't see that. No one saw us on the job."

"Izzy saw us afterwards. He saw us bring the furs to his shop. He knows what we look like."

"The splits don't know we went there."

"Oh, yes, they do. They copped Izzy a couple of hours ago."

"How d'you know that?"

"A woman at his house told me. May have been his missus, I don't know. There was a copper outside his shop."

"If he doesn't talk, what the hell does it matter?"

"He's done a squeak all right. I know his sort. As long as things go all right and he gets all the fat, you're safe, but when he's nabbed, look out! The splits'll tell him that if he spills it they'll look after him and make things easy. They won't have to ask him if he'd like to make a statement after that. He'll write a book about it."

"And that's why the splits are at Rivers's shop?"

"Of course it is. I don't know how they tumbled to Izzy, but that doesn't matter. They have. And now there's no knowing where they'll go next. It's a damn' good thing for us we cleared out of Napier Terrace." Spike moved back to the window, shielding the glow of his cigarette in his cupped hand.

"Look! D'you see that? There's one of 'em going down the back street now. No, there's two—and a copper!"

CHAPTER FIFTEEN

THOMPSON HAD smoked two pipes before Leith came back with the information that Joe, the man who worked for Rivers, lived down by the canal.

"I found a man who knows him," Leith said. "He thinks Joe lives in Napier Terrace."

"Where's that?"

"Only a few hundred yards from here."

"All right, we'll walk. Perry, you wait here. I'll take Leith and a constable."

They walked down the back street, their footsteps ringing loud on the cobbles, to the turning which led to the canal path in front of Napier Terrace.

"Do you know the number?" Thompson asked.

"No. But I think it's one of the middle houses."

"All right. Let's have a go here." Thompson strode up a path and banged on the door. He repeated the summons a couple of minutes later, but there was still no sign of life. "We'll go on to the next." Thompson stepped over a low fence and knocked at the neighbouring house.

A window sash was thrown up overhead and Mrs. Benson put out her head.

"Who are you?" Thompson asked.

"My name's Benson, and if you don't go away I'll call the police. I've had enough of this—"

"We are police officers," Thompson interrupted.

Mrs. Benson was suddenly silent. "Police officers," she said in a voice which had lost its force. "Oh!"

"We want to have a word with you."

Mrs. Benson said "Oh!" again, faintly, and backed from the window. A minute later she opened the door, clutching at the collar of her dressing-gown.

"Sorry to trouble you, ma'am, but can you tell me where a man of the name of Joe lives? He works for a Mr. Rivers."

"You mean Joe Kemp."

"I expect that's the man we want."

"He's next door." Mrs. Benson came out on to the step still holding her dressing-gown together, and pointed over the fence.

"Thanks. Sorry to have troubled you."

"There's been goings on at the Kemps," Mrs. Benson said.

"What do you mean?"

"Oh, I don't know, but I was woke up an hour ago. There was a man trying to get in. He broke a window."

"Oh, yes, I see." Thompson looked at the black gaping hole in the window of Mrs. Kemp's front room. "What happened?"

"Mrs. Kemp let him in." She paused and added: "I think he must have been drunk."

"All right. We'll look into it. Good night."

Mrs. Benson retreated into her house and watched while Thompson knocked up Mrs. Kemp who offered no resistance. She led the police down the passage to the back room. If they had come an hour earlier, however, their reception would have been very different.

"Will you take a chair?" she said to Thompson, who refused. He stood, and his bulk made the room look very small.

"Is your husband in?"

"He's in bed and asleep."

"Tell him to come down," he said, and whispered to Leith to go with her. "Don't let 'em talk together," he ordered.

Joe appeared, a pathetic figure, blinking in the light.

"Is your name Joe Kemp?"

He answered "Yes," hesitantly, as if he wasn't quite sure who he was.

"I believe you work for Mr. Rivers?"

"That's right."

"Where is he?"

"Who?"

"Mr. Rivers."

"I don't know. He's gone away."

"When did you see him last?"

Joe ran a hand through his streaky hair. "It was the back end of last week. Saturday, I think it was."

"Are you sure of that?"

"It was Friday," Mrs. Kemp prompted.

"Friday. That's right. That's when it was. He gave me my money that night, and when I went round on the Saturday morning he was gone."

"What time was that?"

"About nine o'clock. We was going to do a market. The Lower Marsh, I think it was to be."

"What about the shop? Was there any one to look after it?"

"Alma was to do that."

"Who's Alma?"

"She's a girl who was stopping with us."

"Is she in the house now?"

Mrs. Kemp smiled. "No, she's gone, too. A gentleman friend of hers came for her to-night, and took her away."

"Was that the man who kicked in your front window?" The smile began to fade, and then came again as Mrs. Kemp explained. "Well, he was a bit impatient, and when I didn't come down quick enough to suit him he tried to get in at the window, and broke it."

"What was the rest of the girl's name?"

"I don't know. Alma. That's what we called her."

"How long had she been here?"

"Since last Monday."

"Where'd she come from?"

"I don't know."

"That doesn't make sense to me."

"Well, I don't care if it does or it doesn't, but it's the gospel truth. She came here looking for a room, and I fixed her up." Mrs. Kemp's voice had a dogged, defiant note, and Thompson realized he was up against a stone wall. He took Joe by the arm.

"How long have you been working for Rivers?"

"About a year."

"Is he in the habit of going away?"

"No. I've never known him leave his place for a night before this."

"Did he tell you he was going?"

"No."

"What time was it you got your money from him on Friday night?"

"Half-past six, as near as I can recollect."

"And he didn't say anything then?"

"No. He said as I was to be round at the usual time the next morning."

"Where was he when you saw him?"

"In the room over the shop."

"Was he alone?"

"Yes, but Alma was in the shop."

"Did you see any one hanging about when you left?"

"No."

Thompson moved towards the door. "I want to have a look around upstairs."

"That's all right." Mrs. Kemp was almost pleasant. He could look all he wanted to now that Spike and Len were out of the house. She lit the gas lamp in the passage and began to climb the stairs slowly. When she reached the first-floor landing she halted and pointed to a door. "That's my room. Mine and Joe's."

Thompson looked in on a big double bed. The clothes were rumpled and thrown back. A candle was burning on the mantelpiece. He looked under the bed and into the wardrobe. Then he came out on to the landing. "What's in there?"

"That was Alma's room. It's a bit untidy, too." Thompson saw another bed which had obviously been slept in, a pair of slippers under the dressing-table, and a basin half full of dirty water. There was a dress hanging in a cupboard. He touched it. "Is this Alma's," he asked.

"Yes. I don't know how she came to forget to pack it. But she was in a hurry, and I didn't have time to look round to see if she'd left anything."

Thompson bent down and picked up a short length of chain. "What is this?"

Mrs. Kemp stared at it. "I'm sure I don't know. I don't remember having seen it before."

Thompson put the chain in his waistcoat pocket and completed his examination of the room.

"There's another floor, isn't there?"

"Yes, but there's nothing there to see. Only one room. We haven't used it for I don't know how long."

"I'll have a look at it." Thompson mounted the next flight of stairs and opened the door of the room which Spike and Len had used. There were two beds which took up most of the floor space, a wicker table in the window, and two chairs. The seat was out of one of them.

The beds had been stripped, and the blankets had been folded and piled at one end.

"Who's been sleeping here?" Thompson asked.

"Nobody, except Joe. And that's only when he snores and keeps me awake."

"There are two beds."

"Yes. You see, I used to take in lodgers."

"How long is it since any one has used this room?"

"Oh, weeks, I should say."

Thompson told Leith to fetch Joe, and while he was gone made a careful search of the room. His only find was a man's felt hat on the top of a wardrobe. By the mark it had made in the layer of dust it had not been there long.

Mrs. Kemp wet her thick lips with her tongue and said, "That's Joe's," before Thompson asked the question.

"Well, here is Joe. We'll try it on him."

The hat sank down on to Joe's ears.

"It doesn't seem a very good fit, does it?" Thompson said dryly.

"Well, I thought it was Joe's," Mrs. Kemp said. "I don't know who else's it could be."

Thompson ignored her explanation and said to Joe, "Do you ever sleep in this room?"

"No. Never."

"Oh, yes, you do, Joe. When you snores." Mrs. Kemp spoke with a force and directness which penetrated Joe's thick head.

"That's right. I have slept here," he said, speaking quickly, nervously.

But Thompson wasn't listening to him. He was looking out of the window across the canal to the coal yard. There were four or five barges tied up in the basin. He turned Mrs. Kemp and Joe out of the room and shut the door. "That's where the body was found, wasn't it?"

"Yes, that's the place," Leith replied. "The barge was lying under that right-hand crane."

Thompson turned and surveyed the room. "I wonder what the blazes has been going on here? That old woman's lying. She's had some one in this room quite recently."

"How do you know?" Leith asked.

"There's a pile of fresh cigarette ash by the head of that bed, which she didn't see when she cleared the room."

"She missed the hat, too."

Thompson picked it up. "There's no name in it, except the maker's, and it's an ordinary sort, so I don't suppose it'll tell us anything." He opened the door. Mrs. Kemp and Joe were still standing outside. "You two go to your room, and stay there." He went downstairs and into the back room. "Leith, you can wait here and see they don't try to get away."

Thompson went into the back kitchen. "I'm going to see if there's a way out through the garden. It'll be quicker." He unlocked the back door and walked up the path, his torch casting a dancing circle of light ahead. The door in the wall was locked, but the wall wasn't high, and there was a scraggy lilac bush in one corner.

Before he had taken a couple of steps through the rank grass, he knocked his shin against something hard, and fell sprawling over a wooden wheel.

He got up swearing, and flashed the torch about to see if there were any other hidden traps. There was another wheel and, a little farther on, the body of a coster's barrow. He ran his fingers along the side of it, and felt the grooves of a name cut deeply into the wood. By the light of his torch he read the words, "J. Rivers, Camden Town."

"Damn' funny place to keep a barrow," Thompson muttered to himself, and lifted one wheel. By the look of the grass underneath it hadn't been there long. He'd have to ask Joe Kemp about this, but that could wait. He wanted to have another look at Rivers's room first.

The constable on duty in the yard of the shop saluted Thompson as he came in, and said that Hilton had finished his job and was getting ready to go.

"Where is he?" Thompson asked.

"In the street."

"Tell him to wait." Thompson went up the stairs to the top room. He told Perry of the result of his visit to Napier Terrace, and of the discovery of the barrow.

"I don't know what to make of it yet, but we'll try and get something out of the Kemps later on. Meanwhile, I want to have another run through this room."

Perry looked at Thompson curiously. "You've got an idea?" he said.

Thompson nodded. "Half one, but it's so damn' silly I won't tell you what it is, just yet." He walked to the end of the room and looked at the floor. "These rugs have been shifted. You can see by the light patches." He moved one, and then the next, until he had got them all into what appeared to be their original positions.

There was a light square left, to the right of the walnut table. Perry measured it.

"Two foot six by four foot two, as near as I can make it."

"Now do you see what I'm getting at?"

"No."

"That body in the barge had a Persian rug round it, and it measured about the same."

"But it's quite a way to the canal from here," Perry objected.

"Not if you go the back way through the yard."

"But dammit, no one in their senses would have risked carrying a corpse even through a back street. Besides, it would have taken at least two men to do the job, and pretty hefty ones at that."

"I dare say you're right, but still, there it is. The canal's not far away. A barge moored up on this side. And the rug found was the same size as the one which appears to be missing from this room."

"All right, then, suppose Rivers's is the body in the barge. How did it get there?"

"I don't know, but I have an idea how it was taken from here."

"How?"

"In a barrow. The one Rivers used for taking his junk to the markets."

"Why do you think that?"

"I found the barrow in the back garden of the Kemps' house in Napier Terrace. The front of the house isn't forty feet from the canal."

"Still, that would take a nerve. Think of the risk of being stopped by a policeman."

"It's been done before. Do you remember that Henderson case in Tooting?"

"Yes, I know, but—" Perry was still doubtful. Thompson knelt down and looked at the floor from different angles. "Come here a minute."

Perry joined him.

"These boards have been washed. Can you see where I mean?"

"On this side of the table?"

"Yes, and it's over quite a big area."

"Go down and get Hilton. I told him to wait."

Hilton came into the room a few minutes later. "Found another job for me?"

"Yes, I think so." Thompson pointed out the mark left by the missing rug and the signs of washing. "Do you think you can photograph that?"

Hilton looked at the floor, thought for a moment and then said, "I don't think it would come out, but I can try."

"Have a shot at it."

Hilton sent for his camera and lights. Thompson watched him as he moved them about from place to place. At last, Hilton was satisfied, and made two or three exposures.

"That's the best I can do," he said, and asked, "What do you think it was that's been cleaned up?"

"I've an idea it might have been blood."

"Then what about the cracks in the boards? We might find something there."

"I hadn't thought of that."

"Let's hope whoever cleaned the floor didn't think of it, either." Hilton opened his case and took out a hammer, a chisel, and a packet of seed envelopes. "I'll take a sliver off the side of each board."

When he had finished his work he sealed up the pieces of wood in envelopes and marked them.

"That'll give some one in the lab. a job of work. I'll get them on to it as soon as I get back."

"And the photographs of the car. I want them as soon as possible."

"They won't take long. Where'll I be able to find you?"

"Either here or at the Yard," Thompson replied. "I'm working a twenty-four-hour day."

CHAPTER SIXTEEN

WHEN HILTON had gone, Thompson and Perry made a further examination of the room, but found nothing more of interest. Then they went down to the yard and paced out the distance from there to the back garden and door of the Kemps' house. It was roughly two hundred and seventy-five yards, and there were four street lamps on the way.

"I still can't believe it," Perry said.

"You mean taking the body all this way on the barrow?"

"Yes. If there hadn't been any lamps it would be different."

"Then why was the barrow in the Kemps' back garden?"

"Joe has probably got a perfectly reasonable explanation of that. He worked for Rivers."

"We'll go and ask him about it."

Thompson and Perry walked on to the end of Napier Terrace and along a path which ran off at right-angles to the lane at the back. It led to the canal path. Thompson pointed to a couple of empty barges moored up alongside the path. "You see how easy it would be. There are no lamps within two hundred yards, and from the bridge you'd see nothing."

"Yes. This part of it's all right."

Thompson looked over to the warehouse and to the coal heaps on the other side of the canal. "There's no one there after working hours." He walked on to No. 3, and knocked.

Leith opened the door.

"Everything all right?" Thompson asked.

"Yes, they're upstairs. I put the man in the room on the top floor so as he couldn't get talking with his old woman."

"Good."

"Shall I get them down?"

"No. I want to have a look at the room at the back first. That's the one they use, isn't it?"

"Yes, there's nothing but photographs of Great Uncle Ned and Aunt Louisa, and a lot of presents from Margate in the parlour."

By the hard white light of the unshaded gas mantle Thompson and Perry made a systematic search of the back room. They found the bottle of whisky, which was almost empty, the pile of rubbish and papers under the settee, some of which were slightly charred.

Then they worked from the back door through the kitchen, the back room, and the passage to the front of the house looking for bloodstains. They found none.

"I'll have a go at the man," Thompson said, when they had finished their examination. "Bring him down here."

Joe came into the room like a crab with gout.

"Now what the hell d'you want?" he grumbled.

"Sit down."

Perry pushed him forward, and forced him into a chair.

"Where's Rivers's barrow?" Thompson asked.

"Barrow? Why, in the yard back of the shop, where it always stands."

"No, it isn't."

"That's where I left it on Friday night."

"Are you sure about that?"

"Of course I am. You can ask that girl. She was there when I come in. She helped me unload."

"Where was Rivers then?"

"I think he was in his room. I saw him there later when he give me my money. But I've told you all that already."

"Never mind what you've said, just answer my questions. What happened on the next day, Saturday?"

"I went to the shop and found it locked up, so I came away."

"Was the barrow in the yard then?"

"I suppose it was."

"You didn't see it?"

"No. I didn't bother about it, seeing the shop was shut—what was the use?"

"If I told you it was in the back garden, what would you say?"

"You mean out there?" Joe turned his chair and looked at the window.

"Yes."

Joe laughed. "Don't be silly. You couldn't get it through the gate in the wall."

"You could if you took the wheels off it."

"I never did that. Why should I?"

"Some one put Rivers's barrow in your garden."

Joe opened his mouth to voice a denial, and then changed his mind. "If they did, I don't know nothing about it. That barrow was where it always is, in Mr. Rivers's yard, on Friday night."

Thompson changed his ground. "Who's been living in this house and using the room on the top floor?"

"There's been nobody here except me and my missus and Alma." Joe leaned forward in his chair as though to give force to the denial.

"We know there was a man here," Thompson said. "When did he leave?"

"I dunno anything about it. I've been out all day."

"There was a man in this house," Thompson persisted. "And his name was Spike Morgan."

Joe's lips moved tremblingly, but he didn't speak. "There's no harm in Spike being here. What's got you scared?"

"I'm—not—scared." Joe spoke the words slowly. "We'll look after you. Now, come on, and tell us all about it." Thompson opened his cigarette-case and held it out.

Joe took a cigarette clumsily. Perry struck a match. "You'll feel better when you've got it off your chest," Thompson urged.

"Maybe you're right. But there's not much to tell."

"Well, let's have it."

"I hardly saw him."

"You mean Spike?"

"Yes. He stopped upstairs most of the time except when he was out."

"Where'd he go?"

"I don't know."

"Did you ever hear him talk about Larry's?"

Joe shook his head.

"Or Hyams? Izzy Hyams?"

"No, neither of them."

"When did Spike come here first?"

"He slept here Thursday night."

"What did he do on Friday? During the day, I mean?"

"He went out early. Soon after breakfast."

"When did he get back?"

"In time for supper, I think, or perhaps it was later. I can't be sure."

"Did he stay in that night?"

"No, he went out with Alma after supper."

"When did he get back?"

"I dunno. I didn't hear him."

"But he did come back here?" Thompson asked.

"I suppose he did. I know the missus took his breakfast up to his room on the Saturday."

Thompson found out very little more of Spike's movements except that he stayed in his room all Sunday and finally left the house some time before Thompson's first visit an hour or so before.

"I didn't know where they went to," Joe said in answer to a further question.

"They! Who was with Spike?"

"A pal of his. I never saw him."

"What was his name?"

"I dunno. All I know is he came here Saturday night." The clock on the mantelpiece struck two. Thompson yawned. What a damn' game it was, screwing information out of men like Joe. And when they'd finished with him, there was his wife. She was going to be a different proposition to Joe. He told Perry to go and get the police car outside the back door.

Joe had smoked his cigarette down to the cork tip. Thompson gave him another and asked: "What about the man who took Alma away?"

"I woke up when he was having a row at the front door with the missus. He came up the stairs and put his head into my room. 'Where's Alma?' he says, and I told him. He went to her room and tried the handle. Alma called out and he came back to me and wanted the key. I hadn't got it. Then the missus came along and they started slanging, but he didn't take much notice of her." Joe grinned a little. "She met her match that time all right." He puffed at his cigarette and coughed.

"Did he get the key out of her?" Thompson asked.

"No. He was trying all the time to get a run so as he could bust it open, I suppose. She kept getting in his way. And then Len came down the stairs—"

"Len!" Thompson interrupted. "That was Spike's pal, I suppose?"

"That's right."

"You've remembered his name at last. And you told me you never saw him."

"Not properly," Joe hedged. "There wasn't much light."

"What did he do?"

"He put his hand in his trouser pocket and then this bloke what had broke in landed him one. Len didn't take no more interest in what was going on after that. The missus wasn't too keen either."

"What did the other man do then?"

"He got in a kick on the lock and it bust. Alma came out. He said: 'pack your bag, quick,' and then he got the missus by the shoulders and shoved her into our room. God! She weren't half savage. If it hadn't been that she was scared of rousing the neighbours and them calling the police, I believe she would have had a go at stopping 'em."

"Did she stay in your room?"

"Yes, she sat on the bed and cussed me and him and the girl. When the two of 'em had gone, Alma and the man that was, she got on to me good and proper. Who the hell did I think I was not to give her a hand? On and on she went. When you came along she stopped."

Thompson heard the back door being opened and footsteps in the kitchen.

"Have they gone, deary?" a woman's voice asked.

When she received no answer she trod more softly and slowly put her head round the door. It was Mrs. Benson, ready to risk anything to satisfy her curiosity.

At first she only saw Joe sitting with his back to her. "Mrs. Kemp about?" she asked and advanced a pace into the room. Thompson got up from his chair and kicked the door shut behind her. She gave a frightened squeak and groped for the handle.

"Now you're here, won't you sit down?"

"Sit down?" Mrs. Benson repeated stupidly.

Thompson turned a chair round. She lowered herself gently on to the edge of it and pulled her shawl more tightly round her shoulders.

"I've seen you before, haven't I?"

Mrs. Benson nodded.

"What d'you want here at this hour?"

"Well, you see, I haven't been able to sleep since that man broke the window. It gave me a nasty turn. Then I heard you tell Mrs. Kemp you was the police, and when I thought I saw you go away along the garden path, I said to myself: 'Well, I'll just pop in and see if there's anything I can do!'" Mrs. Benson smiled and tried to look like a very good Samaritan. She didn't succeed.

"Smarmy old toad," Thompson thought to himself. He looked coldly at Mrs. Benson and the smile left her face.

They sat in a painful silence until Perry came back to say the car was outside. He'd had to go to the station to get it, he explained.

"All right," Thompson said, "take the Kemps to the station and send the bus back for me."

Perry went upstairs and came back a few minutes later with Mrs. Kemp who carried two grey blankets. She'd had experience of police stations and the scanty bedclothes they provided.

When she saw Mrs. Benson, her mouth twisted in an ugly grin. "Come for your sixpence, I suppose."

Mrs. Benson put the table between herself and her creditor.

"It's all right. I won't touch you." Mrs. Kemp looked contemptuously at Thompson. "You've got good protection."

Perry opened the kitchen door and said a little wearily: "Oh, come on, for God's sake." He touched Joe on the shoulder. "And you."

When they had gone, Thompson drew a chair up to the table and told Mrs. Benson to sit opposite him.

"Well, what do you know about all this?"

"You mean about that man what broke the window?"

"You can start with him."

"Well, I saw him trying to get into this house, or heard him rather. There was a terrible noise that woke me up and I came down and out at my front door." Mrs. Benson spoke slowly. It wasn't often that she had such an exciting story to tell, nor a police officer who would listen to her.

"Did you see the man?"

"Sort of. But it was dark, and when Mrs. Kemp saw me she let him in." The story ended tamely.

"You're a friend of Mrs. Kemp's, I suppose?"

"Well, I am and I ain't, if you get my meaning." Mrs. Benson leaned across the table and became confidential. "We're neighbours and I sometimes drops in for a chat." She was not quite sure if it was a good thing to be thought a friend of Mrs. Kemp's or not.

"What's this talk about a sixpence?" Thompson asked. He wasn't really interested in Mrs. Kemp's borrowings, but he felt that the question might produce an answer which would throw some light on her character.

Mrs. Benson laughed a little and said: "I'll tell you how it started"; and told of her meeting with Mrs. Kemp in the Green Man on the Saturday morning. "She said that Mr. Rivers had gone away, and Fred—he's the potman there—was kind of surprised and so was I."

"Why?" Thompson asked. This was interesting.

"Fred said Mr. Rivers had told him he was going to try the Lower Marsh the next day. And I'd never known him to be away of a night-time. I could see his light from my bedroom window and I could have set my watch by the time it was put out. Ten o'clock to the tick every blooming night. Fred and me said it was funny Mr. Rivers going away so sudden-like without saying nothing to nobody."

"What did Mrs. Kemp say to that?"

"She seemed a bit put out and drank up her beer and went."

"Did she say where she was going?"

"No. She never says what she's a-going to do. She's like that."

Mrs. Benson sniffed. She had little use for people who minded their own business.

Thompson threw the stub of his cigarette into the fireplace and got up. "Give me your name and address and then you can go back to bed."

"Mrs. Benson. Number four, Napier— Oh, there's something else I'd forgotten to say. On the Saturday night I came in here to see if I could borrow one or two odds and ends, a pinch of tea I think it was, and some sugar. Well, they were none of 'em too warm, if you knows what I mean; in fact they practically turned me out of the house. Of course, I'm not one to bear malice and if I'm owed a tanner what of it? I'll get it back some time. I'm not worrying, but there's just one thing I think I ought to tell you."

Mrs. Benson told the tale she'd recounted to Mrs. Tibbett about the "goings on" in the Kemps' back garden on the Friday night. Compared to Mrs. Tibbett, Thompson was much better value as an audience. He asked questions and the story grew.

"They was carrying something when I first saw them. The man and Mrs. Kemp. I couldn't see what it was."

Thompson wrote down a précis of Mrs. Benson's story.

When she could tell no more he thanked her and made an appointment for a meeting at Scotland Yard at 10 A.M.

Mrs. Benson wriggled with excitement. She was going to Scotland Yard! My! Wouldn't she have something to tell her old man when she got back?

Thompson let her out by the back door, locked up, and put the key in his pocket. Mrs. Benson stepped over the low dividing fence between the two back gardens and watched him go out through the door in the wall. She heard a car start up and move off, before she went to bed, a thoroughly happy woman. She had talked her fill.

Thompson found Mrs. Kemp at the police station, sitting bolt upright on a wooden bench. Joe was beside her, apparently in a coma.

The sergeant on duty slipped off his high stool and said: "Perry's in here," and opened a door. Perry was sitting on a chair at a long deal table with his head on his hands. He was sound asleep. Thompson shook him and he looked up drowsily, and said: "What's the matter?"

Then he saw Thompson. "The old woman's outside."

"Yes, I know. I'm going to see her now. I want you to get hold of Leith and find a man called Fred, who works at the Green Man in Cable Street. Bring him here."

Perry left the room and Thompson called out to the sergeant to send in Mrs. Kemp.

She came and sat on an inadequate chair. Silent, statuesque and disapproving.

"You knew Mr. Rivers, I believe."

"What if I did?"

"He told you he was going away?"

"He might have done."

"You told the barman at the Green Man that Rivers was going away?"

Mrs. Kemp gave a grudging "Yes," and stared at a crack in the white plastered ceiling.

"When did Mr. Rivers tell you he was going away?"

"Friday night."

"What time?"

"About half-past six."

"Where?"

"At his shop."

"What were you doing there?"

"Nothing. I was passing and looked in."

"Was there any one with him then?"

Mrs. Kemp was a little doubtful. "I don't think there was," she said. "But I can't be sure."

"Did you tell your husband that Mr. Rivers was going away?"

"I may have done. I can't remember."

"He says he was expecting to go to a market next day with Rivers."

"Then maybe I didn't say anything to him."

"Why not? It would be of interest to him to know that his boss wasn't going to be there next morning."

"Well, I didn't tell him."

"You say you went to the shop at half-past six?"

"That's what I said."

"Was there any one else there?"

"No."

"Are you sure?"

"Of course I'm sure."

"And Rivers was in the shop?"

"That's right."

"What was he doing?"

"I can't remember."

"If your husband said he saw Rivers in the top room at half-past six, would that be incorrect?"

"I didn't say I was there exactly at half-past six. I said 'about half-past six.'"

"Was Alma there then?"

"No. I went straight home and she was getting the supper ready."

Thompson pulled out his wallet from his pocket and took from it a half-sheet of note-paper. He unfolded it and spread it out on the table. "Have you ever seen this before?" It was the letter which Alma had written to Will Dorset.

Mrs. Kemp leaned forward and an expression which Thompson could not define skimmed across her face; then her eyes took on a codfish-stare, and she read the words slowly. When she had finished she resumed her upright pose and folded her arms. "No. This is the first time I've ever seen it." She looked squarely at Thompson and there was a hint of defiance in her gaze as though to say: "Prove that's a lie if you can."

"Part of it has been torn off."

Mrs. Kemp looked at the rough edge. "I don't know nothing about that."

"You say you never handled this letter?"

"I said I'd never seen it before, so how could I have touched it?"

"That's what you say?"

"It's the truth. That's what you want, ain't it?" Thompson did not speak for a moment or two. He read the letter through and then said:

"According to this, Alma was to meet Will Dorset at Hornsey Rise Tube Station."

"That's what it says."

"Didn't she say anything to you about it?"

"She may have done. I can't remember."

"Did she go out that night?"

"I think she did."

"Did she? You must know that."

"I can't remember."

"It was last Friday. That's not so very long ago."

"She may have gone out."

"Where is Hornsey Rise Tube Station?"

"I don't know."

"There's no such place."

Mrs. Kemp was silent.

"Did she ask you how to get there?"

"If she wrote it I suppose she must have known where it was."

"It's rather curious, her making an appointment at a place which doesn't exist, isn't it?"

"I don't know nothing about that."

Thompson put the letter back in his wallet.

"What were you doing on Friday night?" Thompson snapped out the question. He saw Mrs. Kemp stiffen, and then relax, but her expression of stolid indifference did not alter. He waited seconds and then said: "Well?"

"On Friday night?"

"Yes."

"I went to bed early."

"What time?"

"About ten."

"Did you have any visitors that night?"

Mrs. Kemp hesitated and then said: "No."

"A man came to the house late on Friday night."

"That's not true."

"He came the back way. Through the door in the wall."

"I never saw anybody."

"You met him and, between you, you carried something into the house."

Mrs. Kemp shook her head. Her hands were clutching tight at the cloth of her coat.

"If some one said they saw you carrying something down the path to the back door, what would you say to that?"

Mrs. Kemp laughed. "If any one said that, I'd say they was off their blooming nuts. I never stirred out of the house any time on Friday night."

"Or on Saturday morning?"

"I put the dustbin out afore breakfast on Saturday."

"But before that. Early. About one or two o'clock."

"What the hell'd I be doing mucking about the garden at that time in the morning?"

"That's what I want to find out."

"I never did no such thing."

"All right, then, we'll go on to something else. You know Spike Morgan?"

Mrs. Kemp was on her guard and she made no sign at the mention of the name except to say that she didn't know who Thompson meant.

"He stayed in your house on Thursday night and was out all day on Friday."

"I don't know what you're talking about. Who the hell is Spike Morgan, anyway?"

Thompson ignored the question and said: "He went out with Alma after supper on Friday."

"Alma might have met him outside somewhere."

"But she was going to meet Will Dorset."

"Perhaps she changed her mind."

"Then she did go out on Friday night?"

"I'm not answering any more questions."

"If your husband said that Spike Morgan stayed at No. 3 Napier Terrace from Thursday till last night, would you say he was lying?"

"He'd say anything."

"And that a man called Len shared the room on the top floor with Spike Morgan from Saturday night till Monday."

"You're talking nonsense."

Thompson got up and opened the door. "Mrs. Kemp is to be detained," he said to the sergeant. "Take her away." He beckoned to Joe who had woken up and was staring straight ahead of him. "I want you."

Joe walked in slackly. He was very tired.

"You remember Friday night?"

Joe nodded.

"You told me Alma went out with Spike Morgan?"

Joe nodded again.

"Do you remember her saying anything about Hornsey Rise Tube Station that night?"

"Hornsey Rise?" The words struck a warning note in Joe's brain. He remembered what his wife had said to him. "You take a walk to Hornsey Rise."

"What do you want me to do there?" he had asked, and she had laughed fatly and said: "Nothing. When you get there come back again."

The Green Man had seemed a much better place than Hornsey Rise and so it had proved to be, for he had managed to scrounge a pint of beer out of a man he'd never seen before but who was providentially drunk.

"I don't know nothing about Hornsey Rise," he said in answer to Thompson's question.

Thompson became friendly. "You've told me the truth up to now—don't spoil it."

But Joe stuck stubbornly to his denial.

Thompson showed him Alma's letter.

"Never seen it before," he averred.

Then Thompson produced the envelope.

"What about that?"

"I posted that, I think. Let's have a look." He studied the address. "Yes, that's right. The missus sent me out with it. I put it in my pocket and forgot about it till I got back almost."

"Pity you hadn't forgotten altogether," Thompson said to himself.

"What's that?"

"Nothing. Mrs. Kemp told you to post it? Quite sure about that?"

"Yes." Joe was puzzled.

"When?"

Joe thought for minutes. "It must have been Wednesday."

"All right." Thompson dismissed Joe to the jailer's care. Then he borrowed an evening paper and read and smoked and dozed until Perry brought in Fred Stables, barman at the Green Man.

He was not as talkative as Mrs. Benson but he answered questions directly and without qualification. What he had to say corroborated Mrs. Benson's account of the conversation in the Green Man on the Saturday morning.

When he had gone, Thompson got out of his chair slowly. He was stiff and cold. "Leith, I want you to go to Napier Terrace and see if you can find any pieces of stamp paper."

He picked up the notice which he had taken off Rivers's door. "That's the kind—with a red line."

"Shall I take it with me?" Leith asked.

"No. If you find anything like that, bring it to the Yard. I'll be there. Now, Perry, have we got all the exhibits?" He checked them off. "Glass from the picture. Bits of china. Hair out of the car—"

"Yes, all correct," Perry replied. "And the magazine?"

Thompson looked at the torn cover. "Spike was staying at Napier Terrace," he thought to himself, and then he said aloud: "See if you can find the missing half of that cover, Leith. If it's in the house, it'll probably be in the living-room at the back. Take the magazine with you." Thompson felt in his pocket for his pipe and filled and lit it. "Well, that's all we can do here. Report to me direct, sergeant, if anything turns up."

When he arrived at the Yard Thompson rang through to the information room and asked if there was anything for him.

"Yes, sir, just come in. A message from Crowley to say that William Dorset left by the 9.20 train from Snailsham. Believed to have gone to London."

"All right; get through to Snailsham and tell them to bring Dorset to me here as soon as he gets back. And the girl as well. Have you got that?"

The message was repeated back and Thompson rang off. He looked at Perry and smiled. "When we get those two we'll hear something interesting."

"You mean Dorset was the bloke who took Alma away from Napier Terrace?"

"Must have been."

"But how could he have known she was there?"

"She might have written to him or wired."

"The Crowley business is getting tied up," Perry said. Thompson agreed. "There's no doubt in my mind that Spike did it. We'd better find out about this man who seems to have been working with him. The guy in the yellow coat. First name Len."

Perry went to the Records Department and returned twenty minutes later with a typed sheet. He put it on the desk before Thompson. "It doesn't help us much," he said.

Thompson read the brief report. "A man known as Len is suspected of being concerned in a raid on a jeweller's shop in August of this year. He drove a stolen car, later found abandoned in Brixton. A child was run down and killed while this man was escaping. Description: Height 6 ft. Slight build. Boyish appearance."

"No wonder they never got him," Thompson commented.

"I remember the case," Perry said. "The man drove like hell, mounted a pavement and that's how he got clear. The street was blocked with traffic."

"I hope that yellow coat fits him. If it does he'll have something to answer for. Send out that description. It's better than nothing. And now I'm going to have some coffee and turn in for a couple of hours."

CHAPTER SEVENTEEN

MRS. TIBBETT went to the grocer's shop near the bridge as soon as it opened on Tuesday morning. She had nothing for breakfast. "Three bloaters, please," she said and laid the money on the counter.

"You're up early, Mrs. Tibbett," the shopman said, as he slapped the bloaters on to a sheet of brown paper. "I suppose you've heard about what's been happening along at Napier Terrace?"

Mrs. Tibbett wasn't interested; her mind was running on breakfast and her hungry husband, to say nothing of Barney.

"No, I haven't," she replied and held out a hand for the parcel.

"It's Mrs. Kemp and her husband. The police have taken them."

"Not before their time," snapped Mrs. Tibbett.

The shopman was determined to interest, if not to thrill his customer. "It's my belief they know more about what happened to Mr. Rivers than anyone else."

"Nothing's happened to Mr. Rivers. He's gone away, that's all."

The shopman turned and took a folded paper off a shelf. He pointed to a headline running right across the sheet.

"Body found in Barge at Napier Wharf. Foul play suspected." Mrs. Tibbett read the words slowly. "Napier Wharf," she repeated and looked up. "That's just across the other side of the cut, ain't it?"

"That's right." The shopman put his elbows on the counter and leaned across. "Opposite Napier Terrace." His voice was hoarse and confidential.

"What are you getting at?"

"Well, it's like this. Mr. Rivers has disappeared. That's right, ain't it?"

Mrs. Tibbett said yes, she supposed it was.

"There was a body took out of a barge. It says so in the paper. The police are up at Mr. Rivers's shop at this very minute *and* they've took the Kemps."

"Well, I never did like that there Joe Kemp, but he never killed no one. Hasn't got the guts." She took her parcel out of the shopman's hands. "I've got breakfast to cook." She took a step towards the door and then stopped. "Could you give me a loan of that paper? My old man might like to see it. We didn't get one last night."

"I'm sure you're welcome, Mrs. Tibbett," the shopman said, and handed it over.

Mrs. Tibbett walked back so quickly that she was quite out of breath before she got to the caravan. She wasn't a gossip and didn't take an interest in other people's affairs, but still—the Kemps arrested! And a body found over by the Napier Wharf! "Roger!"

Mr. Tibbett put down his hammer. "Got them bloaters?"

"Read that." Mrs. Tibbett thrust the paper into his hands and stood looking at him.

"Bride of a day runs away," read Mr. Tibbett.

She took the paper from him impatiently and refolded it.

"No, not that." She put her finger on the headline. "There."

"Well, I'm jiggered," said Mr. Tibbett. "They say here that it's murder."

"Of course it's murder. People don't cut their own throats and then tie themselves up. At least, I've never heard of it being done before."

Mr. Tibbett read on slowly, spelling out the words.

"This was yesterday morning. Must have been just after Barney got back."

"Where is Barney?"

"Inside, feeding that blinking mouse of his. She's got five."

"Five what?"

"Young 'uns."

Mrs. Tibbett mounted the steps and opened the door of the caravan. "Barney!"

He looked up; a smile crinkling his face.

"Hullo. Like to have a look at 'em?" The door of Fanny's box was open.

"That niece of yours, Alma. She's stopping with the Kemps, ain't she?"

"Yes, she's been there since last Monday."

"Then you'd better go round and find out what's happened to her."

"Why?" Barney asked without interest. He was watching Fanny nibbling a piece of bread.

"The police have took the Kemps. Both of 'em."

"The police!"

"That's what I said." Mrs. Tibbett lit a burner in the oil stove and unwrapped the bloaters.

Barney fastened the door of Fanny's box and stood up. He wasn't smiling. "What's happened?"

"I don't know. It's in the paper. Roger's got it."

Barney hurried down the steps.

"What's this about the Kemps?" he asked Mr. Tibbett.

"Read it yourself. Seems as if they're for it. The police don't arrest people for nothing."

Barney was still reading the paper when Mrs. Tibbett called to him that breakfast was ready. He came and picked at his bloater, ate half a slice of bread and drank a cup of tea.

"Now, you take a good breakfast," Mrs. Tibbett urged him. "It's no use starving yourself at a time like this." She set him a good example. So did Mr. Tibbett, who ate three slices of bread.

When he had finished, Barney sat on the steps smoking. He couldn't figure it out at all. He did not connect the bolster, which he had seen to drop from the lips of the grab, with the body found in the barge, nor with Mr. Rivers.

He tried hard to screw up his courage to go and see about Alma, but when Mrs. Tibbett had finished washing up he was still sucking at his cigarette.

"Ain't you going?" she asked.

"Soon," said Barney and stared at the ground.

"That poor girl. There all alone, and she's your own sister's child too, ain't she?"

Barney nodded heavily.

Mrs. Tibbett looked at him in silence for a minute. "I'll go if you'd rather."

Barney's face lightened and the wrinkles round his mouth were smoothed out. "Would you?"

"Of course," replied Mrs. Tibbett briskly. "As soon as I've finished tidying things up, I'll pop round."

Barney went on smoking and was halfway through his second cigarette when Mrs. Tibbett came out of the caravan. He watched her go. She was a good 'un, all right. He drew comfort from the thought, but he was very much afraid. Spike had been stopping with the Kemps. Had he been in this business? And had the police got him? If they had, he might talk and tell them about the Crowley job.

Barney got up and slouched down to the canal bank. He stood looking morbidly at a barge. Maybe that was the one in which they'd found the body. He shivered slightly and turned away.

Mr. Tibbett was engrossed in his work; the construction of a frame of wood battens which was to take the back sheet of a coconut shy next summer.

He got Barney to hold it for him while he drove in the nails. Captain came and watched them for a short time and then went to sleep. Fine to be a dog, Barney thought, and looked up the path for Mrs. Tibbett.

She returned sooner than he had expected. She was alone.

"Did you see her?" Barney asked.

"There's no one in the house but policemen," Mrs. Tibbett replied shortly. "I asked them if there was a girl about and they started asking questions. 'What did I want with her? Did I know her? What was my name and where did I come from?'"

Mrs. Tibbett was very angry.

"And she wasn't there?"

"No, she went away last night. I met Mrs. Benson and she told me. She said a man had come the night before and taken Alma away. He smashed the front window too. I saw it; glass all over the front bed."

"Where did Alma go?"

"I'm sure I don't know. You'd better go and find out yourself." The impertinent questions of the policemen were still rankling in Mrs. Tibbett's mind.

Barney got up. "I think I'll go for a walk round," he said and walked up the path.

Two policemen in plain clothes were standing on the bridge. They gave Barney a glance and went on talking. Spike Morgan was the man they were looking for.

Barney boarded a bus, took a ticket all the way and landed up somewhere in Brixton. He'd never been there before and he walked aimlessly through endless streets.

Then he saw a card in the window of a frowsy little house next door to a sweet shop. "Apartments." It didn't look much of a place but it was quiet. He went up two steps and rang the bell. A woman's face appeared at the side window behind a dirty lace curtain.

Barney heard footsteps and a moment later the door opened. "I want a room," he said.

"Come in." The woman was as dingy as the house but her charges were low. "Sixteen and sixpence, and that'll include breakfast and supper."

"I'll want dinner too. I won't be going out much."

"Then I'll have to ask another three bob."

Barney scrabbled in his pocket and produced the money. He had forgotten to get the notes he had left with Mrs. Tibbett. His heart sank. He couldn't go back and get them now; not with all these blinking coppers hanging about. He sat down on a chair in the room that was to be his for a week and put his head in his hands. He wished he'd brought Fanny and her family with him.

Thompson was called at seven o'clock and told that Leith was waiting to see him.

"Well. Did you have any luck?" he asked when Leith came into the room.

"I couldn't find any stamp paper, but I got the other half of the cover of the magazine."

"Where was it?"

"Among a lot of litter under a settee in the living-room."

"Let's have a look."

Leith put the magazine on the desk and fitted the torn piece in place.

"That's it all right," Thompson said and asked: "Are you sure there was no stamp paper?"

"Positive."

"You'd better take some time off. Report to me at two o'clock."

Thompson went out and had a shave and breakfast. When he got back there was a telephone message from Snailsham to say that Alma Robinson and Will Dorset would arrive in Town at nine o'clock.

He sent Perry to meet them at Waterloo and waited impatiently. There was still no news of Spike. The telephone bell rang. It was Hilton.

"That hair in the car was black fox all right," he said.

"What about the floor scrapings?"

"Human blood. Group B."

"Have you tested blood from the body in the barge?" Thompson asked.

"Yes. It's the same group."

"Well, that's something. Did you get any fingerprints?"

"One or two; smudgy. I don't think they'll tell us much."

"Are there any like Spike Morgan's?"

"No, nor the corpse's."

"Right. Let me have your full reports as soon as possible." Thompson rang off and sent for a matron. "I've got a girl coming in for questioning. I want you to be present," he told her. "Would you mind waiting in the next room?"

Half an hour later Perry came in with Alma.

"This is Miss Robinson," he said.

The matron placed a chair facing the window.

"Dorset can wait outside," Thompson said to Perry, and then he turned to Alma.

"I want to have a long talk with you." He opened a box of cigarettes and pushed it across the desk.

"I don't smoke."

"That's something new. I thought every girl did, these days."

"My aunt would never let me."

"I'd like to meet your aunt."

"She died. Only a fortnight ago."

"You lived with her at Crowley, didn't you?"

"Yes."

"How long have you known Will Dorset?"

"We were at school together."

"And when are you going to get married?"

Alma blushed. "I haven't thought about it," she said.

Thompson laughed. "When a man goes breaking windows in order to rescue his girl from the clutches of a dragon, the next thing is wedding bells. That's obvious."

"She was rather a dragon. When I heard Will's voice I cried."

"Start at the beginning. At Crowley. Why did you leave there?"

"Well, after my aunt died I had nowhere to go and then my uncle came down and said that I ought to go up to London."

"Who was this uncle of yours?"

"Uncle Barney." Alma laughed. "It's wicked of me to make fun of him but he is rather odd. He wears a big black hat and he always has his mice with him. One's rather nice. She's called Fanny."

Perry, sitting silent in a corner, thought of the fat brown mouse he had found in Rivers's top room.

"Was his name the same as yours? Robinson?"

"No. Withers."

"And he brought you to London?"

"Yes, to Napier Terrace. After Crowley, it was horrible. There was a canal and coal heaps. I hated it. It was raining, I was awfully tired and I felt I'd treated Will rather badly. I hadn't really, but I thought I had."

"And you went to stay with Mrs. Kemp at 3 Napier Terrace?" Thompson prompted.

Alma looked surprised. "Yes, but how did you know?"

"I've been hearing quite a lot about you. The dragon kept you locked up in a room."

"Go on. You seem to know it all."

"And one day, or night rather, you escaped. You met a man who admired the fur you were wearing. Then you got frightened and ran away. The catch broke and you lost your fur."

"How d'you know all this?"

"That's what happened, wasn't it?"

"Yes."

Thompson leaned back in his chair and felt in his waistcoat pocket. "Ever seen this before?"

Alma put out her hand and took the short length of chain Thompson was holding. She looked at it for a moment and then at him. "Where did you find this?"

"In your room at Napier Terrace."

"Yes, I remember now. The catch broke when the man snatched my fur. It fell on the pavement and I picked it up. And when I got back to Napier Terrace I put it on the dressing-table. But still—I don't understand. How do you know about the man who took my fur?"

"Ordinary police work with a bit of luck thrown in." Thompson opened a drawer and drew out a black fox tie. "Do you recognize that?"

"It's like the one Spike gave me."

Thompson felt along the inside of the fur and found a broken chain. He held the two pieces together. They were identical. "When did he give it you?"

"On Saturday night."

"Had you know him long before that?"

"No. I saw him first last Tuesday."

"That's a week ago to-day."

"Yes. It was the day after I came up from Crowley. He was the only one who was really nice to me; he took me to the pictures. He said then that he'd like to give me a fur but I didn't think he meant it."

"Did you see Spike Morgan on Wednesday?"

"At breakfast, yes. We had it early as he was going off somewhere. He was away all day."

"What about Thursday?"

"He was out most of that day too, and Friday. He came back about supper-time on Friday. He asked me to go out with him that night but I said I couldn't."

"Why not?"

"Because Will was coming up. I'd arranged to meet him at a tube station."

"Hornsey Rise?" Thompson suggested.

"Yes. How do you know?"

"Dorset showed me the letter you sent him." Thompson spread a sheet of paper on the table. "You wrote that, didn't you?"

Alma looked at him; there was a puzzled frown on her face; then her gaze fell on the letter. She read it through. "Yes, I wrote that."

"There isn't any address."

Alma picked up the letter and said: "I can tell you about that." She opened her bag and took out a strip of paper. It bore the words, "No. 3, Napier Terrace, Camden Town."

"Why did you tear this off your letter?" Thompson asked.

"I didn't. It must have been Mrs. Kemp or Joe."

"How did you get a hold of it?"

"I found it just inside Mrs. Kemp's room and I was frightened. I realized then that there were things going on in this house I didn't know about. I'd had my suspicions before that."

"Did you go to meet Will?"

"No, Mrs. Kemp sent Joe to Hornsey to meet him and bring him to the house. Joe came back and said that Will had never turned up so I went with Spike to a theatre and on to a restaurant afterwards where we had some sandwiches."

"What was the name of the restaurant?"

"The Domino."

"Do you know where it was?"

"No."

"How long did you stay there?"

"About twenty minutes, I should think. Spike was tired and acted funny, so I suggested we should go home."

"What did he say to that?"

"I think he was rather relieved."

"So you went back to Napier Terrace? What time did you get there?"

"At about midnight. Mrs. Kemp let us in and I went straight to bed. I couldn't sleep, and after about an hour, but it may have been two, I heard a noise out in the garden."

"Could you see anything?"

"No. The roof of the shed was in the way and, of course, it was dark. There wasn't a moon."

"Did you do anything about it?"

"Well, I thought of telling Mrs. Kemp because I thought it must have been burglars but the noise stopped before I'd made up my mind. I tried to go to sleep but about half an hour later I heard some one downstairs in the hall. I was frightened then and went to Mrs. Kemp's room. She wasn't there. Only Joe. He asked me what I wanted. I didn't answer him but went to the top of the stairs and called out."

"Was there any light in the hall?"

"The gas wasn't lit but there was a light shining out from the door of the back room. I saw Mrs. Kemp."

"What was she doing?"

"I think she was carrying something, but I couldn't say for certain. She came up the stairs and made me go back to my room."

"What was she like? Angry?"

"Yes. Very."

"What happened after that?"

"I went back to bed and I didn't hear anything more."

"Was Mrs. Kemp alone when you saw her in the downstairs passage?"

"Yes, I think so."

"Did she say anything to you about this next day?"

"Yes, she told me to say nothing about it."

"Did you notice anything unusual in the back room that morning?"

"No." Alma smiled. "It was in its usual state of untidiness. You know. Crumbs on the table, ash on the carpet and papers littered about everywhere. I had suggested to Mrs. Kemp before that I should give the room a good clean up but she wouldn't let me. There was a whole lot of old papers and rags under a settee which I wanted to clear out."

"Yes, I saw them," Thompson said. "Some of them were charred."

"Oh, I know how that was. They were in the grate when I came down on Saturday morning. Some one had been burning them."

"Have you any idea who it was?"

"Not the slightest."

Thompson spoke to Perry. "Give me the haversack. It's in the cupboard under the window."

The haversack in which John Brook had packed his clothes on Friday morning was laid on the table in front of Alma. It had been cleaned of the coal dust with which it had been covered and there could be seen signs of burning. There were two small holes and patches of scorching. "Did you see this at Napier Terrace?"

"No. Did you find it there?"

"Near there." Thompson took a slip of paper out of a drawer. There were scraps of stamp paper sticking to its corners. "Can you tell me anything about this?"

Alma gave it one glance and said: "Yes, I wrote that. Mrs. Kemp asked me to."

"When?"

Alma thought for a moment. "I think it was Sunday. No, I'm wrong, it was Saturday morning about dinnertime." She laughed. "I didn't make much of a job of it, I'm afraid, but the pen was awful."

"The paper isn't any too good either," was Thompson's comment.

"It looks like the stuff you line drawers with."

"Wasn't there anything better in the house?"

"Oh, yes. There was a box of note-paper. I used a sheet of it when I wrote to Will."

"And yet she made you use this stuff. Now I want to go back a bit; I believe you were looking after the shop on Friday?"

"Yes."

"Did any one take Mr. Rivers's car out that day?"

"Yes, Spike Morgan. He brought it back some time in the afternoon."

"Had he got anything in the car?"

"Not that I know of."

"Was he alone?"

"No, there was a man with him called Len."

"Len who?"

"I don't know his other name."

"What was he like?"

"Young. About twenty-one or two."

"Would you be able to recognize him if you saw him again?"

"Oh, yes, I'm sure I could."

Thompson picked up a pencil. "Try and give me his description as fully as you can."

Alma looked down at her toes and then over to the fire. "It's rather difficult. There was nothing about him that you can exactly get a hold of."

"What about his eyes?"

The frown on Alma's face disappeared. "They were brown. And his mouth was thin-lipped; small and mean. I didn't like him."

"Nose?"

"Ordinary."

"Complexion?"

"I didn't notice it, I'm afraid."

"Was he tall or short?"

"Tall. He could give Spike several inches."

"And what was he wearing?"

"A light coat. It was almost yellow and had a belt."

"Shoes?"

"I didn't notice them."

Thompson looked at what he had written and read it aloud. When he had finished he asked, "Can you add anything?"

"He was wearing a felt hat."

"What colour?"

"Dark. And that's all I can tell you about Len."

"You told me he came in Rivers's car with Spike at some time in the afternoon?"

"Yes. It would be about one o'clock. Spike was annoyed to find Mr. Rivers wasn't in."

"Where was Mr. Rivers?"

"He was at the Chalk Street market with Joe."

"I suppose Spike waited for him?"

"No, he went away."

"With Len?"

"No, Len went first."

"And when did Mr. Rivers get back?"

"It was about half-past five. Joe came in about the same time. I helped him unload the barrow."

"And then?"

"Well, I stayed in the shop till half-past six, when Mr. Rivers locked up and I went home."

"Did Mrs. Kemp come to the shop at any time before you left?"

"Oh, no."

"You're sure about that?"

"Absolutely. She was getting the supper ready when I got back to Napier Terrace."

"Did any one see Mr. Rivers that evening?"

"Yes. My Uncle Barney. He went up to the top room, but he didn't stay long. That would be about half-past six."

"Did you see Mr. Rivers after your uncle had gone?"

"Yes. He came down and put up the shutters."

The telephone bell rang. Thompson said, "Hullo, who's that?" heard the reply, and then covered the mouthpiece. "I think that's all I have to ask you for the moment, Miss Robinson, but if you wouldn't mind waiting downstairs— Hullo—Sergeant Hawkins? Yes, Inspector Thompson speaking." While he listened he watched Alma leave the room. Then he said, "Yes, I've got that. Thanks." He put down the receiver and smiled at Perry. "I was right, after all."

"What about?"

"The body we found in the barge having been taken from Rivers's shop to the Kemps' house."

"Why? What's happened?"

"You know that yard that runs from the shop to the back of Napier Terrace?"

"Yes, I think I know where you mean."

"It has two gates. The locks on both of them were forced some time on Friday night. The owner reported it to the local police on Saturday morning. They had a look round, but as there was nothing missing they took no action. They put it down to boys."

"The pieces are fitting in—" Perry began, and stopped as the door opened and Leith came into the room.

He was quite excited. "I've seen that girl before," he said.

"Yes, she was the one you stopped and took the fur off," Thompson replied.

"Yes, but before that. Last Friday. I was at a theatre, and she was there with Spike Morgan."

"I know, she told me."

"She told you she was with Spike?"

"Yes, and a lot of other things as well. All you've got to do now is to find Spike. Get busy."

When Leith had gone, Perry asked, "Do you want to see that man Dorset now?"

"No, not just yet. I want to see where we are."

"You've got it pretty well tied up," Perry said.

"Yes. I think Spike killed Rivers, but it's the way a jury'll look at it that's bothering me. We've got some evidence to show that Rivers was killed in his room over the shop on Friday night, and his body was chucked into the lighter."

"Bloodstains on the floor. Persian rug. The barrow in the Kemps' garden. Hicks's yard broken into." Perry went over the points.

"Yes." Thompson walked over to a table in the window where the various exhibits were laid out. He looked at them for a minute in silence, and then picked up a length of cord with which the body had been tied up. "Sash cord," he said, and looked at Perry.

"I don't understand."

"A window in Rivers's room was jammed. This is sash cord."

Perry took it in his hands, stared at it for a moment, and then said, "Good God! What a damn' fool I was not to see that. This has been cut from the window, and then whoever did it fixed it so that it couldn't be opened."

"That's what I was thinking." Thompson sat in a chair in front of the fire and slowly filled his pipe. As he rolled up his pouch he said, "But where do we go from here? We haven't identified the body found in the lighter as being Rivers's, and even if we do manage to establish that fact we're faced with the problem of proving that Spike Morgan killed him. It may not have been him. Either of the Kemps might have done it, or this man Len, who was working with Spike."

"Joe Kemp didn't do it."

"It's not likely. I agree, but we can't rule him out."

"But the girl Alma saw him in his bedroom when she heard the noise downstairs. That was when we assume that Mrs. Kemp and some one else was taking the body through the house."

"Yes. I'd forgotten that." Thompson relit his pipe, which had gone out. "Well, with Joe out of it we're left with three to choose from."

"Will Mrs. Kemp talk?"

"I haven't had much out of her up to date. I'll have another try later on."

"What about Joe?"

"There's no difficulty about him, but I don't think he really knows anything. We'll squeeze him dry, all the same."

"You haven't forgotten Dorset, have you? He's outside." Thompson looked at his watch. "He'll have to wait. I've got to be at Cable Street Police Court in half an hour. The Kemps are being brought up, and I must go and ask for a remand."

CHAPTER EIGHTEEN

AT ABOUT the same time that Alma was being interviewed by Thompson at Scotland Yard, Spike woke up stiff and cold. His legs were numb, and he swore as he rubbed some feeling into them.

He stretched out his hand for his coat and felt in the pockets. The bread was there; half a loaf, hard and unappetizing. He put it on one side. The piece of cheese smelt musty.

"A hell of a breakfast," Spike muttered. He ran his hand over his chin, and looked at Len who was still asleep, sprawled across a heap of sacking. His right arm was bent under his head, his fair hair tousled; he looked very young.

Spike put out a leg and kicked at Len, who grunted protestingly and rolled on his back. The light struck his eyes and he blinked several times and said sleepily, "What's up?" Spike said, "Breakfast's ready," and held up the bread. Len turned over and half rose on a bent elbow. He yawned and blinked again. "Breakfast?" he said.

"This is it." Spike grinned and tossed the loaf on to Len's chest. It rolled a foot on to the floor and lay, a grey-brown lump.

Len put a hand on it. "I want a cup of coffee," he said. "You'll have to wait."

Then Len awoke to the realization of the present. "Hell!"

"That's what I was thinking." Spike got on to his feet and stretched. "How are you feeling?"

"As though I'd been beaten all over." Len felt the sacking which had been his bed. "It's wet."

"We'll air it before we turn in again."

"I'm not stopping here another night."

"Where the blazes are you going to doss?"

"I don't know, but not here."

Spike walked over to a window and looked out. A drizzling rain was falling. Far below was a lighter; a man was pulling her in slowly to the coal wharf. Above it hung, expectant, an open grab. Steam hissed from the safety valve of the crane. Spike saw it, a white jet, spreading and disappearing in wispy clouds over the surface of the water of the canal. Then it was shut off suddenly and there was a slow clanking. The grab dipped into the laden barge.

"It isn't too bad." Len broke the loaf and bit out a mouthful. He ate it slowly. Crumbs dropped on his knees. "Isn't there any water?"

"Plenty. In the canal."

"Where's the cheese?"

"Catch!"

Len smelt it and felt it with his thumb. "I'd want a pint of bitter to get this down."

"There's a drop of water here."

Len got up and brushed the crumbs of bread from his mouth with the back of his right hand.

Spike pointed through a gash in the window at a leaking gutter. Len put out a cupped hand. The water, dribbling slowly, soaked into his skin and then slowly formed a little pool. He raised it to his lips and sucked. It tasted flat and salty.

"Haven't we got anything we can catch this in?"

"The old woman'll be along to-night. We'll tell her to get a tin or something."

Len caught another handful of the water and drank it. Bits of the bread still stuck in his throat. Then he picked his coat off the floor and felt in the pockets. There were five cigarettes in a packet. He lit one and savoured the smoke. It tasted good. "And we'll want some fags as well."

"You'd better make out a list in case you forget anything. Give us one." Spike took a cigarette and lit it. Down below on the bridge he saw two men. They were wearing bowler hats, and had the collars of their raincoats turned up. "Splits, or I'm a Dutchman," he said half aloud, and shifted his position so that he could get a better view. Len was walking about, kicking at the litter of shavings and rubbish.

Then Spike stiffened. A figure, squat at that range and elevation, came out of the turning which led to the settlement. There was no mistaking that hat, nor the walk; a slouching, striding glide. Barney! The damn' fool. Spike's fingers clawed at the sill and gripped it. Barney came on. One of the policemen turned his head towards him but made no further movement. He was abreast of them! He was past!

Spike rolled his cigarette to the other side of his mouth and drew in on it. As he slowly exhaled the smoke he saw Barney stop walking and look up the street the way he had come. A bus breasted the rise up to the bridge, slowed, and drew up at the curb. Barney got aboard.

"Well, I'm jiggered. He's through!"

The bus ground on in low gear, changed to second and disappeared.

Len joined Spike and tried to pick up his line of sight. "What are you looking at?"

"Barney." Spike took the cigarette from his mouth and spat out a shred of tobacco.

"What's he doing?"

"There's a couple of splits on the bridge. Barney's just walked by them."

"Well?"

Spike half turned his head to Len. "If they'd been on to the Crowley job they'd have pinched him. They didn't."

He put the cigarette back in his mouth and smoked for a minute. "D'you see what I mean?"

"No."

"They've found out that the haul was dumped at Izzy's. They know Rivers was connected with it some way, but they don't know about us. We needn't have cleared out the way we did. Maybe we can go back to Napier Terrace to-night."

"I wish to blazes I hadn't eaten that bread. I'm as dry as hell."

"The rain's easing off. You'll have to wait till to-night till the old woman comes along. If she gives us the all-clear we'll knock back a pint or two."

Len saw a public bar. He heard the gurgling, foaming spurt of beer into a pint pot.

"I don't know when I've had a thirst like I have now."

"Give me another fag."

"I've only got three left."

"All right, keep 'em." Spike walked over to the two heaps of sacking which had been their beds. "Let's see if we can't find some place where we can hang this lot up. I'll bet they haven't been aired for a year," he laughed. "The old woman'd have a couple of fits if she saw what we'd been sleeping on."

Joe Kemp and his wife spent the remainder of Monday night in separate cells at Cable Street Police Station. At eight o'clock they were given breakfast, and two hours later they were taken along an underground passage to the cells under the police court.

They were united in the dock and the clerk read out the charge. The magistrate, a scholarly, elderly man dressed in a neat black coat and striped trousers, was writing with a scratchy steel pen. He was wearing a high wing collar and a flowered silk tie threaded through a thin gold ring.

The clerk read out the charge. . . . "As accessories after the fact in that they received, relieved, comforted and assisted . . ."

Joe stared dully at the clerk's face. Received. Relieved. He didn't know what the man was talking about. . . . "Well knowing . . . felony had been committed by . . . not yet in custody."

The words suddenly ceased. Papers rustled, and then a voice said, "Do you plead guilty or not guilty?"

Mrs. Kemp said "Not guilty" firmly and defiantly, and nudged Joe who mumbled under his breath. The jailer leaned over the ledge and whispered to him, "Guilty or not guilty?" Joe said "Not guilty" in a very small voice which was relayed by the jailer.

The magistrate put his pen down and clasped his hands together as they lay on his desk. He looked down at the clerk. "Very well, let's have the evidence."

"James Thompson."

Thompson, who was talking with a police officer at the back of the court, came forward and mounted the steps to the witness box. He needed no guidance from the clerk and picked up the Bible and rattled off the oath. Almost without taking breath he said, "At 2.15 a.m. on the fifteenth instant I saw the accused . . ."

"Both of them?" asked the magistrate.

"Yes, sir. I questioned them and ordered that they should be taken into custody. They were charged at this station. Mrs. Kemp said: 'I know nothing about it.' Joseph Kemp made no statement." Thompson paused.

"Well, go on."

"I ask for a remand for eight days. This is a complicated case and inquiries have not yet been completed."

"Have you any objection?" The magistrate looked at Mrs. Kemp who said, "I suppose not."

"And you?" His gaze switched to Joe.

"I don't mind."

"Remanded for eight days."

The jailer opened the door of the dock. He said, "This way," and shepherded Mrs. Kemp and Joe to a side door into the care of a policeman, who took them down the yard and into a van, the door of which was invitingly but ominously open.

Another policeman signed for them and locked them into separate cubicles. Five minutes later they were on their way to Brixton and Holloway respectively.

Thompson caught a bus which took him to Westminster. He walked along the Embankment to Scotland Yard and up to his room.

Perry put down the telephone receiver as he came in. "I've just been telling 'em to put out a description of this man Barney."

"Good. Anything turned up since I've been away?"

"Hilton says that the cast he took of one of the tyres on Rivers's car is identical with the impression in the gravel pit at Crowley."

"No doubt about it?"

"No. There's a cut across half the tread. It's the same in both casts."

"Anything else?"

"Leith knows Barney."

"What does he say about him?"

"Apparently he's a hawker who works the markets selling some patent medicine. He usually has a couple of mice crawling over him."

"Mice?"

"Yes. And you remember we found one dead in Rivers's room."

"The girl said Barney had been there on the Friday night."

"And left before she did."

"That's what she says. He was her uncle. Perhaps *he* could tell us what happened."

"He ought to be easy to pick up. Leith has given me a very full description."

"Well, that's something." Thompson shuffled the papers on his desk. "Let's have a look at Dorset."

Will came in, and sat uneasily on a hard chair.

Thompson wasted no time.

"When you broke up the happy home at Napier Terrace last night, you slugged a man."

"He was trying to stop me taking Alma away."

"I dare say you had a good reason, but I'm not bothering about that. What was he like?"

"Well, I didn't get a proper look at him. There wasn't much light, but I can say he was tall and thin. He was young, too. I was sorry afterwards that I'd hit him so hard, but I was kind of worked up and . . ."

"Wait a minute," Thompson interrupted. "I want you to think back to the time of the hold-up. There were two men, weren't there?"

"That's right. One of 'em had the gun."

"And the other?"

Will looked blankly at Thompson for a full minute, then a look of surprised understanding slowly came over his face. "They were much of the same build. Very much the same, now I come to think of it. But I couldn't swear the man I saw at Napier Terrace was the same as one of the blokes what held me up. I couldn't swear that."

"That's a pity." Thompson traced a squiggly line on his blotting pad. Then he put down his pencil and got up. "That's all I want from you."

"Can I go home?"

"Yes, and take Miss Robinson with you. Good morning." Perry went with Will to the room where Alma was waiting and escorted them down the stairs to the entrance hall.

"If I were you I'd keep out of Town for the next few days."

"I'm never to leave Crowley again," Alma replied.

She walked with Will through the courtyard to Whitehall and caught a bus which took them to Waterloo. The train to Snailsham was empty at that time of day and they had a carriage to themselves.

"Decent lot of fellows, the police," Will said. "They gave me my fare."

Alma said "Yes," and looked out of the window. She wished the train would start.

"Do you want a paper?"

"No, it doesn't matter."

Doors slammed. A whistle blew. They were off. Alma gave a sigh of relief.

"Are you glad to be going back?" Will asked.

"Of course I am."

"Did you mean it when you said you weren't ever going to leave Crowley again?"

"Yes."

Will went red and his fingers picked at the buttons on the cushions.

"I thought you were tired of the place."

"I never said that."

Will did not argue the point, but said, "Well, if you mean that—if you don't want to stop in London—" Then he stuck and tried again. "You see, I thought you felt it was too dull down at Crowley, but if you don't . . ." He stared in agony at a picture of Corfe Castle. His hand found Alma's. He squeezed it and said in a very low voice, "What about making a go of it? The two of us."

The train, jolting over the points outside Vauxhall, caused Alma to lean towards him. "Will you marry me?"

Alma said, "Of course I will," and began to cry.

Freda Klein was the next visitor to Thompson's room. She was a very different proposition from Alma. Purple-black hair, red, full lips, and a vivacity which made Thompson realize he was no longer young.

Within a minute of her entering the room she had asked five questions. Thompson answered none of them. He waited until she had to take breath, and said, "You work for Mr. Hyams, I believe?"

Freda nodded. "Work for him. Yes, from half-past seven to six in the evening. Oh, yes, I work, all right, but what I want to know is . . ."

"Never mind about that. Do you know Mr. Rivers?"

"Mr. Rivers?" Freda made a song of the name. "Yes, of course I know him. Often he come to the shop to see Mr. Hyams."

"Was he there last week?"

"Yes, on Monday."

"Might it not have been Tuesday?" Thompson suggested.

"Monday. Tuesday. What does it matter which day it was?" Freda was not going to bother herself with such details. "It was last week, anyway." She ran off on a side line, but Thompson blocked her stream of talk with short questions.

"Plenty, plenty people, they come to the shop. Some I remember. Some I forget."

"But you remember Mr. Rivers's visit. Why was that?"

"Why. Why. Why. I do not know why. I remember him. That is all."

Thompson described Spike and Len and asked if she thought she'd ever seen them.

"No, I do not think so."

"They brought a parcel of black fox furs to Mr. Hyams on Friday."

"I did not see them."

"And you didn't see the furs?"

"Of course not. They would be taken in at the back door. I work in the shop with the other girls."

"I'm told you made up a black fox fur as a tie on Saturday."

"I finished it on Saturday, but I started to work on it on Friday afternoon."

"What time?"

"I do not know what time, but it was in the afternoon. That is all I know."

"Who told you to make it up?"

"Mr. Hyams, of course. He pays me."

"Is this the tie you made up?" Thompson opened a deep drawer in his desk and took out Alma's fur.

Freda put out her hand and ran her fingers through the hairs. "But this is a beautiful skin."

Thompson repeated his question. "Is this the one you made up?"

"It is like it, yes."

"Have a look at the other side. There's a name tab on it."

She turned the fur over and stretched the silk lining right between her fingers so that the stitching on the tab could be seen. "This is my sewing."

"Sure about that?"

"Of course I am."

"That's fine." Thompson took the fur out of her hands and put it back in the drawer. "Do you always put tabs on the work you do?"

"Usually. Unless Mr. Hyams says we are not to. You see, we do work for many of the West End shops and they like to put their own name on the lining."

"In this case I presume Mr. Hyams said nothing, and you put on Mr. Hyams's tab?"

"Mr. Hyams say nothing!" Freda laughed. "He said a great deal. How it was to be done and when it was to be finished. And yes, he said not to put on his name. But I was in a hurry on Saturday morning and I forgot what he had said. When I had finished it one of the other girls says to me, 'You have been wasting your time, Freda, sewing that tab. Mr. Hyams did not want it on.' I said to her, 'Well, it can stay. I am not going to take it off.'"

"Didn't he look at the tie before it was sent out?"

"No. I do not think so. He knows my work is good."

"Well, I needn't trouble you any further."

Freda's place was taken a few minutes later by Mrs. Benson. She was oppressed by her surroundings, and nervously fingered her bag, which she held in her lap.

"Mrs. Benson, you told me last night that you saw some one in Mrs. Kemp's garden early on Saturday morning."

"Yes, I did."

"And you also said you thought they were carrying something?"

"I couldn't swear that. It was dark and I didn't see 'em for longer than half a minute."

"Could you really see anything?"

"I could see there was some one there. I heard 'em."

"What exactly did you hear?"

"Well, it's hard to say now, but they was walking slow, like, and shuffling. A man's voice said something about 'keeping it up.'"

"Is that what made you think they were carrying something?"

"I suppose it was. That and the way they was shuffling along just as any one would if they was carrying anything heavy."

"But you didn't actually see that was what they were doing?"

"No."

"Have you got anything else to tell me?"

"You mean about the Kemps?"

"Yes."

"No, there's nothing more I can tell you about them, but . . ."

"Go on."

"It's about my dustbins."

Thompson tried to show an interest and asked, "What about your dustbins?"

"I don't suppose you'll want to hear about it, and I said the same to my old man when we was having our breakfast. 'It's a funny thing to find,' I says. 'Funny,' he says, 'it's a blinking godsend. Don't say nothing about 'em. They'll just about fit me!'"

"What are you talking about?"

"I'm telling you," replied Mrs. Benson crossly. "When I'd put the kettle on to boil first thing, I went out into my garden to put the dustbin into the street, and I noticed the sleeve of a coat hanging out. Of course, I takes off the lid and there's a bundle of clothes sitting right on top. I hadn't put 'em there, and I thought my old man must have done it. But he said he hadn't."

"What were the clothes?"

"There was a jacket, worn a bit, but not so bad. A pair of trousers, two shirts and a pair of socks."

"When do you think they were put in your bin?"

"I dunno. But it must have been some time after nine o'clock the night before."

"Why do you think that?"

"Because I was out after we'd had our supper chucking away half a pail of peelings and muck. The clothes weren't in the bin then."

"Did you hear any one in your garden during the night?"

"No."

"I'd like to have a look at these clothes. Where are they?"

"Outside."

Perry brought in the parcel and cut the string. Thompson ticked off the items. "This is the lot? There's nothing more?"

"That's all that was in my dustbin."

"All right. You can go."

"What about the clothes?"

"I may be able to let you have 'em back and I may not. I can't tell until they've been examined."

Mrs. Benson got up. "Then there's nothing for me to stop for?"

"Nothing," said Thompson. "Good morning."

Before the door had shut behind her, Thompson had lifted the receiver of his phone. "Put me through to Mr. Hilton, please. . . . That you, Hilton? Thompson speaking. I want you to come up to my room. I've got some clothing here which appears to have been washed in two or three places."

"What d'you think has been on it?"

"May have been blood."

"I'll come right up."

Hilton came into the room a few minutes later. He had a small dropper bottle in his hand.

"I can do a quick test," he said.

"That's what I want."

Perry cleared a desk and laid the trousers flat out on it. At a place near one knee the cloth was damp and there was a faint ring a shade darker than the cloth.

Hilton switched on the table lamp and tilted the shade till the light was concentrated on the area to be tested.

He took out the cork from the bottle with his teeth. A drop of the liquid fell, spread, and was absorbed by the cloth. Within a couple of seconds bluish streaks appeared.

"That's blood, all right. May be human. I'll have to make a lab. test." Hilton turned over the shirt and looked at the cuffs.

"There might be something here, too." He gathered up the other pieces of clothing and left the room.

Thompson looked at Perry. There was a pleased grin on his face. "We're getting somewhere."

Perry said, "Yes. And now all we've got to do is find Spike and his pal."

"We'll get 'em, all right. They're lying up somewhere, but when they get through their cash they'll have to make a break for it. That's what always happens. Or else one of their pals gives 'em away. Once we get 'em inside the odds are that one of 'em'll talk. Possibly both. That would give us a chance to fill in the gaps."

"It's extraordinary how it's worked out so far," Perry said. "If Freda Klein hadn't sewn that tab on the fur we would never have got started."

"Or if Leith hadn't run into Alma when she was wearing the fur. That was a bit of luck." Thompson leaned forward in his chair and raked dead ashes from the fire. "Mrs. Benson helped a bit, too. It was she who put me on to searching the top room at the Kemps' house. The funny part of it is I don't think she'd have said what she did if she hadn't been wild with Mrs. Kemp."

"I don't get that."

"She lent Mrs. Kemp sixpence and wasn't paid back. The moral is, don't fight with your creditors."

"There's another 'if,'" Perry said.

"What's that?"

"If Mrs. Benson hadn't noticed the clothes in her dustbin."

"Yes, there's a hell of a lot of chance in this game—and a lot of hard work, too." Thompson watched the fire flicker up and felt for his pouch and pipe.

"This case is going to take a lot of working up," Perry said. "I've got a foolscap sheet of exhibits already and then there's Hilton's reports."

"It's like one of these damn' jigsaw puzzles," Thompson replied. "You've got to have every piece in the right place if you want a complete picture." He turned his chair to his desk and pulled over a stack of papers. "Come on. Let's get on with this little lot and see if we can't get 'em straight. First, there's this statement of Mrs. Benson. It wants pruning a bit if it's going to make sense. . . ."

CHAPTER NINETEEN

BARNEY IN HIS room at Brixton was almost as close a prisoner as Mrs. Kemp at Holloway, or Spike and Len in the warehouse opposite Napier Terrace.

There was no one to talk to. Not even the plethoric George or the more agile Fanny. Funny how he liked the mice.

He raised his head from his hands and looked round the room; at the green-tiled fire-place and the rubbishy, dusty ornaments on the narrow mantelpiece; a paper fan crudely painted; two red-plush framed photographs, one of a gentleman holding a top hat. He was sitting on a most uncomfortable rustic seat against an unlikely back-cloth of painted trees and a rustic stile.

Barney wondered who he was and what had happened to him.

There was a short shelf filled with books, paper-backs, mostly. He took one down and read a page. Then he got up and looked out of the window. It was a very dull and respectable street. There were no children playing in the roadway.

Barney thought of the noise of Chalk Street and the crowd of customers which filled it at every lunch-hour. It was getting on for the time he usually started to go there. He hadn't a watch, and the clock on the mantelpiece was stopped.

A milkman came along with a tray of bottles and rang the front-door bell.

Barney wanted to go out and talk to him and was a little more depressed when he went on his way a pint lighter.

He ate his dinner in the kitchen with his landlady and helped her wash up afterwards.

She was suspicious of his action and he had to retreat to his room. There he slept until it was dark.

The woman woke him by knocking on the door. When he answered she poked in her head and said, "I thought you'd gone out," and asked grudgingly if he wanted a light.

Barney said he didn't care. "I think I'll take a walk," he added.

"I would, if I was you," the woman answered. She had been waiting all day for a chance to go through his "things" and see if she could find out something about her lodger.

Barney let himself out by the front door and walked to the end of the street. He passed only one man, who didn't look at him, and he immediately felt more confident.

Somewhere to the right a tram bell clanged. Barney turned in the direction of the sound. He passed a row of five shops brightly lit. It was the evening shopping-hour of the district, and women with string bags and untidy parcels filled the pavements. They didn't look at him.

It was all right, and he'd known it would be. Silly to think of shutting himself in that damn' room. He smiled and talked to himself.

"Oranges. Two a penny. Jaffa oranges. Two a penny. Five for twopence."

The strident voice guided him to a street market in a side street. Naphtha lamps flared, casting eddying pools of yellow light on the wet pavement.

Now, if he'd only got his stuff he could pick up a shilling or two. But all his little bottles and labels and crock of peppermint-flavoured coloured water were in the Tibbetts' caravan.

He was feeling so very brave now that he had half a mind to go and collect them. No one would notice him if he were careful. He turned and walked back in the direction of the street with the trams and the buses. He had money for the fare, and there'd be enough for a pint as well.

He was walking along rehearsing the opening of his spiel when he felt that some one was following him. He quickened his pace, but did not look round. It was cold, but he began to sweat.

At the end of the side street he stopped for a moment. He'd have to cross the road to get a bus which would take him to Cable Street, but he wasn't sure if he wanted to go there now. He smelled danger.

"Good evening." A man touched him on the arm. Barney didn't look round. "Excuse me, but what is your name?"

"Name!" Barney mumbled something and took a step to the edge of the pavement.

"Just a minute." The hand tightened on his arm. The man repeated his question.

Barney made a sudden effort to free himself. He ducked his head and twisted his body. His other arm was seized, and the two detectives ran him through the crowd to an alley-way. They stopped under a street lamp.

"Do not think he's the bloke?" one said to the other.

"If it's not him, it's his twin brother. We'll take a chance."

They took Barney to the police station, searched him, and sat him on a bench under a bright light. A sergeant in uniform read out a description and the detectives looked at him while he did so.

When the sergeant finished he, too, had a good look at Barney and then asked, "What's your name?"

"Johnson. Bill Johnson."

"Sure it's not Barney Withers?"

The reply was a shaky laugh.

"Where d'you live?"

Barney gave the address of the house where he'd taken the room earlier in the day. A constable was sent out to check the statement. When he had gone the sergeant took up his pen and wrote in his ledger the words William Johnson. Then he asked, "What do you do for a living?"

"Nothing much."

"How d'you live?"

Barney grinned foolishly. "I've got independent means."

"Do you know any one who would speak for you?" Barney thought of Mr. and Mrs. Tibbett. But they wouldn't do. He didn't want the police to start asking questions round Cable Street way. They might discover his connection with Mr. Rivers. Of course, there was Alma, but she'd left Napier Terrace, and the Kemps were inside. None of them was any use to him.

The sergeant said, "Well?" impatiently, pen poised over the book.

"I don't want to give nobody no trouble."

"All right. You'll have to stop here till we make inquiries."

Half an hour later the constable who had gone to Barney's lodgings came back with the information that Barney had taken the room that morning. Nothing was known of him there and he had no luggage.

The sergeant said, "All right," and dialled Whitehall one two, one two.

Leith was sent to see if he could identify Barney and did so without the slightest hesitation.

"We were wondering where you'd got to," he said. "Where are your mice?"

"Lost 'em," Barney replied.

"I know where there's one."

"Where?"

"I'll tell you later."

Leith took Barney to Scotland Yard in a police car. Thompson was waiting for them in his room.

"Barney Withers," Leith announced, and took Barney's hat off and threw it on a chair.

"Give him a chair," said Thompson.

Barney looked round the room vaguely.

Thompson tapped on his desk with his pencil. Barney's eyes focused on him. "What dealings have you had with Mr. Rivers?"

There was silence for two or three seconds before Barney replied, "I don't know Mr. Rivers."

"That's a lie."

"Not to speak to." Barney amended his answer. "Of course, I know who you mean." The smile which was intended to be disarming failed to achieve its purpose.

"You knew him. You went to his shop and you had business with him. We know that."

Barney shrank back in his chair under the force of Thompson's attack. He did not speak.

"That's the truth, isn't it?"

"Well, yes. In a way."

"Think back to last week. Friday."

Barney put up a hand to his mouth. His lips were trembling. "Friday," he mumbled.

"That's what I said. Friday. You went to Rivers's shop that night at half-past six."

Barney was so frightened that he could not utter a word in denial.

"Do you say you didn't see Rivers that night?"

Barney's reply could not be heard a foot away. His right hand was passing and repassing across his mouth. "What was that? Take your hand away."

"I've never been near his place."

Perry, sitting by the window, tilted back his chair and took something out of a drawer behind him.

"This is yours, isn't it?"

Barney's head turned slowly towards him. At first he couldn't see what was hanging from Perry's fingers. Then he got up quickly and took the body of the fat brown mouse in his hand. He was crying.

Thompson and Perry watched him as his thick fingers stroked the fur of poor George Mouse. He had forgotten the room and his inquisitors. He was quite alone with George.

Thompson waited for three minutes and then got up. He put his hand on Barney's shoulder and squeezed it gently. "You were in Rivers's room, weren't you?" he said.

Barney looked up at him as though he had not heard the question. Thompson repeated it, and added, "This mouse was found in the room over the shop."

Tears were drying on the wrinkled skin of Barney's cheeks as he said very quietly:

"Yes, I was there."

Perry took the mouse from him and Thompson guided him back to his chair.

"Now tell us all about it."

"You mean when I saw Mr. Rivers?"

"Yes. How long were you with him?"

"Not long."

"Why did you go there?"

"To get my money."

"Your money?"

Barney wetted his lips with his tongue and put a hand under his jaw. "What he owed me."

"Why did Rivers owe you money?"

"I did jobs for him."

"What sort of jobs?"

"Giving him a hand in the market. In Chalk Street."

"But Joe Kemp looked after the barrow, didn't he?"

"That's right."

"How much did Mr. Rivers give you?"

"Three pounds."

Thompson did not show his surprise, but asked, "What was that for?"

"The Crowley job."

Thompson moved forward in his chair and exchanged a glance with Perry.

"Oh, so it was you put him on to that?"

Barney said, "Yes," in a whisper. "I found out about the fox skins when I went see Alma. I was joking when I told him about them, but he took me serious and that's how it all came about."

"Spike Morgan worked it, didn't he?"

"Him and Len, yes."

"What happened?"

"We all went down to Crowley some time last week. I think it was Wednesday."

"Wednesday?"

"Yes, that was the first time. We went in Mr. Rivers's car to have a look at the place. They fixed on the gravel pit as where they'd put the van, and then we came back."

"That's all you did on Wednesday?"

Barney nodded. "And it was to be the finish as far as I was concerned, but Spike said he'd want me there when we pulled the job. I was to keep a look-out up on the hill."

"Now, stop there. I'm going to caution you."

"Caution?"

"Yes. Anything you may say from now on will be taken down and may be used in evidence. Do you understand?"

Barney said "No," and looked from Thompson to Perry and back to Thompson.

"You were concerned in the theft of a quantity of black fox skins from a van at Crowley."

"I didn't mean to have anything to do with it. I've never done anything like that before. I was forced into it."

"Never mind about that. Listen to me."

Barney looked at Thompson, puzzled.

"I'm going to charge you with theft. Do you understand?"

Barney nodded dumbly.

"If you wish to say anything about it you can, but every word you utter will be written down, and may be used in evidence when you are brought up in court before a magistrate."

"I get you."

"Now, do you want to say anything?"

"I want to tell you all I know. Maybe I'll feel better, then."

Thompson dictated a few lines to Perry, who wrote in long-hand. Thompson took the paper from Perry and gave it to Barney. "Can you read that?"

"Yes, it seems clear enough."

"All right, go ahead. Read aloud."

"I have been cautioned by Chief Inspector Thompson that anything I say will be taken down and may be given in evidence."

"Will you sign that?"

Barney held out his hand for a pen. He scrawled "Barney" across the sheet. "Will that do?"

"No, put your full name."

Barney added "Withers." Thompson took the pen from his fingers and blotted the signature.

"Now then, start from the beginning." And Barney told his story with the simplicity of a child.

Shortly after he had finished the clock struck ten.

Perry blotted the last sheet. "I'll read what I've written."

Thompson said, "Is there any correction you would like to make? Or do you wish to add anything?"

"No. It's all there." Barney signed every sheet.

"Get some one to take him along to the station and lock him up for the night," Thompson said to Perry.

"What charge?"

"Oh, I don't know. Detained on suspicion of being concerned with the robbery at Crowley. That'll fill the bill."

When Perry came back Thompson was standing at the window looking out across the river. He turned and sat on the edge of the desk. "I'm sorry for the poor old blighter," he said.

"Yes. He's rather pathetic. He asked me if he could have the mouse. He wanted to bury it, I think."

"God! You strike some funny ones in this game." Thompson began to fill his pipe. When it was drawing he said. "His alibi on Friday night is the Tibbetts. Get that checked up."

"I've sent a man out."

"Good." Thompson slid off the desk and sat in a chair before the fire. He put his feet on the fender and stared at the glowing coals. "He doesn't help us over Rivers's death, does he?"

"No, it's a pity about that."

"But if he's right about what happened at Crowley we'll have Spike Morgan cold for Brook's death. And the bloke who was with him. Barney can identify them both."

"Yes, but his story doesn't quite fit in with what Will Dorset told us. Barney says he thinks Spike Morgan was the one who went after the other man in the van, Brook."

"Possibly he was mistaken. Don't forget he was a quarter of a mile away at the time. I think it'll work out all right. And if what he said about Len is correct that kid'll talk."

"Let's hope he does."

The phone bell rang.

"You answer it." Perry picked up the receiver.

He spoke a few words and then listened. "All right, keep him there. We'll be along in twenty minutes." He looked at Thompson. "They've got Len at Cable Street."

Thompson reached for his hat. "This looks like the last lap. Come on."

CHAPTER TWENTY

AT TWO O'CLOCK on the Tuesday afternoon Spike saw a police van draw up at the end of the path leading to Napier Terrace. Four men got out and walked to No. 3. A policeman in uniform opened the door and they went in.

Nothing happened for half an hour, and then the door opened again. Two men came out carrying parcels. The others of the party followed them a few minutes later. The policeman shut the door. The four men walked quickly up the path to the van, got in and drove away.

"That's cooked it." Spike tried to think, but could not. His brain was dead. "I've got to think of something." But he could think of nothing. "They must have taken Mrs. Kemp, and Joe as well."

He felt in his pocket and brought out tenpence ha'penny in coppers. Enough for a pint and then—what the hell was he going to do?

Len was walking up and down with his hands thrust deep in his trouser pockets.

"For God's sake keep still. Sit down."

Len smiled. "You ought to have had some breakfast, like me. What time did you say the old woman'd be here?"

"She's not coming. She's been nabbed."

"You mean—"

"You'll have to whistle for your supper."

"And how long is this going to last?"

"I'll think up something. But we've got to stop here tonight."

"Nobody's going to stop me if I want to go." Len took his hands out of his pockets and clenched his left fist. He took two paces towards Spike.

"Stand back!"

Len saw the dull blue of a revolver in Spike's hand and stopped. They stood still, glowering at each other like a couple of angry dogs.

Spike lowered the muzzle of his gun until it pointed to the pit of Len's stomach.

"If we go out of here we go together, and if they come for us there's going to be fireworks."

"You damn' fool. What the hell is the good of that?"

Spike stuck out his jaw. "That's what's going to happen."

"And if they don't find out we're here?"

"We'll work another stick-up, get some cash and shift to some place where it's healthier. We've got to have dough."

"Got any ideas?"

"Yes."

"What is it?"

"Wait and see. You can get your bedding down. Take it over to the corner."

Spike waited till Len had arranged the sacking. Then he put his gun in its holster under his left arm and fixed his bed on the top of the trap-door.

He was feeling weak with hunger and his mouth was dry. His legs crumpled under him and he sprawled across the sacking. It still felt damp and smelled musty and rotten.

Len said, "There's that dob of meat you put on the window. What about getting it?"

"I'd forgotten. I'll go down." Spike opened the trap and went down to the ground floor. He found the glass, but there was not a morsel of the mince on it. He walked back up the stairs, his knees sagging.

"Got it?"

"The rats have scoffed it."

Len swore.

Spike lay on his right side and tried to keep awake. "I could do with some of that bread."

"I've finished it. And the cheese. There's one fag left." Len broke it in two and tossed a half to Spike, who lit it and felt better.

At four o'clock he dozed off for a few minutes and woke with a start. "What's that?"

"Nothing."

"I thought I heard something."

"It was the rats, I expect. One ran over my foot."

Spike kept awake for nearly an hour, then he fell asleep. It was pitch dark when he woke. The windows were faint, grey squares.

"Len!" He listened, but heard nothing. "Len!" He couldn't even hear the sound of breathing. He struck a match. It burned slowly at first and then flared up. Len wasn't on his bed.

Spike dropped the match and lit another, and looked round on every side. Len had gone! Or perhaps he was lying under the sacking waiting for a chance to catch him unawares.

Spike felt for his gun and laid it on the floor. Then he struck another light, picked up the revolver, and walked slowly over to where Len had been lying. He kicked at the sacking. There was nothing there. The match burned his fingers and he dropped it with a curse.

He stumbled back to his bed and sat down. If only he had the guts he'd shoot himself. It would be a quick way out. If only he had the guts!

Len had waited until Spike had sunk into a heavy sleep and then he had started to work on a loose board. When the nails were free he tried the one next to it. The wood was rotten and an hour's work was sufficient to provide him a way of escape.

He dropped through the hole on to the floor below, ran lightly down the ladders, got out into the open, and over the fence into the street which ran up to the canal bridge.

Two women were standing in a doorway talking. Len stopped and asked the way to the nearest police station. The women stared at him for a moment and then laughed.

"Going to give yourself up?" one of them asked.

"Where's the police station?"

"Well, if you really want to know, it's in Cable Street, first to the left and then it's a little way down on the right-hand side."

Len hurried on. The other woman called after him jeeringly. "They've got lovely beds. You'll be ever so comfortable."

The constable on duty at the entrance to the station barred the way in. "What d'you want?"

"I've come to give myself up."

"All right, come along with me." He took Len into the charge room.

A sergeant who was sitting reading an evening paper looked up.

"I was in the Crowley job," Len said.

"Name?" The paper rustled to the floor.

"Len Harmon."

The sergeant stretched out a hand and lifted the receiver of his desk phone. He called Scotland Yard and was put through to Thompson's room.

Perry's voice answered, and when the sergeant had made his report, Perry said, "All right. Keep him there. We'll be along in twenty minutes."

Len was drinking cocoa when Thompson and Perry arrived. The sergeant pointed at him and said, "This is the man."

Len put down his cup, wiped his mouth with the back of his hand and stood up.

"What's your full name?" Thompson asked.

"Leonard Harmon."

The sergeant opened a door and pressed a light switch. He signed to Len to go in.

Thompson asked in a low voice, "Has he told you anything?"

"No. He wanted to, but I stopped him."

The room was cold. Thompson kept on his coat and hat. He told Len to sit down and stood for half a minute looking down at him. "What are you going to talk about?"

"The Crowley job."

"That'll do to start with."

"Start—with! What d'you mean?" Len's fingers scrabbled on the bare wood of the table. He was looking at the floor.

"Rivers," said Thompson. "You knew him?"

"No. I've never seen the man."

"You went to his place on Friday."

"I don't know where he lives."

"I thought you wanted to spill it."

"So I do." Len spoke eagerly and edged forward in his chair. "I'm interested in Rivers."

"I tell you I don't know him. Spike did all the fixing."

"About what?"

"The Crowley job. Spike and me worked it. Rivers was to give us a packet when we'd pulled it, but he never did."

"All right. Let's get on with what you want to say." Thompson administered the customary caution. "And now, don't talk too fast." He jerked his head in the direction of Perry. "Watch his pen."

"I get you." Len paused, and then said, "Spike came to me at the place I was staying last Thursday. He said he had a job and wanted me to go in with him. He'd get the car, but I was to drive. On Friday he met me at Barnes Bridge. It was in the morning, about eight. We drove to Crowley and waited for a bit. A van came along. It had to stop as we were blocking the road. Spike got out and held up the driver. He had a gun."

"Who had a gun?"

"Spike."

"All right, go on."

"There was another man in the van. He got out and ran down the road."

"Towards you?"

"No, up the hill."

Perry made the correction and Len went on.

"Spike went after him." Len hesitated for a moment and then repeated the words. "Spike went after him. He came back pretty soon and did something to the driver. Then he drove the van into a gravel pit. I took our car in and we filled it up with what was in the van, and went back to Town. We took the stuff to a shop down Aldgate way. And that's all I know about it. So help me God." Perry read out what he had written. Len signed the sheets.

"I expect you're glad you've got that off your mind?" Len nodded and took the cigarette Thompson offered him. When he had got it going Thompson asked, "What made you give yourself up?"

Len blew out a stream of smoke and said, "Spike. He's got a gun."

"Well?"

"He'll shoot any one that tries to take him. When he told me that, I thought it was time for me to get going. I didn't want to get mixed up in no murder."

"Where is Spike?"

"In that warehouse down by the wharf."

"What wharf?"

"Opposite Napier Terrace."

"The hell he is! Perry, we'll want every man we can get. Tell the sergeant to call out the reserves."

Forty-eight men formed a cordon round the warehouse. When they were in position, Thompson, Perry, the D.D.I. and two constables searched for a way in. They soon found the broken shutter creaking mournfully in the night wind which was getting up.

Thompson said, "I'll go first. You wait outside." He had a revolver in his right hand, a torch in the other. He stepped in through the broken window and took a side pace, and stood against the wall.

"Come out of it, Spike."

It was very quiet when he stopped speaking. He listened for the sound of bathing, heard none and snapped on his torch. He played it round for half a minute and then called out, "All right, you can come in. He's not here. Probably up top."

But Spike Morgan was not in the warehouse. They found the piles of sacking and the stubs of three cigarettes squashed flat. That was all.

Mrs. Benson gave her husband his supper and when he left for his night's work she piled the dishes in the sink with a promise that she'd wash them in the morning. Then she put on her bonnet and her coat and hurried to the settlement. She had a lot to tell Mrs. Tibbett. What the police had said to her. What she'd told them. What Scotland Yard was really like.

She even forgot to be really afraid of the path or of Captain. His low-pitched growl, however, hastened her steps up the ladder.

Mrs. Tibbett brewed a pot of tea and brought out a piece of currant cake. They discussed the whole business; even Mr. Tibbett, who had hitherto adopted an attitude of superior indifference, joined in.

It was late when Mrs. Benson at last found that she had recounted every word of her experiences. Mr. Tibbett offered to go with her up to Cable Street.

"No. I couldn't think of it. I'll be all right," Mrs. Benson assured him.

Unfortunately for her she was not a bit all right. Before she had reached the end of the path she heard footsteps ahead of her. She stopped and listened, her heart thumping. It wasn't anything. She must have imagined it. She laughed a little to keep her courage up and walked on cautiously. Then her nerve broke and she ran blindly, stumbling towards the lights of Cable Street.

Spike came out of the shadow of the fence and crept on towards the Tibbetts' caravan. He took his gun out and gripped it by the barrel. A crack over Captain's head would settle his hash.

There was a light in the window. Spike could see the shadow of some one moving in front of the lamp. He stood quite still. There was no sign of the dog. Maybe he was dead. But Captain had scented Spike. He crept forward on his belly until he was within three feet of him. Then he crouched back on his haunches and sprang.

Spike staggered a pace backwards and fell. The gun flew out of his hand and hit the wheel of the caravan.

Spike felt for the gun with his right hand, but Captain growled and bared his teeth two inches from his throat.

Spike was lying quite still when Mr. Tibbett came down the ladder with a smoking oil lamp in his hand.

He started to call Captain off. Then he recognized Spike and called out to Mrs. Tibbett to fetch a policeman. He added, "Better get two, when you're about it."

Spike Morgan and Len Harmon were charged with the murder of John Brook at Cable Street Police Station and, after a preliminary hearing before the magistrates which lasted three days, they were committed for trial to the Central Criminal Court. The following is an extract from the summing-up of the learned judge who presided at the trial:

"Gentlemen of the jury, if you are satisfied, having regard to all the evidence, that Morgan and Harmon were acting in concert in pursuit of an unlawful object, and that in order to achieve this common purpose one of these two men did an act which was the cause of the death of John Brook, under such circumstances that it amounted to murder, it is your duty to find both prisoners guilty. It is not necessary that it should be proved which prisoner actually struck the fatal blow; it is sufficient if you are satisfied that one committed the felony and that the other was present, aiding and abetting. That is the law.

"I will deal first with the case against Harmon. Shortly after his arrest he made a statement which showed quite clearly that he took part in this expedition to the village of Crawley with the express purpose of stealing a quantity of furs. I must remind you again that this statement is in no way evidence against Morgan. It is evidence against Harmon alone.

"The story he tells is a curious one. He says, in effect, 'I was a party to the robbery. I drove the car. But I had no idea that violence would be used.' Can you accept that statement? He knew there would be some one in charge of the van. And it is only reasonable to suppose that this man would make some show of resistance and that Morgan would endeavour to overcome this resistance.

"Harmon says that he sat in the car while Morgan presented a pistol at the driver of the van. He saw another man get out of the van and run away up the hill. He says that Morgan followed him and returned a few minutes later and secured the driver with a pair of handcuffs.

"Is that a probable explanation of what occurred? I do not think it is. The driver, Dorset, would surely have made his escape while Morgan was absent. Harmon says that he did not do so.

"Learned counsel has made the suggestion that Dorset may have been a party to this hold-up; that he was what one might call a willing victim. There is no evidence whatsoever which supports this contention and, in the absence of evidence, it is not open to you to come to a conclusion such as this on mere guesswork.

"You have seen Dorset in the box. You have heard his story and have had an opportunity of deciding if he is or is not an honest man giving a true account of what occurred.

"If you believe him, then it would appear that Harmon was the man who caused the death of John Brook. . . . There is no reason why you should not accept one part of Harmon's statement and reject another. . . .

"Then there is the evidence about the yellow overcoat which was found behind the shop in Pelham Street.

"According to the evidence of Chief Inspector Thompson, Harmon, on being shown the coat, said, 'Yes. That is mine. I didn't think you'd find it. . . .'

"A man working in his garden at Crowley said that one of the men in the car was wearing a yellow coat. . . . He thought it was the driver.

"Harmon was identified by the man Hyams as having assisted in carrying the stolen furs into Hyams's shop. . . . At that time Harmon was wearing a yellow coat.

"And you will remember that a skin which was part of the stolen property was traced to this very shop where the coat was found. . . .

"Morgan has made no statement. He has not gone into the witness box. His defines is a very simple one. 'I was not there. I know nothing about it.'

"Let us examine the evidence. First, we have Miss Alma Robinson. She was employed at the shop of a man known as Mr. Rivers. On the Friday morning she says that Morgan came to the yard at the back of the shop. Mr. Rivers was there at the time 'fiddling about his car,' as she puts it. It is, I think, clear from the evidence of the expert witnesses who examined the tyres of this car and who took plaster casts of impressions of tracks at the gravel pit, that this was the car used in the expedition to Crowley. A black fox hair was found in it; also a magazine, half of the cover of which was found in a house near by—in Napier Terrace.

"If you believe Miss Robinson, this car was driven from Mr. Rivers's yard at about eight o'clock on the Friday morning.

"I must break off here to comment on the evidence of Barnabas Withers. On his own story, as told to you from the box, he was an accomplice in the robbery. I direct you, therefore, that you should not convict Morgan nor Harmon on Withers's evidence alone. If, however, it is corroborated in material matters by other independent evidence, you may accept it.

"Withers says that Morgan met him at the canal bridge in Cable Street shortly before eight o'clock. This fits in with Miss Robinson's evidence.

"From Cable Street they drove, that is, Morgan and Withers, to Barnes Bridge, where Harmon was waiting. Harmon drove the car to Crowley, and Withers got out and went up on a hill to keep watch. He gave a signal when he saw the van approaching and he saw, or says that he saw, a man running away from the van up the hill.

"In examination in chief, he said: 'I thought it was Spike,' but when cross-examined by counsel on behalf of Morgan he admitted that he was too far away to be sure who it was. 'I thought it must be Spike,' he said.

This part of his story is supported by Dorset, who is more certain. He said: 'It was the young fellow who had been sitting in the car, who ran after Brook.'

"In cross-examination both Dorset and Withers adhered to their evidence given in chief and were in no way shaken.

"Hyams, whom I have already mentioned, is quite definite that Morgan was the man who delivered the furs to his shop.

"Miss Robinson saw Morgan and Harmon return to Mr. Rivers's yard.

"In short, there is evidence that Morgan started in the car which was used in the robbery and that he drove this car filled with the stolen goods to Hyams's shop. Withers's evidence is therefore corroborated in certain material matters.

"It is true that Dorset was unable to identify Morgan definitely as the man who held him up, but he did say that Morgan was similar in build and 'I thought I recognized his voice,' he says. . . .

"There are one or two other points with which I will now deal. The first is that Morgan has been unable to account for his movements at the material times on that Friday.

"Miss Robinson has told you that he gave her a fur tie on the Saturday evening. You have seen this tie and also heard the evidence of Miss Freda Klein who identified it as the one which she made up at the order of Hyams. Hyams himself has admitted that it was one of the furs which Morgan delivered to him on the Friday afternoon.

"Now it is an interesting and important part of the case against Morgan that the times spoken to by the various witnesses agree with the contention of the prosecution that Morgan was involved in this affair from the beginning to the end. Miss Robinson says that he left the shop at about eight o'clock. That would allow him sufficient time to reach Crowley by the time of the alleged robbery. That time is fixed within limits by Dorset and by the gardener in the village who saw the car pass his cottage. Hyams says that Morgan arrived at his shop at about twelve o'clock. . . ."

The jury retired to consider their verdict. At four o'clock they filed into their places in the jury box and the learned judge took his seat.

The clerk rose to his feet and said: "Gentlemen of the jury, do you find the prisoner, George Morgan, guilty or not guilty of the willful murder of John Brook?"

"Guilty."

"Gentlemen of the jury, do you find the prisoner, Leonard Harmon, guilty or not guilty of the willful murder of John Brook?"

"Guilty."

Leith left the court as soon as the verdicts had been given. He stopped outside and took a note-book from his pocket. In it he wrote: "Attended Central Criminal Court. 10.30 to 4 p.m. Expenses 2/10."

Thompson, who was close behind him, said: "Chalking 'em off your list?"

Leith looked round. "They're a couple of bad eggs all right."

"It's a pity we couldn't get Mrs. Kemp a stretch. But we hadn't the evidence."

"I shouldn't worry," Leith said. "She's got a private hell of her own."

"What d'you mean?"

"Spike Morgan was her son. Didn't you know that?"

THE END